Death at Breakfast

ALSO BY BETH GUTCHEON

Gossip

Good-bye and Amen

Leeway Cottage

More Than You Know

Five Fortunes

Saying Grace

Domestic Pleasures

Still Missing

The New Girls

Death at Breakfast

Beth Gutcheon

An Imprint of HarperCollinsPublishers

HarperCollins books may be purchased for educational, business, or sales promotional use. For information please e-mail the Special Markets Department at SPsales@harpercollins.com.

FIRST HARPERLUXE EDITION

ISBN: 978-0-06-246633-4

HarperLuxe™ is a trademark of HarperCollins Publishers.

Library of Congress Cataloging-in-Publication Data is available upon request.

16 17 18 19 20 ID/RRD 10 9 8 7 6 5 4 3 2 1

For Robin Clements

Death at Breakfast

Day One, Sunday, October 6

Maggie Detweiler, new-minted woman of leisure and not at all sure she was going to like it, had no sense of impending tragedy as she posed in front of the broad stone veranda of the Oquossoc Mountain Inn that bright October morning. She didn't really know what made her say to Hope, "When your picture's being taken, don't you always wonder if it's the one that will run with your obituary?"

"Well, that one won't be," Hope Babbin said, consigning the image to the digital trash can. "Hold still and smile, will you?"

Maggie did.

"And no, of course I don't. What a strange woman you are." Hope showed Maggie her cheerful image now glowing on the screen of her iPad, of a smallish pleasant-looking woman with a warm smile, intense blue eyes, and a halo of feathery white hair.

"Oh, am I? I think it's much better to keep in mind that it's waiting for all of us than to have it come as a surprise," said Maggie.

For Maggie, it was probably something to do with retirement, which already was not at all the way she had once pictured it. To begin with, in the time it took you to get to Bergen, Maine, you could have flown to London. When her husband was alive they had dreamed of retiring to a bedsit in the West End. But in this first unstructured autumn of the rest of her life, she had instead taken a train to Boston to meet her friend Hope who had recently left New York for a Beantown suburb. Together they had trailed out to Logan Airport and after a longish wait for "a piece of equipment," which turned out to be the plane (there had been fog somewhere along its puddle-jumping route), they had flown to Bangor. There Hope insisted on being the one to rent a car, because it was her treat, this whole trip. They drove another hour and a half through the early dusk, past a stark northern moonscape of blueberry barrens studded with vast boulders dropped by haphazard glaciers in the last ice age, then on narrow roads that felt like tunnels cut through blue-black evergreen forests pressing in on them from both sides. By the time they reached Bergen, Maggie had come to fear that Hope had no peripheral vision at all. When you lived in New York, you didn't know what kind of drivers your friends were. Hope never actually hit anything, but Maggie thought it a miracle that the car still had both side mirrors when they finally found the Oquossoc Mountain Inn, the late Victorian stone pile that hulked at the head of Long Lake.

So it wasn't London, but the inn was charming, and it made sense for Maggie and Hope to see if they traveled well together. They'd been friends for years. They made each other laugh. They shared a penetrating curiosity about how people had chosen to live their lives, now and in the past. Maggie's life list of things to do before the rocking chair and the ear trumpet was heavier on museums and medieval ruins than Hope's, and Hope's was longer on palaces and gardens than Maggie's, but both had a yen to see sites of ancient civilizations in uncomfortable parts of the world, which Maggie's much mourned late husband would have loved, and Hope's unlamented ex would have hated.

Hope could afford to travel in far grander style than Maggie, thanks to having years earlier caught the father of her children, a hedge fund monster, in an extremely compromising position with the children's nanny, indeed a position worthy of the Kama Sutra. The husband did not wish the details of their ensuing divorce aired in the New York scandal rags, let alone the *Wall Street Journal,* so he had made a generous settlement with Hope on the condition that she never talk about it, and she never had, which was more than could be said for his next three wives.

So the Oquossoc outing was a trial run. Here, it would be easier to pull the plug than if they were halfway up the Andes when they discovered that it wasn't working out. Hope had signed them up for a cooking course being given by the inn's resident chef, whose food was winning some attention on luxury travel blogs. Maggie remained agnostic about the amusement value of this, since her culinary skills were mostly confined to working the microwave. But retirement is a time to learn new things. They'd been given rooms in the original part of the inn with lake views as recommended by TripAdvisor and had enjoyed a late and excellent dinner in the dining room the night before, where they got a chance to take the measure of their fellow inmates. They had spent this morning canoeing and been thrilled when an enormous blue heron, hidden among some rushes they were plashing toward, had suddenly erupted from its hiding place with a crashing of water and great paddling of wings.

And now, they were happily heading back down the mountain to the village of Bergen, dimly seen the night before, with its two white-steepled churches on opposite sides of the main drag and its interesting Richardson Romanesque public library. Someone in Bergen had had a good deal of money 150 years ago.

On the other hand, Buster Babbin, the deputy sheriff of Bergen, Maine, was not happy this morning. His mother was one of those women with the impact of a battleship; you could see her coming like the prow of the USS *Nimitz*. Hope was tall and slim, with carefully coiffed and blonded hair, an altogether dressier person than her dread friend Mrs. Detweiler. Watching the two of them advancing toward him up Main Street was like being an involuntary spectator at Fleet Week. It mattered little that he knew the objects of his terror thought of themselves as good-natured middle-aged women, salt of the earth and beloved of the young.

Hope and Maggie enjoyed making their way along the uneven leaf-spangled sidewalk, its concrete slabs buckled here and there by the roots of the mighty oaks and maples that lined the streets of the village. There was something so majestic about big trees; you missed that in the city. The sun was bright, and Hope wore huge sunglasses and a broad-brimmed hat. Maggie, who had as usual forgotten her hat, squinted into the sun, shading her eyes with her hand, which made her look to Deputy Babbin as if she thought she was Sacajawea, the Bird Woman, gazing over some rushing gorge, to discern the safest route along which to lead her charges.

"Here they come," said Sandra. She was looking out the front window of Just Barb's, the village diner, which she ran with her mother-in-law. "Man your stations." Sandra had greatly looked forward to this visitation, which would be the town's first sighting of anyone from Buster's heretofore storied family of origin. He had for years prevented his mother and sister from showing up in his life and taking over everything by paying just enough home visits to them at birthdays and holidays to keep them pacified. Some of us are content and at ease in the worlds we are born to, and some of us know we've been raised by wolves and take decades to find our true native landscapes. There is no point in trying to explain this to the wolves.

Buster Babbin stood up from his counter stool and checked to see that his shirt was tucked in. He was wearing his holster and gun, just to make a point. Sandra took her place behind the counter.

A glittering burst of bright fall air came into the room with the ladies.

"Well, don't you look official!" Hope exclaimed, moving to kiss her son, whose given name was Henry, but had been nicknamed by his father, then everybody, because of his genius for breaking things. Buster leaned into Hope with his shoulders and head, keeping his body well out of embracing range, and managed to connect his cheek with his mother's ear.

"Mrs. Detweiler," he said, turning to Maggie with his hand extended. The idea that *she* might try to kiss him as well had presented itself as a possibility.

"Oh, let me be Maggie now, please," said Mrs. Detweiler, in a voice that was far gentler than the sort of prison guard Klaxon tone he thought he remembered. She was now shorter than he was. She wore her hair in a neat no-nonsense cut and had gained a little weight around the middle, but her warm smile and watchful blue eyes were utterly the same, dreadful as that was to contemplate.

Sandra had appeared in their midst, holding menus, and somehow herded all three of them toward the corner booth.

How the hell was he supposed to call this figure of menace by her first name? The last time he had seen her he'd been thirteen years old, his uniform was torn and his nose was bleeding, and Mrs. Detweiler was on the phone to Hope, explaining that everyone at the Winthrop School felt that Buster would really be happier in a setting where he could get more individual support and would not have to take higher math or a foreign language. Afterward his mother had sent him off for a Wilderness Attitude Adjustment Experience in Nevada and he hadn't come back to live on the East Coast for seventeen years.

While he was gone, his mother and Mrs. Detweiler had bonded over the perfections of Buster's younger sister Lauren, who was currently finishing her residency in obstetrics at Brigham and Women's Hospital in Boston and was also mother of twins. This trip to Bergen, he'd been told, was a present from Hope to Mrs. Detweiler, on her retirement after twenty-three years as Winthrop School head and all-around rhinoceros. In addition to the thrill of seeing Buster in situ, they were staying up at the inn, which, though struggling, was by far Bergen's biggest remaining employer. It was, in fact, pretty much the town's reason for being at this point. Once there had been farming and fishing, copper mining and a small factory that made toothpicks, but now there was leaf peeping in the fall, followed by hunting season, followed by old-fashioned Christmas follies with sleigh rides and taffy pulls and caroling, plus skating and cross-country skiing that lasted if they were lucky until mud season. At least this dreaded visit was boosting the local economy.

"Is that thing loaded?" asked Hope. She had her napkin tucked into her pearls.

"No, Ma," he said, with heavy sarcasm, "I just wear the holster belt to keep my pants up."

Hope looked up from the menu at him to see if he was being fresh. Under the table, his knees were jiggling the way they always had since he was small. (He had just remembered it drove his mother crazy, which made them want to jig more.)

"Well how exciting," said Hope.

Sandra appeared and took their orders. When that diversion was over, Hope returned, as he knew she would, to Inquisitor mode, her version of showing motherly enthusiasm.

"And do you have a jail?"

After a pause, Buster said with dignity, consciously holding his knees still, "We have a chair."

The women looked at each other.

"It's pretty heavy. We can handcuff them to the arms until someone comes to take them to Ainsley."

"Well, I'd love to see the chair," said Hope.

"It's over in the town hall," said Buster, gesturing at the squat stone building across the street. "In the selectmen's office." He was not going to spend the week leading these two on a tour of the civic arrangements of Bergen. Sandra arrived with their plates, two on one arm and one on the other.

The large black radio on Buster's belt began to crackle. Buster struggled to get it out from under the table.

"Deputy Babbin here—" He got up and walked outside, where they could see him pacing back and forth on the sidewalk with the zest of a prisoner let out of an oubliette. After he finished his transmission he strode back inside, all business.

"Gotta go," he said. His mother and Mrs. D looked up from their plates. Buster put on his hat, fastened his radio back in place, and hitched his pants as Sandra, with practiced motions, whisked over to their table with a huge roll of aluminum foil, wrapped his lunch, and handed it to him. "Cow on the road out by Laskey's farm. Get to it before there's an accident," he said. Sandra nodded, as if she knew he rarely finished a meal without an emergency, and Buster strode out. They watched him swing into the driver's seat of the patrol car out by the curb as if he were mounting a horse, perfectly aware that the ladies were watching;

then he was off with what seemed like an unnecessary and declarative burst of speed.

"Does he have an office?" Hope asked Sandra.

"Well, here," said Sandra. "Or his car. We all know how to find him."

"I had no idea he knew anything about cows."

"He's real good with 'em," said Sandra. "Goats too. If it's pigs, though, he calls for backup."

"Pigs can be mean," said the one that wasn't Buster's mother. She had a nice smile.

That evening, Hope and Maggie had declined the gentle yoga class that was offered after the opening session of their cooking course. Several of their classmates could be seen at this moment out on the lawn saluting the setting sun, but the ladies were instead contemplating the cocktail menu in the lounge while they waited for dinner.

"I think an apple martini sounds sufficiently in the harvest bounty spirit," Hope declared. They had spent the afternoon learning about the importance of using seasonal produce with an emphasis on the wonders of root vegetables and a spice they'd never heard of, called za'atar.

"I only hope the gin is locally sourced and artisanal," said Maggie as they ordered two.

"You know, it might be," said Hope. "When I was a girl, Poland Spring up here made gin that came in a green glass bottle shaped like a little old man. My father drank it like water. Took me forever to figure out why he didn't make any sense after lunch until he'd had his nap."

Around them, the lounge was slowly filling with gastronomes bathed and dressed for dinner. A couple from Cleveland called Homer and Margaux Kleinkramer was across the room drinking something beige and disturbing-looking from coupe champagne glasses. Albie Clark, a long thin grayish man nursing a secret grief or grievance, or both, was sitting by himself reading his Nook book and pulling at a beer.

"I used to hide my cigarette butts in one of those little old man bottles. I loved to smoke," Hope said dreamily. "It was so glamorous. My friends and I used to spend the afternoon in my brother's tree house, smoking Kents and reading *True Romance* magazines aloud to each other. Do romance magazines even exist anymore?"

"I doubt it. I think it's all sexting and Internet porn these days."

The chicest members of the cooking group, Martin and Nina Maynard, materialized beside them. They both had wet hair, fresh from showers. Nina's dress was covered in printed hibiscus and she wore a bright

lipstick that matched the flowers and nicely emphasized her bright smile.

"May we join you?" Martin asked. He was a well-
buffed African American with the build of a recently
retired football player. He was dressed as if for golf,
which showed off his physique nicely. "It sounded as
if you might know something about D.C. schools. We
need advice."

"Definitely," said Maggie. "And we were hoping to
ask you what you are doing in a cooking class."

Martin laughed as they settled themselves. "My wife
thinks I don't know how to find our kitchen."

"Well, do you?" asked Nina. She was a beauty, elfin,
with caramel-colored skin.

"I'm sorry," said Martin, "I'm not allowed to talk
about it."

"He works for the FBI," said Nina.

"I told my wife she could have anything she wanted
for her birthday and she said she wanted me to come
to this class with her. Believe me, I tried to talk her into
a mink."

He scanned the room for a waiter as Hope, turning
in her chair, asked, "Now what do you think that's all
about?"

Across the lobby, some kind of fuss was building at
the front desk. A huge man in a rust-colored cashmere

tweed jacket was leaning over the counter speaking loudly to the village girl who was trying, apparently, to check him into the hotel. Off to the side, a pair of glossy bottle-blondes who were certainly sisters, maybe even twins, stared into space as if this was nothing to do with them. There was a small stack of matched luggage beside them, and one of the women had a tiny white dog in her arms.

"Don't those women look familiar?" Maggie asked.

Hope took off her glasses so she could see them better across the room.

"Are they from one of those reality TV shows?"

The large man had now turned his back to the girl behind the counter, who was tapping fruitlessly at her computer and making eye contact with nobody. She looked very young in her unbecoming moss green hotel uniform.

The man said something contemptuous to the woman with the dog, who was ignoring him. He leaned back with his elbows on the counter behind him and stared furiously across the lounge, as if daring anyone in it to notice that he had not been served.

Gabriel Gurrell was closeted that evening with Zeke, his head of maintenance. The riding mower was broken again, this time probably fatally. Zeke's brother had already rebuilt it once and he never had got it running quite right after that, though Zeke was in favor of trying his brother again. Gabriel was spared making a decision about it by the call from Cherry downstairs on the front desk. Yet again, she seemed unable to deal with a check-in. Cherry was trying hard but, Gabriel admitted to himself, probably wasn't going to work out. Too bad; he dreaded having to tell her formidable mother. He apologized to Zeke and took off for the stairs at a trot.

"Good evening," he said as he crossed the lobby to the vast man who was blocking all sight of Cherry. "I'm so sorry to learn there's a problem. How can I help you?"

"You the manager?" the huge man roared. Gabriel could see that every stitch he was wearing was hand-tailored; they didn't make clothes out of fabric like that at the Large and Tall shops.

"Manager slash general factotum. Gabriel Gurrell." He offered the man his hand. The man ignored it.

"My secretary made reservations for me for dinner and the night and this idiot . . ."

"I'm so sorry, let me see if I can help." Gabriel whisked behind the counter and took Cherry's place at the computer. "Your name?"

The man slapped the driver's license and gleaming black credit card that were lying on the desk.

After more tapping, Gabe looked up and asked, "Did she reserve by e-mail, Mr. Antippas? Or by telephone?" He had unluckily emphasized the first syllable of the name.

"It's AnTIPPas, and how the hell do I know!" bellowed the man, so that even the Kleinkramers, far across the room, stopped their conversation and turned to look.

"I'm sorry for your inconvenience, and I'm sure I can accommodate you."

"That's what this idiot said, but she was wrong, weren't you?" he turned to Cherry, who shrank back a step.

"Just tell me what you're looking for."

"I reserved a suite with a California king bed and separate sitting room, smoking, and another room for my sister-in-law, nonsmoking, and we want views of the lake."

"I'm afraid all our rooms are nonsmoking, sir . . ."

"Well couldn't you have fucking told me that when I reserved?" he yelled.

Gabriel's eyes flicked toward the lounge. Had they all heard the *F*-bomb? By the look of the raised heads and startled-looking eyes all over the room, they had. Not what his clientele came to Oquossoc for.

After a moment he said, "It's stated clearly on our website, sir, that we are a nonsmoking facility, but I understand your disappointment."

"You think I have time to read your fucking website? Who owns this place, Mike Bloomberg?"

"I can offer you a very nice suite on the mountain side of the building, with a terrace you can smoke on. It's just here," said Gabriel, producing a map of the hotel and grounds and making an X with his pen.

"You think I drove for seven hours for a view of the fucking parking lot?"

The woman with the dog in her arms, presumably his wife, came to join him.

"Alex," she said wearily, "I'm sure it's fine."

The huge man turned to look at her, as if to say *you think it will be fine?*

To Gabriel he snapped, "Is your supervisor here? Who can I talk to? How about the owner?"

Gabriel said, "I am the owner." He was trying not to look as if he'd be glad if they just took their luggage and went out the way they came. In flush times, you could choose whom not to accommodate, but since the crash of '08, he needed every bit of trade he could get and keep.

"Why don't we just go up and have a look at the suite he's got?" said Mrs. Antippas. "I'm tired, and Colette needs her dinner."

"Yes of course," Gabriel said. "I'll phone the dining room and tell them you'll need a table for three in what, fifteen minutes?"

"Colette is the dog," said the second blond woman, who delivered this news, then returned to her wool-gathering. Behind him Cherry was whispering a long self-justifying explanation of the problem she'd been trying to solve. Which involved the dog.

Gabriel seemed to refocus. The woman with the huge man had a dog in her arms.

"Ah. I see." He went back to the computer, as the woman with the dog said with a warning note in her voice, "*I* read the website and it expressly said that this is a dog-friendly hotel."

"Yes it is, madame," said Gabriel. "But we are bound by health department rules. Dogs are only permitted in this wing here; we have guests who are allergic, and all animals have to be kept away from food service."

"Don't you clean the rooms between guests?"

Gabriel was close to losing it. "Yes of course we clean between guests," he said through tight lips. "These are not my rules."

"Then give us a suite in the dog wing."

"I'm afraid I don't have a suite in that wing, madame. I have only one room open there, and it has twin beds and no sitting room."

"Do you mean there are no suites in that wing?"

"There are two, madame, but they are both occupied."

"Well, tell someone they have to move to the one over the fucking parking lot," said Antippas.

"I can't do that, sir. They are booked for the week by people here for the cooking class."

"The chef is giving a cooking class?" asked the sister-in-law, suddenly seeming to come back to earth.

"Well that takes the fucking cake," bellowed Antippas. "I drove nine hours just to have dinner here, and I get to sleep over the parking lot and my wife has to kill her dog."

"I'd like to know more about this cooking class," said the sister-in-law.

"You'll have to leave her in the car," said Antippas to his wife.

The wife said to Gabriel, "You know what? It's fine. I'll sleep with my sister in the dog wing and my husband will take the suite with the balcony. Could you just take us to our rooms now? If I can't get out of these panty hose soon and take a leak, I'm going to wet myself right here. Alex, get the dog's suitcase and just shut up."

"What did you just say to me?"

"The dog is not spending the night in the car. *You* sleep in the car, if you think that's so nice." Gabriel had summoned a bellman without seeming to move a muscle and in spite of his high dudgeon the man mountain had picked up a pet carrier bag and a large tote, in which Maggie could see a red leather leash, and a tiny Burberry plaid dog overcoat.

Day Two, Monday, October 7

In the bracing cold of early morning light, Maggie joined a small group swaddled in fleece that had gathered in the parking lot to climb the mountain. Their guide would be Bonnie McCue, a "fitness professional" and member of the cooking class who was paying her way by offering hikes and exercise classes. Above them the windows of the mountain view rooms were draped in blackout curtains like rows of bandaged eyes. After seeing Alex Antippas in action in the lobby the night before, and again in the dining room, where there had been a fuss when he sent his *truite en croûte* back—twice—because the crumb inside the pastry was not up to his standards, no one wanted to disturb his slumbers, let alone risk seeing him in his nightclothes on his balcony.

Bonnie said in a near-whisper that they were going to do some stretches before taking off, and that a shepherd would bring up the rear so that no straggler would be lost on the mountain. Maggie looked in the direction she indicated and saw the little girl from the front desk last night, Cherry. She was in jeans and a sweatshirt with the hood over her hair and she hunched her thin shoulders as if she was bone cold. She must get combat pay to be here, Maggie thought. Surely not doing it for pleasure.

When they finished with their warm-up, Martin Maynard stripped off his fleeces, and after kissing his wife on the top of her head, he took off running. On his feet he was wearing something that looked like rubber socks with toes.

Bonnie looked after him, nonplussed.

"Don't worry," said Nina Maynard. "He does this wherever we go. He's an Ironman."

"They don't really like the guests to go off by themselves unless they know the area."

"He's got a map. And a cell phone with GPS."

"That's fine, if he can get a signal," said Bonnie, too late. Martin had disappeared into the trees above them. Bonnie squared her narrow shoulders and set off toward the mountain. Her little band fell in behind her and soon established their paces. Nina was right on Bonnie's flank, her legs taut and strong, her arms pumping. Behind them, Albie Clark, wearing a wool cap and mittens and big earphones, made his solitary way.

"The cat who walks by himself," said Teddy Bledsoe, an enthusiastic young man from San Francisco, gesturing toward Albie. He fell into step with Maggie. "Yes," said Maggie. "I've dealt with parents like that, all sealed up in their own silos. You wonder what it is they're keeping so close to the vest."

"You're a teacher, right?" Teddy asked.

"Former. And you're a writer?"

"A food blogger. I grew up cooking and I thought I'd write a cookbook, but they're over."

"Cookbooks?"

"Yes. Now if you want to cook something you just pull up a recipe on the Internet."

"How do you know the recipe is any good?"

"That's where I come in. I'd give you my Web address, but good luck getting a signal here. I'm in withdrawal. You know those people in the dining room last night?"

No need at all to ask which people. In twelve short hours the new arrivals had managed one way or another to annoy almost everyone in the hotel.

"I swear I know who they are, it's driving me crazy not to be able to Google them. It's like having a phantom limb. Before I went to bed I heard the sister chewing on Mr. Gurrell, demanding to join the cooking class. He kept saying Chef Sarah closed the class months ago, and the sister said 'Do you know who I am?'"

"I didn't think people really said that," Maggie remarked, stepping around some porcupine scat on the trail. "So what brought you all this way for this class? You must have plenty of food to write about in San Francisco."

"Chef Sarah came from San Francisco. She used to cook at a little bistro out in the avenues. She made a lobster ice cream you could kill for. Kill."

"I think that sounds completely disgusting."

"It was a first course. People would taste it and swoon, you could hear them hitting the floor all over the dining room. I was crushed when she moved east."

By the time Maggie had had her posthike shower and eaten breakfast, Teddy had been into town to Just Barb's, which had a wi-fi hotspot, and returned with a wealth of Internet gossip and a copy of the *Boston Herald*.

And the two blond sisters had joined the cooking class.

Mr. Rexroth was in Gabriel's office, spluttering in a rapid, pressured way that was frequently interrupted with explosions, like a car running rough with occasional backfires. His forehead was wrinkled with distress and his bald head had gone pink. He was wearing his summer uniform, a seersucker suit that had seen much better days.

"We met them in the hall last night and everything was *fine*, they seemed like lovely girls and Clarence sniffed and it sniffed and everyone *wagged* but then this morning just as I settled down to my *sermon* it started to yap and it *yapped* and that made Clarence *howl* and I don't know I just don't know, I can't work with a racket like that and the text is from *Jeremiah* and you know what that's like, I mean it's hard enough and they're up there this minute *yapping* and *howling* . . ."

"I'm so sorry this is happening, Mr. Rexroth. As you know we love our four-legged guests . . ."

"Yes but, yes but . . . is there no other place you could move them to? How long are they staying? I mean I can't . . . I *can't* . . ."

"I understand," said Gabriel rather desperately. "You know what a valued friend of the Mountain Inn family you are. I don't know what I can do this morning except to offer you another room to work in, but . . ."

"Can Clarence come with me?"

"As I was going to say, I don't have another room open where we're allowed to accommodate pets. As soon as I can I'll try to arrange a trade with another guest."

"I hope you have one who's deaf as a fence post," said Mr. Rexroth bitterly.

Gabriel had already thought of that and had no idea what he was going to do about it. There were a limited number of rooms where animals were allowed, all occupied, and the guests were out for the day. Except for Earl, the stable manager who had had an accident and fallen on very hard times. Gabriel allowed him to live in the smallest room in exchange for some light gardening and taking care of the horses. Earl had already been to Gabe's office to mention how much the yapping in 6G was upsetting his parrot.

"I wonder if possibly Clarence could wait for you in the car, just for this morning? The weather is mild and we could—"

"In the *car*? Clarence? In the CAR? He did not *start* this, it's that tarted-up little . . . he would feel he was being *punished*! And *that's* not fair! Where is its mother?"

Gabriel wished with all his heart that its "mother" was at the bottom of Long Lake along with her huge fat bully of a husband, but if wishes were horses, beggars would ride.

"I promise I will speak to her as soon as she comes in. They swore that the dog never barks. Mr. Rexroth, would it help if I find someone to take Clarence on a good long walk this morning, while you get on with your work?"

Mr. Rexroth paused and flapped his arms as if to say no, that won't work, but he couldn't think of why it wouldn't. "It would have to be someone Clarence knows. Clarence is particular."

Gabriel suspected that like most people, Mr. Rexroth preferred almost anything to actually having to write, and was now inventing excuses. "Tell me who he likes."

"He likes Chef Sarah," said Mr. Rexroth. Of course he did. Sarah was a dog whisperer. She knew just where they most liked to be scratched, and she saved delicious table scraps for Clarence. But she couldn't be asked to exercise the guests' pets.

"I'm afraid she's busy with her class this morning."

A long pause. Mr. Rexroth said, "He let that little girl at the front desk pat him once."

"Cherry Weaver?"

"The one with the hair like this." He made a motion with his hands.

"I tell you what, she just came on duty. I'll take over the desk for her and she can take Clarence for a walk along the lake. I'm sure she'd enjoy the exercise."

Mr. Rexroth agreed, though as if with grave doubts, that that might solve the problem for the time being.

"Let's go talk to Cherry, then," said Gabriel. Just to make him look like a complete liar, the first person they saw coming toward them in the hall was Chef Sarah, with her handsome auburn hair pulled up in a bun, looking far from busy. There was something he wasn't used to in her manner, though, as if she wasn't feeling well, or had gotten bad news. She greeted Mr. Rexroth before saying, "Gabriel, could I have a word?"

He looked at her a little wild-eyed, thinking, Damn, I hope this isn't about Cherry. Cherry's mother worked for Sarah in the kitchen, and neither one was a woman you wanted to piss off. He said, "One thing at a time. Come see me in the lobby in ten minutes, could you?"

Sarah said, "Never mind. Come find me when you're free."

The cooking class was on a visit to a local apple orchard. Because they were now too many to fit in the hotel van, Hope and Maggie had volunteered to follow in Hope's rental car. It was another gorgeous day, sweater weather but warm in the sunshine, and although it was early for the full autumn leaf panoply, there were blazes of scarlet and of bright ochre in the hardwood stands along the road.

At the orchard, the farmer, a young woman from Oregon who talked a good deal about "slow food," had laid out samples of different varieties of heritage apples, neatly sliced and labeled Maiden Blush, Pound Sweet, St. Edmund's Russet, and Whitney Crab. There were ten little notebooks and ten sharp pencils with the name of the farm on them ready for the class to make their "tasting notes," as if they were sampling wine. Teddy Bledsoe and Margaux, who arrived last because they had detoured to see if the Concord grapes in the arbor were ripe, were taking their notes on the backs of deposit slips Margaux had found in her purse, since the flossy blond newcomers to the group betrayed no sense that it was they for whom no notebooks had been provided.

The taller of the blondes looked at the rather gnarled slice of the Whitney Crab apple she was holding. She showed it to her sister and the corners of their pretty pillow-lipped mouths turned down.

"What is this black stuff," the taller one asked the farmer. She held out her apple slice and pointed.

"Oh that—excuse me, what's your name?"

"Glory."

"That's a little sooty blotch, Glory. It won't hurt you."

Glory had returned her untasted slice to the plate and was sorting through the rest to find one that was unblemished.

After the apple-tasting the farmer demonstrated the use of the cider press. Then the farmer's husband gave them all samples of an organic apple sweetener he was trying to market as apple molasses, and ten of them were given paper sacks of apples in all the varieties they had tasted. Hope and Maggie offered to share a bag, and everyone was appreciative except Glory's sister, who declined her bag, saying apples really weren't her favorites.

Teddy caught up with Maggie and Hope. "Can I ride back with you? I've got to tell you what I learned in town."

"Absolutely," said Hope.

"Still no service," Teddy said. "I found some amazing video . . . oh well." He put the cell phone away again. "I knew they were ringing some bell in my reptile brain."

"What is her name? Glory?" Hope asked.

Teddy didn't seem to notice Hope's driving, so intent was he on bringing the wonders of the Internet to them. He was in the backseat where there were no air bags, and didn't even have his seat belt on.

"Her real name is Gloria. The other one is Melisande, known as Lisa."

"Goodness, aren't we literary."

"They're twins, but not identical. From Ontario. They were 'it' girls in Toronto for a while, and then Glory went to Hollywood. She had some parts in B movies and had a talk show on cable TV."

"What about Lisa?"

"She went west too. They cut quite a swath. Some gossip column said they moved through the L.A. party scene like lionesses looking for zebra. All tanned, with big blond manes and matching boob jobs. Designers lent them clothes. David Yurman gave them jewelry. Their father is Victor Poole, do you know who he is?"

"I never heard of him," said Hope. An elderly golden retriever choosing that moment to stroll down to the road from his front yard escaped with his life, but not by much.

"He made a fortune with duty-free shops in airports," Teddy said. "But you know the pop singer Artemis?"

Everyone in the world had at least heard of the singer called Artemis. "My daughter, Lauren, just worshipped her when she was on that Disney show," said Hope.

Maggie said, "There was one year when every single girl in my fourth grade went as Artemis on Halloween.

They must have been freezing with their little bare midriffs."

"Lauren had Artemis dolls," said Hope "and she and her friends would dance around in the bedroom with their T-shirts rolled up to their armpits singing Artemis songs, with bananas for microphones."

"I *worship* Artemis," Teddy declared. "She's an icon. The husband is Artemis's father."

"What?"

"No!"

"Wait, which husband?"

"Lisa's husband, the great fat thing who kept sending his dinner back last night. He's Artemis's father. Albie Clark knows him from Southampton too."

After a moment, Maggie said, "Well, that poor child."

Teddy said, "You won't believe how gorgeous he was when he was young." He tried again to see if he had cell phone service.

Hope said, "Did you know that after all that fuss over the trout last night, he demanded that the chef come out so he could congratulate her?"

"You're kidding."

"No. But Sarah was so mad she wouldn't go. She sent Oliver out to say she'd gone to bed."

Clarence was a bloodhound. It wasn't a popular breed, nor a very beautiful one. The bloodhound has a wrinkled face as if his skull was once about twice as big as it is now, and no one thought to have the skin resized when the skull shrank. He has droopy eyes and jowls that don't quite seal even when his mouth is closed, so drool is more or less a constant. Back in the day when hunting large game on horseback was a sport of kings, the bloodhound was useless as a member of the pack, though he was quite good at locating the scent of quarry in the first place. One can picture him standing, fecklessly drooling, with his big feet splayed out, watching as the hounds gave tongue and sped off with joyous zeal after deer or elk, and the riders galloped after them. The bloodhound's work was done at that point and he was ready for lunch and a nap.

The only thing a bloodhound is really good at is finding and following a scent, even a cold and not very fresh one, even over water. Particularly human scent. So when Cherry tried to take Clarence for a walk around the lake, he weighing a hundred pounds and she about ninety, it was not a very great pleasure for either one of them. Cherry was not from a background that valued recreational exercise, and she had already been up and down the mountain once today. She was now dressed in her hotel uniform and wearing high heels, which hurt her feet. Clarence did not care much for recreational exercise either. He wanted to go back to the hotel and track Mr. Rexroth to wherever they had taken him.

But Cherry battled onward, hauling on the leash. Cherry had had a checkered employment history and she could not fail here. She had been on the vocational track in high school and hoped to work in a hair salon. She had done well in her apprenticeship at Upper Cuts, a beauty shop in Ainsley. She was the shampoo girl, and was learning to do color. It was sort of like magic, the way the color developed on the hair. She didn't even mind the smell. But Mrs. Pease had told her she had two rules that no one was allowed to break. One was don't smoke in the shop, and the other one was don't talk politics with the customers. Cherry explained at length to a woman from New York how wrong it was for people in the cities to keep people like her father, who was a hunter, he hunted for *food*, from being able to buy the guns he needed. And also he had a gun repair business, and selling parts of a gun to a friend who needed them was really a public service. The customer spoke to Mrs. Pease about it. When Mrs. Pease asked her what part of rule number two she didn't understand, Cherry stood mute and sullen. She couldn't say out loud that she didn't know guns counted as politics.

Her father was a hunter. And a volunteer firefighter. He worked as a house painter sometimes, but hated it. He wasn't too good at anything where he wasn't his own boss. He and her mother were divorced. Or maybe never married, anyway she lived with her mother. Her mother used to cook at the elementary school, plain cooking. Mac and cheese, franks and beans. Chowder. Now her mother worked for Chef Sarah at the hotel, and it was the best job she'd ever had. She did prep work and cleanup, but when they had time Sarah showed her how to make things she'd heard about on television. At home now she watched cooking shows. She had health insurance. She had promised Gabriel that Cherry was a good worker. She wanted Cherry to rise in the world.

The cooking class spent the afternoon in the kitchen with Oliver, the sous-chef, and Chef Sarah. One group made a black bean soup with ginger and apples. Maggie and Hope, working with Albie, made an apple confit with caramelized onion threads. Albie sliced the onions tissue-thin with a mandoline he'd been taught to use. His absorption in his task was rather touching, Maggie thought. The confit was to form a bed for chops from local fresh-killed young pork. Albie had perked up and asked if Sarah ever taught a class in butchering, and she said she'd be glad to if there was interest. Glory said she was a vegetarian and this conversation made her want to hurl. Oliver asked if Glory ate fish and would she like salmon instead of pork at dinner, and she asked if it was wild and line-caught. Glory, Lisa, and Mr. Kleinkramer were making kohlrabi salad and curried sweet potato oven fries. The last group was making a classic apple pie with heritage apples and homemade cinnamon ice cream.

Hope and Maggie invited Albie to join them for a drink before dinner, and to their surprise, he accepted. The evening was warm for the season, and they settled themselves outside on the west veranda where they could watch the sunset over the lake.

"They live on the same beach as I do," Albie suddenly said. "We all see each other at the farm stand and the post office. Here I am right down the hall from them and they don't even recognize me."

"Who?" asked Hope.

"Where?" asked Maggie.

"Those bitches," said Albie, and the bitterness of his tone took both women by surprise. "In Southampton. They tore down a beautiful shingle-style house on the beach and built a thing that would be gaudy on Rodeo Drive, let alone in a potato field. They speed in and out in huge black cars with tinted windows. They don't know the neighbors. They don't join the community. I don't even think they know where they are."

"We had neighbors like that in our building in New York," said Hope. "They renovated their apartment three different times in four years. Imagine the dirt and noise. They put in a steam room that leaked through to the apartment below and the super couldn't get in to fix it because they wouldn't give him a key. The people below them had to live in a hotel an entire year while the damage was repaired."

"I hope someone had them murdered," said Albie.

"We didn't have to, we had an act of god. Right after their third renovation, Hurricane Sandy blew in their fancy new French windows and the whole place was wrecked. They put it on the market and moved to Santa Fe."

"Well that story makes me feel all warm and fuzzy," said Maggie.

"Southampton was my wife's place," said Albie. "She inherited the house from her parents. Spent all her summers there as a child. Our children did too, they loved it. There's something about the light . . . My wife was a painter. Mostly landscapes, some portraits. A very delicate colorist." He got out his cell phone and fooled with it for a long minute, then passed it to

Hope, to show her a lovely watercolor of herring gulls on a beach. Hope swiped through and looked at more pictures, then handed the phone to Maggie.

"Beautiful," said Hope.

"Yes," he answered. "She worked in pastels too. I don't know what I'm going to do with all her . . . there's a chest this high, filled with different shades of blues, greens, pinks. Yellows. I never thought about how many yellows there are in the world. Give it to a school, I guess, but . . . and the brushes and sketchbooks and her smocks . . ."

"How many children do you have?"

"Two. Al and Selena. Nothing's been right since Ruth got sick. The children aren't speaking to me."

Hope reached across and gave his hand a pat. "These things happen after a hard death. They pass." Albie looked at her, grateful.

He said, "When she finished chemo, I moved her out to the beach full-time. My daughter was upset about it; she said it was too far from the hospital and too far from *her*. She was always needy. Selena. But Ruth could see the ocean from our bedroom window, and to her, it was medicine. We knew there was no hope. You see. But she seemed to feed herself through her eyes, with that light, and the changing colors of the sea."

After a pause, Maggie said, "I'm so sorry."

"Were you there for the hurricane?" Hope asked after silence.

Albie nodded.

"The storm hit hard out there."

He gestured with his hands, as if to say there were worse kinds of damage. "Not bad. Power went out, but we had oil lamps and candles and a fireplace in the bedroom. We stayed for two days, then our son came and made us go home with him to Oyster Bay till the power came back on. During those two days we kept to that bedroom, wrapped in blankets, sitting over the fire, and I read to her while she watched the sea out the window."

"What did you read?" Maggie asked.

"*Middlemarch*. Ruth loved that book."

"Yes," said Maggie, agreeing with Ruth.

"And she loved the storm. I was afraid a tree would come down onto the roof, but she seemed thrilled. By the power of it, the huge seas, the rain lashing. It was raining sideways." Albie seemed back in the memory of the wild rampaging disaster inside his wife's body, the disaster going on outside the house. "As if for that period of time, it was all one thing, and not evil, but majestic."

"Did it damage your beach?"

Albie seemed not to hear at first. Then he refocused.

"Yes. That was on her mind. That the beaches were washing away and there would be no place for our grandchildren, or their children to . . . that there wouldn't be the future we always pictured. There were town meetings. The first few were at our house, once we moved back; people came to us so Ruth could be part of it. Then *those* people started building their own seawall to protect "their" beach." He made quotation marks with his fingers. "Of course it isn't their beach. It's everyone's beach below the high-water mark. We had hired engineers, we were going to act together so that . . . Oh never mind." He threw back the last of his drink.

"No. Finish," said Hope.

"The point is if just one little piece of beach is protected, the damage is twice as bad for the people around it. With the next storm, and the next and the next, the sand along the outsides of that seawall drain away . . . our dunes began to collapse, and she couldn't stand to watch it. She died in a downstairs room at the front of the house, with her back to the ocean. Watching that beach degrade was like watching her own body leaving her."

Finally he added, "She was a very visual person."

The cooking class ate dinner together in a private dining room, all except for Glory and Lisa, who were eating with Alexander the Great, as Glory called her brother-in-law. Chef Sarah joined the class. She was looking a little pinched, Maggie thought, but this dinner with her was part of the program they'd signed up for, and she was a woman who hit her marks, they were learning. Maggie knew all too well about having to carry out the schedule, no matter what the state of your heart or your health, and admired her style.

They had apple wine with the pork, and Martin Maynard proclaimed it not at all bad. In fact, quite good. In fact they had to call for several more bottles. By dessert, a rumor went around the table that Chef Sarah had once been a professional singer.

"Will you sing 'Every Time We Say Good-bye?'" Margaux Kleinkramer called down the table. "I worship Cole Porter."

"Growing up means the death of many talents," Sarah said, and went back to her conversation with Teddy Bledsoe about San Francisco.

"Where *did* you grow up?" Teddy asked Sarah.

"Western Pennsylvania."

"Did you really?" Maggie chimed in. "I'm from Ambridge!"

"You were from the big city," said Sarah, and they both laughed. Ambridge was a smallish blue-collar steel town down the river from Pittsburgh. "I came from farm country in Washington County."

"Do you remember the roller rink in Moon Township?"

"I had my tenth birthday party there!" said Sarah. "And how about Kennywood?"

"Kennywood! Countryman!" cried Maggie, and she and Sarah slapped each others' hands.

"How did you learn to cook like this in Washington County?" Maggie asked, but Margaux Kleinkramer had begun to sing "Every Time We Say Good-bye," and people were joining in. They had forgotten some of the words but at the far end of the table Nina Maynard and Homer Kleinkramer suddenly swung into the Michigan fight song, having just discovered that they were both Wolverines.

"You know it's been a good party when people start singing fight songs," said Maggie.

"I wonder what fight songs Glory and Lisa know," said Teddy.

"Why don't we invite them all in here?" asked Margaux, reaching for the wine.

"Why don't we not," said Sarah sharply.

"Of all the gin joints in the world, they have to walk into this one," said Albie, and he looked at Hope and Maggie.

"Of all the gin joints in all the towns in all the world, they walk into mine," Sarah corrected.

"My favorite movie of all time," cried Margaux. "Let's sing the 'Marseillaise'!" Some version of that happened. Maggie was near enough to pick out Sarah's contralto, and it was gorgeous, rich, and velvety. Before the song ended the kitchen door opened and several of the cooks came to listen.

"What is going on in here?" one of them asked, looking delighted.

"I'm going to bed, is what," said Sarah, and left them.

"Fight songs," said Maggie.

"Did your parents really name you Marg-ox?" Albie asked Margaux.

"Of course not," said Margaux. "But a little self-invention is good for the soul."

Martin said to Maggie, "Were you married to Paul Detweiler?"

Maggie, who had been about to go to bed herself, turned to look at him. "I was. What made you ask?"

"It just occurred to me. He was a very big deal in our community."

"Did you know him?"

"Met him once. I'm sorry about what happened."

"Thank you," said Maggie. "I am too."

On their way to their rooms, Hope asked, "What did he mean about Paul, 'a big deal in *our* community'? What community?"

"Intelligence, I imagine."

"Paul was a spook? You told me he sold irrigation equipment!"

"He told *me* he was retired."

"From selling irrigation equipment?"

"Irrigation equipment in the Middle East, yes."

Hope looked at Maggie with narrowed eyes. "I can't believe you never told me this."

The elevator door opened and released them onto their floor. "Well," said Maggie, "the retirement part may have been an exaggeration." They reached their bedroom doors, found their key cards, and wished each other a good night.

Day Three, Tuesday, October 8

Alexander Antippas was sitting in an Adirondack chair in the weak October sun, reading yesterday's newspaper. The lawn sloped down to Long Lake, where colorful kayaks and dark green canoes were laid out on the edge of the beach. In the flower beds, chrysanthemums glowed orange and rust, and leggy joe-pye weed waved pale purple heads in the morning light.

Up near the kitchen there were herb and vegetable gardens, still producing late tomatoes, many colored peppers, and neat rows of chard and spinach and kale. There were silvery sage and bushy basil plants, and spindly cilantro and dill trying to bolt. He'd been monitoring them when the Cooking People weren't swarming. Food interested him.

He'd had a wife with a green thumb once. She had taught him all the American names for these plants, and he loved the dark, bitter greens of autumn especially. In the Peloponnese, in his boyhood, he had tended goats from a stone house above a village of almost unimaginable poverty when considered from where he sat now. Bare stone houses cut into the sides of slopes so steep that they seemed nearly vertical, scarcely reachable except by footpaths, and never entirely safe from rock slides from above or the danger that the track beneath your feet would crumble and send you hurtling thousands of feet down the gorge. They had kept chickens and grown garlic and onions. His mother was dead, had always been dead, but when he was little his aunt had made goat cheese. She taught him and his sister to gather wild chervil and greens that resembled spinach, and she would trade eggs for dried cranberry beans and olive oil down in the hamlet. When his sister died and his aunt left for Athens and there were no more women in the house, the diet was bleak and unvaried, designed for subsistence rather than pleasure. Ever since, food had meant more to him than it seemed to mean to other people.

His wife's dog was attached to the leg of his chair by a leash. In Greece dogs didn't live inside. They didn't really belong to anyone, though children were indulged if they wanted to feed and play with them. One grew accustomed to the keening of dogs on the hills outside at night, hungry or cold or just bored. You lived with it, unless you decided not to, and then the dog in question disappeared. In the cities now, with rich tourists so important to the economy, the state had grown either sentimental or pragmatic about dogs. They still lived outdoors but they had addresses on their state-issued collars, and were regularly picked up, taken to the vet or who knows what, maybe to the dog shampoo parlor, then returned to the street where they spent their days. There was a surprisingly fat and contented-looking mutt lolling outside the Grande Bretagne the last time they'd been in Athens. It amused him to see The Wife sweep into the grand lobby with Colette on her rhinestone leash, while the placid unkempt street dog lay outside in the sun, paying so little attention you could doubt they belonged to the same species. If you stayed at the very best hotels, they understood people who thought their dogs belonged inside. Otherwise it was a problem. Like here.

Alex had reached the part of the paper that concerned itself with the private lives of public idiots, which today, oh surprise, was in a busybody ecstasy over the spectacle calling herself Artemis.

Artemis. That child knew as much about Greek mythology as this poodle. Here she was, doing a perp walk into the Brentwood police station, having crashed her Jaguar at three in the afternoon on the way to a rehearsal for her latest "comeback" tour. She'd been released from her third court-ordered stint at Betty Ford ten days ago.

Comeback tour. What the hell had she done to her hair, it looked as if it had been boiled and left to mat, like felt. Who were these geniuses who thought she was actually going to be able to lose fifteen pounds and stay off drugs long enough to remember the words to her songs, and prance around onstage in her little spangled hooker costumes in city after city, and sing the way she sang these days, that sounded as if she was shredding the inside of her larynx? Without blowing her pipes out, if nothing worse? Twerking, would that be next? She made him physically ill.

Look at that hair. When she was three she'd had the hair of a Botticelli Venus. If she were right in front of him, he'd hold her down and shave her head, let her spend a few months looking like a hairless monkey, maybe she'd learn to respect the gifts she'd been given.

He turned to the Sudoku. At his feet the dog had gotten up and was wandering around, incapable, apparently, of realizing that it was tethered. It seemed to smell something interesting. He shifted his bulk, put down the paper, and turned his attention to the scene before him again. There was a lone catboat out on the lake, skimming lazily across the path of the sun. A herd of fat white clouds, drifting like great "*îsles flottantes*" on that marvelous nursery dessert, were breaking up the sheen of light on the water. And over on the other side of the perennial bed, there was now a figure moving.

It was crawling along the edge of the bed on all fours, stopping to work at the stalks of things to strip away crisp and curling leaves, to pinch or behead the spent flowers. Putting on his sunglasses to cut the glare, Alex could see that the figure was a small, slender man, not a boy as he'd thought at first. A slight old man in a very old flannel shirt, towing a large rubber bucket behind him, into which he threw his cuttings. Alex thought of bonfires of the cuttings from grapevines and olive trees in his childhood, how the stinging smoke scented the air and your hair and clothes and made your eyes feel burned. He'd love the times of year that he went with the others to work on the rich farm down the slope that belonged to people from Argos. When he first grew rich he took The Wife and daughter, who was still called Jenny, back to Greece to see where he'd come from. But when he got to Argos, it looked like a grubby market town, not the glowing metropolis he'd thought to startle with his newfound glory, and when they reached his home village, he didn't even stop to look for the "rich" farm. Instead he pointed out a substantial house in Stemnitsa as they drove through without stopping and afterward The Wife enjoyed telling people she'd seen where he grew up and it was an absolute hovel.

The fleshless little man was standing on the near side of the flower bed now, frankly watching him. His version of erect was painful to see; there had been a man on the rich farm who'd misunderstood the fancy farm machinery and had an accident that left him much like that. Something bad had happened to this one, anyway.

"That's the dog," said the bent figure, looking at Colette.

"It's certainly *a* dog," said Alex. He was admiring himself as if watching this scene from one of the floating cloud islands, the prosperous man of affairs making time to be civil to a rude mechanical, who would never guess that he had once been such a one himself.

"That's the dog upset my Walter," said the man. His tone was surprisingly aggressive, for a menial addressing a guest.

Alex looked at the poodle. She was lolling in the grass, now that the figure had approached and been accepted, and as if she knew they were speaking of her, she rolled onto her back with all four paws in the air and her bottom teeth just showing, her ears lying open and pink on the grass like hair bows.

"And you are?" said Alex pleasantly.

"Earl."

"And how did the dog upset Walter?"

"Yaps."

"Ah. Well, I don't doubt that," said Alex. "Fortunately my room is too far away for me to hear her." He picked up his newspaper.

"Shouldn't be left alone in the room," said Earl.

"And you see, she hasn't been. She's out here with me. Please tell Walter I'm sorry he was inconvenienced." As an afterthought, he reached into his pocket and peeled a twenty off a roll of bills. "Please give this to Walter and tell him to buy himself a drink. If he's old enough to drink." Maybe this person was supporting a grandson.

"He's eighty-seven," said Earl. He did not take the money. Mr. Antippas looked at him, decided he must be a little deranged, and put the bill back in his pocket. Then he hoisted himself out of his chair and towered over Earl, just to make the point that he was not, in case his good manners had deceived this troll, someone who could be toyed with. Then he unhooked Colette's leash and said to Earl, "I see you're busy." He walked back toward the hotel, let himself in the side door to the wing he thought of as the Animal House, ascended to the room shared by The Wife and her sister, and tossed the dog in. The door locked behind him, and as he went down the stairs, he heard Colette take up her howls of complaint.

Cherry Weaver was in the kitchen, sitting on a stool near the salad prep, eating a curried turkey wrap and sobbing. It was not an attractive sight. Her mother was elbow-deep in steaming sudsy water, cleaning the stockpots.

"It wasn't my fault," she said, "and he was like he knew that but he could only keep me until the end of the month. So I could make my plans."

Her mother turned around to look at her daughter, now sporting oily dressing on the skirt of her moss-colored Oquossoc Mountain Inn uniform. Mrs. Weaver snapped a paper towel off the nearest roll, and handed it to Cherry. "Blow your nose," she said and turned back to her work. It was nearly impossible to cry and eat at the same time and keep your mouth closed while doing it, and Beryl Weaver didn't really feel she had to see what that looked like. She thought about what a pretty little thing Cherry had been. And very sweet, always the one to make you a ceramic ashtray or bring a handful of candy corn to you from her treat bag at Halloween, in her grubby damp hand. But that had been quite a time ago.

"And he said anyway it had nothing to do with that reservations thing, it just like wasn't working out. But I know it did."

Mrs. Weaver kept scrubbing. She wished Cherry hadn't grown up to look so much like her father. Her children didn't seem to know the meaning of work, and this one had never had more than a teaspoonful of brains, but she had been biddable. She was going to end up emptying bedpans and wiping wrinkly old behinds over at Ainsley Nursing just like her feckless sister. She'd hoped, she really had, that this one at least wanted to *try* for something you could do in life without wearing rubber gloves.

"Couldn't you ask Chef Sarah to talk to him?" Cherry snuffled, while chewing huge bites, rushing, since technically, her lunch break was over.

Mrs. Weaver turned to look at her.

"So we can both get fired? I like my job, thanks."

"She'd never fire you for asking."

"You don't keep good jobs by asking for special favors."

Mrs. Weaver finished rinsing the big stockpot and reached for a clean kitchen towel. She looked at

Cherry, then pointedly up at the wall clock, which stood at two minutes past one. Cherry stuffed the last inch of turkey wrap into her mouth, jumped up and took her plate to the sink, and hurried out, chewing. Her mother hoped she would stop in the ladies' and fix her smeared eye makeup, but she wasn't going to bet the farm on it.

Sarah, as it happened, had already talked with Gabe about Cherry Weaver. It was the eighth of the month, so she had taken his lunch tray up personally. Gabe proposed to her every month on the eighth, and every month she laughed, but they both knew she enjoyed it. She'd told him the first time that she would never marry again, and she had her reasons. He had told her that *never* was just a word, and that he was persistent. He had no idea how close she had come to accepting him this morning, but instead of answering him immediately, she happened to ask if he had any idea why Cherry Weaver was weeping in her kitchen, and he had dropped his head into his hands.

"I hate firing people," he said from behind his fingers.

"I was afraid of that," said Sarah, and gave him a chance to explain why he felt he had to do it. And felt, as she left him, that perhaps it was just as well that the moment had passed. There would be other months, and this was not the best of times.

Maggie and Hope were playing honeymoon bridge in the lounge at the cocktail hour. The Maynards and Bonnie McCue came in together, having just finished Walking Meditation on the lawn in the violet light of sunset. Lisa and Glory and Alexander the Great were nearby, sharing a baked herbed goat cheese Glory had made in the afternoon.

As goat cheese went this was rather good, Alex thought. Too bad The Wife hadn't learned this trick, he loved goat cheese. He put a large mound of it onto a cracker and popped it into his mouth like dropping a letter into a mailbox. It slipped out of sight with barely a movement of the great jowls, as if he had swallowed it whole.

How did he even taste things? Maggie wondered. She watched Glory recross her long tan legs and flip a lock of silky multihued blond hair over her shoulder. She was wearing a buff-colored suede jacket and a very brief matching skirt (surely it was rather cool for so much bare flesh now that the night chill was coming on). Maggie noticed Alex watching the legs, as if they had been put on earth for his benefit.

The Wife was chattering about the pumpkin polenta gratinée she had made, which they would have for dinner. What, could someone please explain to him, was the point of pumpkins? Great tedious starchy things, he didn't even like the color. And he wished his wife wouldn't wear pants. Glory never did, at least not around him. She knew what a man liked and she liked to see that he got it. Especially in bed, not that he'd had that pleasure lately.

The young moron from the reception desk was coming toward them, oh god, she had food stains on her skirt, carrying a dark red retro telephone, with a dial and a long cord dangling from it like some article of clothing the girl had neglected to tuck in.

"A call for you, Mrs. Antippas," Cherry Weaver said. She shoved things around on the cocktail table to make room for the phone, then dropped to her hands and knees to plug the line into a jack somewhere behind Glory's chair.

"How adorable, it's just like the old days at the Polo Lounge!" Glory said. "Where did they get the phones?"

"Flea markets," said Lisa.

"People's cells don't work here, so," said Cherry, and left them. Lisa picked up the phone, looking as if she doubted such instruments still conveyed human speech.

"Hello?"

On the other side of the continent, her son Jeremy was a mess of resentment and relief. "Finally! Mom! I've been trying to call you for a day! Where *are* you?"

"We're in a wrinkle in time," she said. "It's kind of adorable. Nothing invented since 1980 works here. Why, what's up?"

"Jenny's dead," yelled Jeremy.

"Jenny's what?" she said stupidly, her eyes suddenly wide and stunned. "She's *dead?*" Glory and Alex went stiff and said "What?" at the same time.

"She's dead, it's in the papers, they keep calling me and I didn't know what to say. Where *are* you?"

"But . . . ! Was there an accident?"

"She hung herself in her cell. She was arrested again."

"I know that part. Are you sure?"

"Well of course I'm *sure*, Mom, that's why I've been calling you!"

Alex grabbed the phone from his wife.

"Who is this, Sophie?"

"Jeremy. Dad, Jenny's dead. I don't know what to do!" and he started to cry.

"Hang up, I'll call you back from my room." He slammed the phone down, heaved himself out of his chair, and left the lounge moving more swiftly than Maggie would have thought he could.

The women stared after him. Then Lisa jumped up and followed, walking as quickly as she could in her high-heeled sandals. Glory looked as if her brain had frozen and she was waiting for it to reboot. Then she too got up abruptly and hurried after her sister, holding her hand over her mouth.

Bonnie McCue hurried across the room and dropped into the chair beside Hope.

"Did you hear that?" she asked. "She's dead! Artemis!" She looked as if she might cry.

Hope looked up from her hand. "Wait, who are we talking about?"

"The pop star, Artemis. She killed herself last night."

Hope put her cards down and looked at Bonnie. "How really terrible," she said. "I read the *Boston Herald* this morning, in the library. She had just been arrested."

"That was yesterday's paper. The papers don't get to the village until afternoon. Mr. Rexroth drives down for them every evening."

"Who is Mr. Rexroth?"

"The old guy with the drooly dog? You've seen him. They're out on the porch most of the day because Lisa's poodle is driving his dog crazy."

"The seersucker guy, the minister?"

"He wears the backward collar but he's been retired for years. Or maybe *retired.*" She made air quotes with her fingers. "He may be just a little bit cracked. He's been writing the same sermon since Hurricane Irene."

"How do you *know* all this?" Hope asked, frankly fascinated.

"I got visiting with the girl who was cleaning my room this morning. I love a Chatty Cathy. Mr. Rexroth came here a few summers ago and sort of never left. He goes to Florida for a couple of months in the winters, but otherwise he lives here. He does errands for Mr. Gurrell for a break in his rent."

Just then, as if to illustrate the lecture, Mr. Rexroth strolled in from the front veranda with a bundle of newspapers under his arm. Eyes followed him hungrily as he crossed the lounge to the library. Then in ones and twos, people rose to follow him, like ants converging on a ribbon of syrup.

The Antippas group did not appear for dinner, and everyone agreed that they must be going, or gone, back to California. The papers said the family was "in seclusion," which was sort of true. Jeremy, Sophie, and Ada, Jenny's half-siblings, had been mobbed by paparazzi and had stopped going outside.

The entertainment press were now making a great rhubarb about a funeral, clamoring for an extravaganza, and running placeholder stories about Michael Jackson's death and even about the national grief convulsion at the demise of Rudolph Valentino.

Mr. Rexroth was looking piously pleased during dinner, which he ate alone with his own copy of the *New York Post*. The terrible yapper was leaving and he could resume his quiet pattern of writing in his room in the morning, and strolling with Clarence after lunch by the lake.

Earl took his meals in the kitchen, sometimes early with the kitchen staff, sometimes after the dinner rush. Usually Sarah would make a plate for him and keep it in the warming oven, but tonight she had forgotten and was not in the kitchen herself. Oliver, the sous-chef, said she had a migraine and had gone to bed. Mrs. Weaver assembled dinner for Earl and sat with him while he ate.

"I had about all I could take," Earl said to her. "That dog upset Walter. It upset everybody. Oughtn't to have pets if you can't teach 'em."

"No, that's right, Earl."

"Sorry what happened to their girl. But I won't be sorry to see the back of them."

"I don't think you're alone there. Would you like more chicken?"

"Is there pie?"

"Yep, I saved some."

"I don't think I'm alone either."

She took his dinner plate away and served him a slice of pie.

Day Four, Wednesday, October 9

When Lisa and Glory were girls, Lisa was the effortlessly pretty one. Glory was the fat competitive one. Their mother had been a beauty, and a model. Like most people, Mrs. Poole valued most what particularly distinguished *her* in the world. She took her daughters to have their legs and armpits waxed when they were barely into puberty, convinced (incorrectly as it happens) that if they never shaved, eventually they wouldn't have to. Waxing hurt, but it was fun to have a spa day with their glamorous mother once a month. They'd all have their faces cleansed and hydrated, their feet pumiced and massaged, and their toenails painted while they ate watercress with minuscule scoops of chicken salad served to them on trays with pink linens. Mrs. Poole also made sure that her daughters were, like her, accomplished equestriennes. Riding clothes were so becoming to a woman. Theirs was a sunny, sporty childhood, uncomplicated except that being a twin is never uncomplicated.

Gloria was her father's girl. One summer when Lisa was confined to a darkened bedroom, not allowed to read or watch TV or think, basically, as she recovered from a severe concussion suffered in a horse show accident, Mr. Poole took Glory on a trip all the way to Vancouver on the TransCanada Rail Express train, just the two of them. They played backgammon for hours as the scenery streamed by, and ate fancy meals in the dining car. She had her own roomette. They saw the Rockies and Beautiful Lake Louise and Vancouver Island. Then they flew down to L.A. for a couple of days, because her father had some business there. What the business was Glory never knew, but they had dinner every night with a woman named Marie Elise whom her father seemed to know extremely well. Marie Elise was chic, funny, and apparently rich in her own right; Mr. Poole reported with something like awe that she was on the boards of several major corporations. Glory learned that everyone in Los Angeles was thin and beautiful and drove exciting cars. The last night they were in town Warren Beatty, a movie star whom their mother had a fantastic crush on, joined their table for dessert; Marie Elise was his financial adviser.

When Glory got home from that trip, she knew what world she wanted to conquer. By the time she was twenty, she was slimmer than Lisa, had had two years of acting classes, and knew all about her best camera angles. A man who had briefly loved her once described her to a casting director as being like a smart animal. Glory assumed he meant she was talented, instinctive, and valuable, like a racehorse, and rather liked it, though the casting director never called.

Wednesday morning, when the mists were hanging low on the hilltops and Maggie joined the morning hikers, there was Glory, in becoming velvety sweats, doing her own set of stretches while she waited for the hike to start. It took all Maggie's restraint to keep from staring at her as Bonnie led the rest of the group in a warm-up routine. After Martin Maynard took off on his run, and Bonnie led the hikers toward the mountain at a brisk clip, Nina Maynard and Maggie fell in with Glory.

"I'm so sorry about Artemis," Maggie said.

"It's really sad," said Nina. "So much talent."

Glory was very fit and it was going to be a strain to keep up with her and still be able to talk.

"You know, it's probably a blessing," Glory said. "She was a mess, that girl. Trouble as long as I've known her."

Maggie and Nina looked at each other, but Glory had her chin up, and her gaze was on the hills, from whence her help might or might not cometh.

"Have you been able to learn any more . . . I mean, do they know why she did it?"

"Was there a note, you mean? It seems not. But the girl *was* an addict. I think she just saw no way out. There wasn't ever going to be a good way for it to end."

"Addicted to what?"

"She never *met* a drug she didn't like. The first time she got drunk, she was like eleven. Found a bottle of some disgusting melon-flavored booze someone had given my sister and drank the whole thing. The nanny found her passed out in her bed covered with vomit."

Nina said, "Wasn't she on that Disney show when she was eleven?"

"Exactly," said Glory. "She had everything a child could want. I mean, what other children *dream* of. Every comfort. Beautiful parents, adorable brother and sisters. And she was famous. She was earning a fortune before she was a teen."

"Sounds like a lot, for a child," said Maggie.

"Exactly," said Glory, missing her point. "She had it all. But you can imagine what it was like for my sister, trying to raise her own children, with Miss Eleven Going on Thirty living down the hall. There wasn't any way to control her. Her manager gave her anything she wanted. Before she could drive, she'd just call a limo. She kept running away from home. What teenager wouldn't, if she could afford anything in the world? The Disney people kept as much of it quiet as they could, but after she aged out of their deal and started making her own records, it was Katie Bar the Door." That was what people had been saying for years in Hollywood about Artemis. Katie Bar the Door.

"Why would anyone do that to a child?"

"Who, the manager? He wanted her working. If she didn't get what she wanted she might get difficult, so he kept her happy. He killed her, really."

There was a silence but for the thud of their shoes on the mountain path, and somewhere an excited blue jay complaining.

"This must have been awful for your sister."

"You have no idea. She was trying to raise her own children with some values, you know? We weren't brought up like that. Our parents were strict. We couldn't date until we were sixteen. Got grounded for swearing or bad grades. Dad had money, I guess, but we didn't know that growing up, there were lots of people in our school richer than us. And the worst thing was, Lisa's kids seemed to idolize Jenny. Lisa had visions of them all following her footsteps. I blame the manager, I really do. He should be arrested."

"Her father must be terribly upset."

Glory strode silently for some time before answering. "He probably is. But he hides it. She's been such a nightmare, and of course, he has three other children to worry about."

They paced onward. The sun was fully up now and the mists were dissipating. Dew sparkled underfoot like scattered crystals, and spiderwebs were etched out in the grasses, and then suddenly, when the sun rose above a certain angle, they disappeared.

Nina asked, "Is her bio mother in the picture? I noticed she's never mentioned."

"She is *long* gone. She just disappeared when Jenny was hardly out of diapers. Never called, never wrote. I'm not even sure what her name was. That was probably the primal wound, if you know what I mean. That was probably the thing that Jenny was never going to get over. My sister tried, she really did, but . . ."

Nina said, "Didn't anyone try to find her, ever? I mean these days . . . Facebook and Google . . ."

"No idea. As far as I know, Jenny wanted nothing to do with her. That was one of the reasons she took a stage name. 'I'm Artemis, I'm Greek, I'm my father's daughter.' She didn't want some awful woman showing up saying 'Mummy's here, where's the money?'"

They had reached the peak of the hill, where Bonnie was waiting. They paused to breathe and drink from their PCB-free water bottles as the others huffed up the last grade and joined them. The view, a sea of evergreens punctuated with hardwoods in their glowing fall gowns, was a rich reward for the effort. Far below them was a farm with a big red barn surrounded by fallow fields, rows of dry yellow corn shocks, and pumpkin patches.

Little Cherry in her gray hoodie, bringing up the rear, told Bonnie she and Mrs. Kleinkramer had seen a snake on the path, sunning itself.

"There are no poisonous snakes in Maine," Bonnie said. "In case you worried."

"That's interesting," said Margaux Kleinkramer.

"I know," said Cherry, looking as if she hadn't enjoyed the experience much anyway.

They started down the back side of the hill, falling into the same groups in which they had climbed.

"I'm so glad I got to see that," said Nina.

"Me too," said Glory. "You miss that in California. Fall colors."

"What time are you all leaving?"

Glory looked confused. Then she sorted it out and said, "Oh we're not leaving. Until the end of the cooking class anyway. It's a perfect place for us to be, really. Who's going to come bother us, the *Bangor Daily News*?"

The morning class was all about soufflés. Savory ones, coffee ones, fruit ones, chocolate ones, of course, and crème anglaise to go with.

Maggie was working with Lisa and Albie Clark, who couldn't get the hang of separating the egg yolks from the whites. He poured the yolks back and forth between the broken halves of the shell, which Sarah had made look so easy, but he kept piercing the yolk and leaking yellow droplets into the bowl of transparent egg slime.

"The whites won't whip if you do that," said Lisa impatiently, and Albie snapped, "I know!" Putting these two together on this of all mornings might not have been Sarah's best idea, Maggie thought. Meanwhile Lisa was on a talking jag.

"My husband's had no sleep at all. We've been on the phone, getting our lawyers to try to stop this circus.

Her goddamn manager is going to milk it for every dime. Death is a great career move, that's his take. He's busy arranging a tribute concert in I don't know, the goddamn Hollywood Bowl or something. It's disgusting. Meanwhile the children have gone all sentimental, Oh poor Jenny, and they want a *funeral,* with the body there. I'd go, I mean she is their sister, not that she ever did anything in her life except disappoint them. But Alex says absolutely not. It's a sin, what she did. Life is all we have. He grew up very poor, you wouldn't think it but I mean *dirt* poor. In Greece. He lived in like, a hovel. It's hard for him, to see how much these kids have. He says he gave Jenny everything and she treated it all like garbage. Him, me, the children, herself, garbage. That's what he says. I guess he's broken up but he isn't showing it, and you know what? I admire him. So we're not going back. Not for some funeral circus, anyway. The children can do what they want. I remember when the twins had their Sweet Sixteen, it was out in Southampton. We had a tent, and some famous band, the Black Eyed Peas, have you heard of them? And all their boarding school friends came out for the weekend, it was the party of the summer, I mean it, and at midnight on the best night of their lives my girls were in tears because *Jenny* wasn't coming. They told all their friends she would be there. Jenny was in *New York* that weekend. It wasn't like she was in Outer Oshkosh. It was always like that. Their birthdays, Christmas—she sent expensive presents. Tickets to her shows, backstage passes. But she was never there when it counted, when it wasn't about her. I think that time her excuse was some guy had broken up with her. Please."

Albie said, "The music from that party went on until three in the morning."

Lisa looked at him. "Oh did you read about it? There was a lot of ink. My husband is very generous to the Suffolk County police, he says it always pays, and he gave them a really nice present the day of the party."

"I know," said Albie. "I called them."

Lisa looked blank.

"You called the police?"

"At one in the morning, yes."

"Why?"

"I live two lanes over from you."

There was a long silence. Finally Lisa said, "Oh."

Maggie found that Oliver, Sarah's assistant, was with them. He said "Does anyone need any help here?"

"He does," said Lisa, and pointed to the egg whites with splats of yolk in them. Maggie resumed shaving chocolate into a mound of fatty brown shards.

Oliver set Albie's bowl aside and said, "This will make a delicious egg-white omelet. Let's start over. Go wash your hands." When Albie came back, he showed him how to separate the eggs by cradling the yolks in his cupped hands and letting the whites slip through his fingers.

"So I assume you gave Jenny a Sweet Sixteen party too," Albie said to Lisa as he cracked his third egg sharply on the bowl's edge.

Lisa whirled to stare at him. Then said, "You know what? I just lost a child, so fuck you. Just fuck you." She threw down her dish towel and marched out of the kitchen.

Hope had nipped out to the herb garden to gather some thyme to scent her cheese soufflé when Lisa emerged from the side veranda, weeping. Her husband was sitting on his Adirondack chair in the sun, smoking a cigar and looking out over the lake. Hope couldn't help but overhear the angry sobbing. Nor could she help being more than a little curious.

"We have to go home" was Lisa's main theme. Her husband, impassive, took out his handkerchief and handed it to her to mop her streaming eyes and nose. "I don't want to talk to that prick ever again. And that's how everyone will be, they're all going to say it was our fault. That asshole practically said no one loved her."

"I'm not sure I even liked her, after she got to twelve," said her husband.

"You can't say things like that! They're going to be like, 'what kind of Sweet Sixteen did little Jenny get,' for the rest of our lives!"

"So what?" asked Alex.

"So what?! So what?! What is the matter with you?"

He stood up swiftly and suddenly, so that they were almost nose to nose.

"There is nothing the matter with me," he roared. "I know who I am, and where I stand, and how I got here, and that's all there is. What's the matter with *you*, that you care so much what other people say? Are you so empty?"

"The goddamn queen of England cared, when people were like 'She's so cold, she doesn't care Diana died, she probably had her killed,' " yelled Lisa.

"Nobody thinks we had Jenny killed. It was all too clear that she was doing a fine job of that herself!"

"Stop being an asshole! Don't you see what it's going to be like? Tomorrow, or the next day, my children will be walking into some chapel at Forest Lawn, or wherever, with every fucking news truck in California filming, and if we aren't there with them . . ."

Alex slapped her, hard across the face. "You don't call me an asshole. Ever," he said.

With a whap, she slapped him in return. "And you don't hit me! Ever!"

He started to laugh.

"Jesus, you are a sick bastard," she yelled, starting to cry again. "We are going home. I'm going to take the car into town, where I can see the news and use my phone and then I'm going to charter a fucking plane, and we are going home."

Alex took car keys from his pocket and tossed them to her. "Suit yourself," he said, and sat down. "She was *my* daughter and I'm not going. Not just to put on a show. And I think your sister is enjoying her cooking course."

Lisa had started away, but now she came back and stood over him. "Oh, is that your plan? You and Glory stay here and this will give you a chance to get into her pants again?"

Alex paid her no attention. He was concentrating on relighting his cigar.

"Sometimes I hate your fucking guts!" his wife yelled, and she stalked off in the direction of the parking lot.

Deputy Sheriff Babbin was lounging around, shooting the breeze with Janet, the Bergen town clerk, when the call came. It was a lady from OnStar. Janet handed Buster the receiver.

"We have a disabled vehicle on the Kingdom Road in Bergen," said the OnStar operator. "GPS puts her about two-thirds of a mile out of town, right before the Dump Road turnoff."

"Is the driver hurt? Called an ambulance?"

"Driver is conscious but confused. Air bags deployed."

"Roger that. I'm on my way," said Buster. "Better call the ambulance just to be safe. And get ahold of Pete at the Lakeview Garage. Send a truck." He hitched his pants and put on his sheriff's hat. "Accident up the Kingdom Road," he said briskly to Janet.

"Drive safe," she said, knowing Buster liked nothing better than to turn on the siren and drive eight hundred miles an hour to answer a call about a cat in a tree. Even though it was the firefighters who got cats down.

When Buster reached the car, a huge Cadillac, he found the lady at the wheel still talking to her dashboard. She had been crying, and one side of her face was beginning to swell.

"I don't think it's broken," she was saying as she rotated her wrist in the air, wincing. She was pretty in a sort of plastic way, like people on television. She had clearly taken a curve too fast. Her rear wheels had clipped the guardrail and started a spin, he guessed. The guardrail was torn out and the right front tire was hanging entirely in the air over the drop. The nose of the car was crumpled against a power pole, the hood accordioned, but the pole had saved her life.

"A policeman is here," the lady said to the dashboard.

"That's good," said the dashboard. "Do you want me to stay on the line?"

"Did you just tell me you called a tow truck?"

"I did, ma'am. It's on the way. And an ambulance."

"Okay. Okay. Thank you."

"You're welcome, ma'am. You have a nice day."

The woman looked up at Buster. "I'm alive," she said, as if really asking for confirmation.

"You are," he said. "Do you think you can get out of the car?"

She considered. "I don't know. Do you think I should?"

"If you can. I think it'd be safer."

She was talking as if she were translating each word he uttered from a foreign language. "Safer. Oh."

"Have you tried opening the door?"

She shook her head no. She pushed a button to unlock the doors and the buttons popped. So the electricals were working. He wasn't sure that was a real good thing. If the gas tank was breached or the . . . well, he thought of sparks and he thought of gasoline and it seemed to him it might not be good. He tried the door. It was jammed, but not as badly as the door on the other side of the vehicle. He was weighing the possibility that really putting his weight into getting the door open might dislodge the car and send it farther over the edge, when Pete arrived in the tow truck.

The cooking class was eating a late lunch in the glassed-in porch looking out toward the mountains. Oliver was telling a story about catering a private fundraiser in San Francisco for the president when Maggie said, "Isn't that a police car coming up the drive?"

Everyone stopped chewing and turned to look at the sedan, with its blue roof light revolving silently to announce the urgent business of the officer at the wheel. Buster parked directly at the front steps, beside the NO PARKING sign. As if he felt eyes or a camera on him, he left the car, hat firmly on his large round head, and marched importantly into the inn.

The table started to buzz with questions. Accident? Crime? Accident?

Cherry Weaver came to the door of the porch with Buster right behind her.

"That one," Cherry said, pointing to Glory.

"Miss Poole?" said Buster, stepping forward.

Everyone looked at Glory, who had covered her mouth with her hands when Cherry spoke, and gone rigid. Her eyes filled with tears.

"Everything's all right, ma'am," said Buster, sounding like a policeman on television.

"My sister?"

"She's going to be fine, ma'am."

Glory sprang up and hurried to Buster just as Mr. Gurrell rushed up behind them. "You can use my office," he said. "Come this way."

When they had gone, the buzz of curiosity resumed. "Accident!" "Lisa?" "Hospital?" people asked each other.

"What was that sign you were making to Buster?" Maggie asked Hope.

"I was trying to tell him to take off his hat."

"Who's Buster?" asked Nina.

"My son."

"The sheriff is your son?"

"Deputy sheriff. And it's a long story," said Hope.

No one knew what to do next. Dessert had not yet been served, and apparently no one was dead, except for Artemis. Yet to resume chattering about whether it made a difference to whip egg whites by hand or in a mixer seemed wrong.

Oliver said, "All right, troops. We need an organizing principle. Hope is the mother of the local sheriff. Now everyone tell something about themselves that the rest of us don't know."

This was met with a murmur of relief. Oh good, parlor games. Oliver turned to Martin, who was on his right. "You're up."

Martin's wife looked delighted. "This'll be good. There's nothing I don't know about you."

Martin said, "I can play the tuba."

"Shut *up*," said Nina. "You can not."

"I played tuba in my junior high school marching band," he insisted.

"You are lying."

"If I am, no one can prove it because no one ever has a tuba handy."

Nina bopped him on the head with her napkin as she said, "In high school I was junior runner-up sewing champion of Indiana."

No one doubted her and all were pleased. Teddy Bledsoe said he could do the tango. Margaux Kleinkramer was a level 90 orc shaman in World of Warcraft. "Whoa," said Oliver, impressed.

Homer Kleinkramer had gone helicopter skiing in Alaska in a group that included the king of Spain. Bonnie McCue said that Billy Joel once kissed her on the lips. Albie Clark had been a nationally ranked squash player. Oliver was fluent in Japanese. Maggie said she had once expelled a boy from school whose mother then came into the building and tried to shoot her.

They all saw Buster's car pull off down the driveway. Mr. Gurrell came back to the door.

"Mrs. Antippas had an accident on the way down the mountain," he said. "I knew you'd want to know. She's been taken to the hospital in Ainsley. The EMTs said she didn't appear to be badly injured but she's in shock, and she might have a concussion. She's asked for her sister to come and to bring her some things."

"Does Glory need a car?" Martin asked, reaching for his keys.

"No, Mr. Rexroth will drive her. Miss Poole will be in touch with me as soon as she knows more, and I'll let you all know."

As he left, a girl arrived with a tray of dessert soufflés, and Oliver said, "Hope, it's your turn."

"I already went. My son is the deputy sheriff of Bergen," she said, and chose a coffee soufflé.

He made a buzzer sound, like a wrong answer noise on a quiz show. "We all already know that."

After a pause, she said, "You're cheating, but all right. I can read astrological charts."

Maggie stared at Hope. Hope shrugged. "I used to be sent to my grandmother's in Maryland. There was nothing on earth to do there. Her Catalan cook had a little business going out the back door, doing readings. She didn't want me to tell, so she offered to teach me."

"I think you're going to have to prove it," said Teddy Bledsoe.

"Fine," said Hope. "You're a Pisces."

Teddy gave an appreciative hoot and slapped the table. "I am a *triple* Pisces!"

"I'm not a bit surprised," said Hope.

"What does that even *mean*?" asked Maggie.

"And you," said Hope to Nina, "are a Sagittarian."

"I'm a what?"

"When's your birthday?"

"December first."

"I rest my case," said Hope.

The head of housekeeping was in Mr. Gurrell's office. Mrs. Antippas's dog had been in room 6G yowling, since midmorning. When the girl went in to clean, it snarled at her, and then went to the bathroom on the carpet. She had just gone to ask Mr. Antippas to take the dog, so the room could be ready for when the sisters came back, but he had his DO NOT DISTURB sign out, apparently taking a nap after lunch. His room reeked of cigar smoke, by the way. She'd found a cigar butt floating in his toilet yesterday, disgusting, like he forgot to flush. Someone had to get the dog out of the room, and *she* wasn't going to do it, she drew the line, he knew when he hired her that she wouldn't deal with animals . . .

Gabriel Gurrell was pinching his knees under the desk to distract himself so he wouldn't shout at her. She was a very good housekeeper, but high-strung, and once she got going like this you practically had to tackle her to get her to stop.

"I'll take care of . . . Mrs. Eaton, I'll . . . Mrs. Eaton!" he finally raised his voice. Then he added, "I'm sorry. I know it's been difficult. I will have Cherry take the dog for a walk, and please apologize to the staff for me. There was an accident this morning, you know, and we're all upset."

Mrs. Eaton knew all about the accident. Everyone in the house did. They all knew about the girl's death in California too, the singer, and they thought Mr. Antippas was a . . .

"Thank you, Mrs. Eaton," Gabriel said. "Everyone is under strain."

"They are. Chef is very upset. Earl is upset."

"I'll take care of it. Thank you for coming to me." He was on his feet, guiding her to the door. When she had disappeared up the stairs he went down to find Cherry.

Cherry was lounging behind the reception desk, reading a magazine and chewing gum. She jumped up when she saw him coming, stowed the magazine, and spit the gum into her hand and hid it behind her back.

"Cherry," he said.

"What?" No more 'Yes, Mr. Gurrell?' Now that she knew she wasn't staying on she'd reverted to the sullen manners that were apparently her default mode.

"A couple of things. When the deputy arrived this morning, you should have called me rather than dealing with it yourself."

"You said I was to take initiative."

"But this was rather a special case, don't you think?"

"Yes I do. I did. Buster said he needed to see Mrs. Antippas's sister right away and I knew where she was so I took him. Anyway it wasn't morning."

Now she was just being rude. She was really a very hostile little item, Gabriel thought. He sighed impatiently and hitched his shoulders back. Stand straight.

Maintain your dignity. You're the one who always has to eat the crow if you're in the hospitality business. Clearly the Cherry situation was deteriorating fast, but at this minute, he needed her, if he didn't want a domino effect cascading through the staff.

"Afternoon then. You're right about that."

"I know."

"I've come to you about something else though. With Mrs. Antippas in the hospital, and her sister gone, I need someone to walk the little dog. The maid hasn't been able to clean the room and—"

"You know what, I quit. I quit right now. I know you already fired me but I still quit, I am not a fucking dog walker. I don't even like dogs."

"Cherry! Remember where you are!" Gabe was trying to whisper.

"That slobbering horse you made me walk last time dragged me halfway around the lake, I've still got blisters on my feet, you try it in fucking high heels!"

"That was unavoidable and I told you how much I—"

"Oh shut up. I know you think I'm stupid, you blame me for everything. Walk the damn dog yourself." Suddenly she started to cry and began to unbutton her Oquossoc Mountain Inn jacket.

"Cherry! Please!"

Furiously, Cherry threw the jacket onto the reception desk. There was a gob of chewing gum stuck to it. She began unzipping her skirt. Gabriel was horrified.

"Cherry!" Gabriel cried helplessly. "You're in a public space!"

She took off the skirt and threw that on the desk. Then she took off one tan faux patent leather pump and threw it at him, and found it so satisfying that she did the same with the other one. Then she stalked off in her blouse and ragged slip, through which you could see her magenta thong underpants.

The cooking class had a rather antic quality in the afternoon of that day. With both blond interlopers gone, the mood was oddly bubbly. People kept asking Hope if she would do their charts.

"I *knew* this would happen, that's why I never tell people. Anyway you need to know what time of day you were born."

"I know mine," said Teddy. "March eighteenth, 1965, Houston, Texas, four-thirteen A.M."

"I'll call my mother and find out," said Nina.

"I'm February fifteenth," said Margaux Kleinkramer, "and I know I was born right after midnight because my father said I had a red ribbon in my hair. I'd just missed Valentine's Day."

By the end of the class Hope had everyone's birth date and place, and she had promised to take her laptop to town and see what she could do. She also had no idea how to make the ceviche or gravlax the rest had been working on but Maggie said she'd teach her. And that, by the way, her own birthday was October 16.

"I know," said Hope, "and you have Scorpio rising. I did your chart ages ago."

"You did?"

"I was on the search committee that hired you, re-member?"

"You mean you chose me based on my *sun sign,* or whatever it's called?" Maggie was offended.

"Of course not, we chose you because you are won-derful. I just find it a useful tool."

Maggie was slightly cool to Hope the rest of the class.

It was teatime when Mr. Rexroth's seedy Grand Marquis made its way majestically up the drive. He parked in front of the steps, then got out and started around the car to help Lisa get out, but Glory got to her sister first. Maggie and Teddy Bledsoe, playing bridge with Bonnie and Nina, watched the arrival from their table in the bow window of the lounge. The whole right side of Lisa's face was black and blue and swollen, the eye nearly swallowed within puffy purple-green bruising, the skin stretched shiny and taut. Both her right wrist and foot were in high-tech splints involving a lot of Velcro. Glory put her arm around her sister and acted as her crutch as she negotiated the porch stairs. Neither woman seemed to be speaking to Mr. Rexroth. He busied himself with producing a wheelchair from the trunk of the car and setting it up for Lisa at the top of the porch stairs.

Mr. Gurrell hurried out from behind the reception desk to see if he could help.

"Just send a bucket of ice up to our room," said Glory shortly. "And tell Mr. Antippas his wife is back."

Ten minutes later, Glory reappeared.

"Did you find Mr. Antippas?" she demanded.

"We're looking for him."

"How hard could it be? He isn't small."

"We think he may have gone for a walk," said Mr. Gurrell.

"That would be a first," said Glory acidly.

"I'm a little short-staffed at the moment but someone has gone to look."

"And has the rental car arrived?"

"Yes, Miss Poole. It's in the parking lot. Would you like the keys?"

"Yes. I'll bring it around and you can send a bell-man for our bags."

Glory swept out.

A few minutes later, she was back, furious. "They brought a stick shift! It's a fucking stick!" she yelled at Mr. Gurrell. He looked rather frightened.

"I'm sorry—I'm sorry, did you tell me you needed an automatic? I'm afraid I didn't hear that, this was all they had in Bangor. It's an Escalade. I thought you'd be so pleased . . ."

"I can't drive a fucking stick, and my sister can't drive at all for at least a month. They'll just have to bring another one. The plane will be waiting for us."

"But this was the last car they had, at least the last sedan, and you said . . ."

"Oh for Christ sake, well obviously if they didn't have a sedan I could drive you should have ordered something else."

Mr. Gurrell didn't answer, though he looked un-happy, and after a silence even Glory seemed to realize that this wasn't his fault, though she wanted it to be somebody's.

"Then call us a taxi. There must be a taxi in this shit hole."

"Well—no. I might be able to get one to come from Ainsley, but at this time of day, she's usually having her supper. Mr. Rexroth might be willing . . ."

"Forget that. That guy is creepy weird and his car is a death trap."

"Miss Poole, do you really think your sister should travel tonight? She didn't look as if she . . ."

"She wants to go home. That's what she wants. She's going to that funeral if she has to go on a gurney. Call the rental people and have them send another car."

"Miss Poole. This was all they had. I'm afraid they'd have to find someone to come from Portland, four hours both ways . . ."

"Look. If the president of the United States wanted a car here tonight, they'd get one here, right?"

"I imagine so . . ."

"Well then get one here. That is all. Make it happen."

Mr. Gurrell looked as if he didn't think it was going to help, but he started to dial.

He was on the phone, saying, "Three people, I think. And a dog. Wait, I'll ask. Miss Poole?" when Earl shambled up to the desk.

"Found 'im," he said sourly. "Last place I looked. His wife's room. Heard them yelling at each other from a floor below."

The elevator doors opened, and Mr. Antippas appeared, half-smoked cigar in one hand.

"This is like a three-ring circus," said Teddy happily. Then returning his attention to the game, he added, "The rest are mine," and swept up the tricks on the table.

In retrospect, there were people who might have offered to make the drive to Bangor with the sisters. Martin Maynard could have done it, but he didn't hear about the scene in the lounge until he was halfway through dinner and well launched on a very nice bottle of zinfandel. Hope could have offered, but she'd already spent several hours in the village using the library wi-fi and wanted her supper. No one felt much inclined to devote the evening to solving the Antippas family's problems.

Mr. Gurrell couldn't leave the front desk, and it didn't occur to him to see if someone else on staff was willing to go. The hotel van was in the shop for inspection and now the garage was closed. The staff parking lot was full of junkers, and you never could tell who was or wasn't keeping up their insurance. Much as he wanted all three of them gone, four counting the dog, he assumed the family would be litigious, and the last thing he needed was an accident laid at his door, followed by a lawsuit. Besides, no one who had seen Mrs. Antippas thought she should be traveling. She had looked as if she should still be in the hospital. Her face was a mess—could the pressure of a flight be good for that? And concussions were tricky.

Chef Sarah had another migraine. The cooking class members had broken into small groups and were taking their dinners in the dining room. Mr. Antippas was at a table for two against the wall, by himself, eating steadily with his napkin tucked into his shirt to protect his tie, and his full lips were bright with grease from the roasted pork on his fork. Maggie and Hope were at a table for four with Albie Clark. About halfway through the meal, Glory came into the dining room. Maggie, who was facing the door, saw her take one look at her brother-in-law holding a piece of crisp pork skin in his fingers and ripping at it with his even white Hollywood teeth, and then head straight to Maggie. She dropped into their open chair and said, "Can I sit with you?"

All three expressed welcome, whatever they may have felt.

"How is your sister?" Maggie asked.

"Fucked. I don't think she'll ever look the same. She wanted a mirror but I wouldn't give her one. A double gin martini, rocks, with a twist," she said to the waiter who had materialized beside her.

"And to eat?" he asked.

Glory made a dismissive gesture. "Anything. Whatever they're having." As all three at the table were eating different things this didn't help him much. "One cheekbone is two inches higher than the other, she looks like a Picasso," said Glory. "The nerves on that side of her face are crushed. They don't know if they'll come back or not." Glory's own makeup was smeary, and she looked raddled. She loves her sister, Maggie registered, with a little surprise.

"*He* was a big help," she added bitterly, jerking her head toward her brother-in-law. "I could really kill him. He *laughed* at her for wrecking the car, and stone-cold refused to drive us to the airport, even though the plane is waiting. She just wants to go home. She was crying," said Glory, and she began to cry herself.

The martini arrived and she gulped it. Hope patted her shoulder. After a bit Glory found a ratty Kleenex in her pocket and blew her nose. "She's asleep now. It was bad when the pain meds started to wear off. She didn't want to take more, she really doesn't like drugs, but I made her, and she did feel better and then she went to sleep. They told me not to say the name of the pain meds out loud, for fear someone will mug her for them. Around here it's called redneck heroin. Did you ever just want to stick someone with a knife and twist it?" She looked over at Alex Antippas, who was solemnly pondering selections from the cheese cart with the air of one whose decisions could bring peace to the Middle East.

Hope signaled to the waiter and ordered lobster bisque and a bowl of pasta for Glory.

"You need comfort food," she said kindly. Glory ignored her and ordered another martini.

Buster Babbin lived in a trailer in a clearing just north of Bergen. His neighbor owned the land but was glad to let Buster live there. The neighbor was getting on in years and none of his children had stayed in the area to farm, so it was good to have a young man nearby, especially a deputy sheriff. It deterred people from jacking deer in his driveway, right up by the house the way they used to, scaring his wife, and it meant their road got plowed out right quick during snowstorms. The town paid good money to have Buster on the job, and he wasn't any use if he couldn't get out of his driveway.

Also Buster was handy. He had got his trailer up on cement blocks, and set about building a thing he called a studio onto the back of his house, and it was handsome. Had a high ceiling with a skylight in it, and a big wood-burning stove to heat it, and he'd put in a well and septic, all improvements to the property. The studio was where Buster would paint his watercolors in the evening. He was real good, the neighbors thought. When you looked at Buster's pictures, you could tell right away what it was a picture of. Also he had a dish on his roof that gave him TV from Bangor, and an Internet signal. He didn't put a password on it either, so when their children came to visit they could sit in their cars outside Buster's house and pick up their e-mail, which was a big improvement over hearing them bitch about having to drive into town to use the library wi-fi, or up to the Subway shop in the Tradewinds Market in Bergen Falls.

Buster was contracted to the town—well to the three towns, Bergen, West Bergen, and Bergen Falls—from the sheriff's department in Ainsley. He was a peace officer more than anything, parking his cruiser near the high school when school let out, or when there was a game, driving around in the evenings to watch for DUIs, responding to domestic disputes and animal control calls. He'd joined the Bergen Grange and the Oddfellows, and was well liked in the village. He was real good with the teenagers, who tended to get into trouble just out of being balked and bored. Mostly minor scrapes but you didn't want them becoming major. Kids with no place to go would break into hunting camps to party

and leave a mess. They'd make off with peoples' out-
board motorboats in the summer and zoom around the
lake at night. Sometimes crash somewhere, but mostly
just run it out of gas and leave it full of beer cans. The
kids in town tended to tell Deputy Babbin the truth,
even when they'd screwed up and knew there was pun-
ishment coming. It didn't hurt that everyone knew he'd
been a bad boy himself at one time.

There were a couple of hard cases in the neighborhood, guys who'd gone to Iraq or Afghanistan and come
back wrecked, who stockpiled guns, and beat up their
wives and children, and knew they were driving away
the people who loved them but couldn't stop. One guy
had disappeared into the woods where he was probably cooking meth, and another one flew the American
flag upside down outside his house, marine in trouble,
and man, was he ever. His wife had taken the children
and moved back in with her parents in Totten, and he
would get a snootful and drive to their house and stand
on the lawn roaring that if she didn't come back he
would kill all of them. When he was sober he could
understand what was wrong with that strategy, but he
was rarely sober. More than once Buster had talked
him down, locked up his guns, and let him sleep in his
studio until he sobered up because he knew that most
of all, the guy shouldn't be alone.

There had been only one capital crime in Buster's bailiwick since he got the job: two summers ago, after a night of drinking, a young woman had pushed her boyfriend out of the car and run over him on purpose. Twice. She rolled over him going forward and then she put it in reverse and gunned it backward until she'd made two sets of tracks across his T-shirt, right below where it read DO I *LOOK* LIKE A FUCKING PEOPLE PERSON? Buster caught that call.

This call, from the Oquossoc Mountain Inn at 2:14 in the morning of Thursday, October 10, was not for police, but for the fire department. Buster's radio crackled to life on the kitchen table. His girlfriend Brianna, who was a light sleeper, heard it first. She pulled up her sleep mask, peered at the clock, then gave Buster a poke. She resettled the mask and felt for the yellow earplugs that lay beside the clock. Buster made an awful lot of noise crashing around the tiny room getting dressed in a hurry in the dark.

He was in the cruiser heading up the hill when the Bergen fire truck passed him. He already knew it was a structure fire up at the inn. When the fire truck from Bergen Falls caught up with him and sped past, sirens screaming, he knew it was no paint fire in the garden shed.

Day Five, Thursday, October 10

It was 2:18 in the morning when Maggie was roused by a pounding on her door.

"Fire!" shouted a panicky voice she thought was Mr. Gurrell's. "Leave everything, close the door behind you, and come down the stairs at the end of the hall." She'd been wakened from a strange but vivid dream about a fire drill in her school in Washington thirty years ago. Somewhere a smoke alarm was shrilling.

She shouted to tell him she was on her feet, and she heard him move down the hall, banging and shouting. "Shut your door behind you! Don't use the elevator! Hurry!"

By the time Maggie got outside there was an orange light in the sky from the mountain side of the building. Mr. Gurrell, with Clarence the bloodhound on a leash, stood looking at the dancing light above the roofline of his hotel. Maggie wondered where Mr. Rexroth was. Hope, who had come out right behind her, was wearing her own flimsy blue velour dressing gown, while Maggie was in the terry cloth bathrobe provided by the hotel. Quite a few evacuees were wearing these white bathrobes, which made the lawn look like an odd convention of nurses or nuns.

"The fire seems to be on the other side," said Hope. "Do you think we can go back in and get warmer clothes? I'm freezing."

"I doubt it," said Maggie, who had supervised about a million fire drills in her time.

The night was chilly and the moon about to set. The only illumination they had came from the porch lights and a lamp beside the side door. As her eyes adjusted, Maggie discerned Mr. Rexroth emerging from the fire stairs half-carrying Lisa Antippas. Lisa was weeping, either from pain or resentment of Mr. Rexroth. Glory was right behind them, carrying the little dog and her sister's jewelry case. Behind her came that gardener man, Earl, who was, oddly, fully dressed and had a parrot peeking out from inside his jacket. *He* seemed to be crying too. His gait was painful to see. Maggie watched him hurry in his bobbing way around the end of the lakeside wing toward the wing of the building where the blaze was.

After a cold stretch that felt like an hour but was probably about fifteen minutes, Hope spotted Chef Sarah wearing blue jeans and a parka. She was carrying a stack of blankets she must have taken from the housekeeping room.

"Thank God," said Hope. "Someone thought of something useful. It's all I can do to keep from tackling her and taking them all."

When Sarah got to Hope and Maggie, Maggie said, "How come you get to wear a parka and we're all wearing our stupid bathrobes?"

"You forget, I live here," said Sarah. "Winter clothes always at the ready. Blanket? Can you share?"

They accepted a blanket, and Hope said, "I'll give you a million dollars for those gloves. Look at my fingers." She turned on the flashlight in her cell phone, and Maggie and Sarah could see that the fingertips were pinched-looking and white with a greenish tinge. "I have Tourneau's syndrome."

"Raynaud's," said Maggie. "Tourneau is where you bought your watch."

Sarah said, "Make it two million."

"Done," said Hope. Sarah gave her the gloves.

"I'm putting you in my will," said Hope. "How's the migraine?"

"Horrible," said Sarah. Hope and Maggie wrapped themselves together and watched Sarah move on, offering blankets.

"She's a class act," said Maggie.

"I'm in love with these gloves," said Hope. "I hope she never wants them back."

"How are your feet?"

"I have no idea, I've gone completely numb below the ankles."

"Well, I think we're all accounted for, here," said Maggie having checked the group on the lawn for the rest of the cooking class. "I'd like to go see the fire." They could hear sirens now, in the distance but approaching fast.

"Let's do it," said Hope. It took them a minute to figure out how to walk together without wrenching the blanket from each other. "A little like a three-legged sack race," said Maggie, who had also presided over about a million of those. They made their way around to the mountain side, arriving just in time to see the fire truck from Bergen race into the parking lot, sirens screaming, followed by Buster in his patrol car, who bathed the scene in lurid blue light from his revolving roof lamp. He skidded to a stop, and his siren died with a disappointed sigh. Hope and Maggie watched Buster rush to the volunteer fire chief and commence a powwow. They were pointing up at the second-floor windows as the fire hoses began to shoot mighty streams toward the blaze.

Maggie counted windows, left to right. The place where the flames were best established was not hard to spot.

"I bet it's Mr. Antippas's room," said Maggie. She and Hope looked at each other. They knew they hadn't seen him in the group at the other side of the building. "Those disgusting cigars," said Hope.

They watched in silence as more and more of the group from the lake side of the building came around to see the damage. Lisa (Maggie learned later) had been wrapped warmly and installed in one of the Adirondack chairs on the lawn, but Glory appeared in the parking lot. Maggie had been watching for her, and observed her carefully as she looked at the site of the blaze. Her expression was oddly blank, Maggie noted.

In the meantime, Deputy Babbin was taking pictures.

The flames were declared extinguished by 3:30 A.M. The firefighters had been through the building and pronounced it safe, all except the section where the fire had started, where there was smoke and water damage and the roof was compromised. The ruin was confined to a fairly narrow area, and Mr. Gurrell was begging the firemen to let him send his guests back inside to their rooms in the other wings.

"Come on," said Hope, and she started the sack-race process with Maggie toward where the deputy sheriff now stood with the fire chief and a number of the firemen.

"Buster, what's going on?" she asked, then turned to the firefighters. "You all did a magnificent job, thank you *so* much. Can we go back to bed now?"

The fire chief looked at Buster, unsure how to respond.

"I'm Hope Babbin, Buster's mother," said Hope, extending her hand. "Pardon my glove," she added. He shook it and said, "Denny Robertson." Since things were suddenly taking on the aspect of a debutante tea, Maggie extended her hand from under the blanket and said "Maggie Detweiler." Chief Robertson shook her hand too.

"Please let us go. My feet are blocks of ice."

The two men looked at each other.

By this time most of the onlookers had gathered around the two who seemed most likely to be able to make a decision.

Buster turned to Mr. Gurrell. "Gabe, is there a place where we can meet inside? No need to keep these people out in the cold any longer."

"The dining room has the most chairs," said Gabe. He looked to Chef Sarah, who nodded her agreement. She was looking ashen and ill. Migraines are no fun, thought Maggie.

"Do you want just the guests in there?"

"No, everyone on the premises." Deputy Babbin went to his car for his portable megaphone.

"Attention," he said through the megaphone, which broadcast at earsplitting volume. "Attention everyone. This is Deputy Sheriff Babbin speaking. It is safe to reenter the lake view wing of the building. Please proceed directly to the dining room. Please use the—" He stopped and asked Mr. Gurrell how to get to the dining room without going through the halls of the affected area of the building.

"Please proceed to the door over there, and Mr. Gurrell will direct you inside."

"Can I just go back to my room and put on a pair of pants?" asked Margaux Kleinkramer, making herself perfectly audible by raising her voice.

"Please do not go back to your rooms first," said Buster through his bullhorn. "Please proceed directly to the dining room," but in spite of his magnified authority, at least a dozen people had already left the group and were hurrying into the hotel.

"Poor Buster," said Hope, as she and Maggie moved toward the building. It was a good half hour before the guests were all reassembled in the dining room, almost all of them in more dignified garb than their bathrobes. The dining room was warm and bright, and Oliver was serving coffee and hot boullion and had put out plates of petits fours and macaroons.

After confirming with Mr. Gurrell that everyone was present, Buster called the meeting to order. Maggie and Hope took seats toward the back so as not to distract Buster in his moment of glory. Also Maggie automatically liked to be where she could see the whole room, just to keep track of who was passing notes or making spitballs or texting when they shouldn't be; it was instinctive. There were a couple of staff people present whom she didn't recognize, who must be on duty through the night in case of housekeeping or other emergencies. The cooking class she knew of course, and Mr. Rexroth and Earl, Mr. Gurrell. There were two young couples who had arrived the afternoon before to spend the night on their way to Montreal. Glory and her sister were missing, and there was a boy/ man she'd never seen before sitting near them, taking feverish notes. That would be a member of the fourth estate, she guessed. Either the Ainsley weekly paper had a stringer in town, or this was a high school kid hoping to get lucky and sell his first bylined story.

Buster introduced himself.

"You've all had a long night, I know, and I'm sorry to have to detain you further, but there was a casualty this evening. The fire started in the bedroom of Mr."—he consulted a piece of paper—"Alexander Antippas and I'm sorry to tell you, the gentleman did not survive."

There was an electrified stir and murmur at this news, although many had expected it, having seen for themselves where the fire had been, and noted that he was not among them.

"Chief Robertson and I have examined the site, and we have no choice but to designate it a crime scene. There's a forensic crew on its way from Augusta, and no unauthorized persons will be allowed into that part of the building until the Major Crimes Unit has done its work. Until we can tell if there's been foul play or not, we must ask you all to remain in the hotel."

There was a roar of response. For How Long? Did he mean they couldn't even go outside? People had other plans. They had travel arrangements. They had grandchildren coming to visit, doctor's appointments, were called for jury duty. They had important jobs and busy lives. Gabriel Gurrell wondered, if people were prevented by the police from leaving the hotel, did they have to pay for their rooms and food while they were kept here? And was anyone going to settle Mr. Antippas's enormous bill? Into the middle of this strode Glory, looking to be at the end of her rope.

"My suitcase has been stolen!" she said loudly. "My sister is in pain and my suitcase is gone!"

Knocked off script, Buster seemed to forget what he was doing.

"Wait, Miss Poole, your suitcase was . . . where was the suitcase?"

"In our room."

Buster took his pad from his back pocket and made a note. "And where exactly in your room? Was it in the closet or out in plain sight?"

"In the closet."

"And were there items of value in the suitcase?"

"My sister's pain meds were in it."

"Excuse me, officer," said Martin Maynard. "I have to be in Washington without fail by tomorrow evening. Could we get back to the point here?" And as others piled on with questions and claims about their schedules, the young man with the notepad reached Glory.

"Excuse me, Miss Poole? Are you the sister of Mrs. Antippas?"

Glory agreed that she was.

"So Artemis was your niece?"

With the dawn came the paparazzi. There were several print reporters from Portland, more from Boston, and even one enterprising photographer from New York. There were film crews from the major news channels doing stand-ups in the parking lot with the charred wall of the hotel in the background. A picture of Alex Antippas in happier times, younger, much slimmer, holding a six-year-old Jenny by the hand, was being featured on all the morning news shows. In the picture, both are in bathing suits and both are smiling. There is a turquoise swimming pool glittering behind them.

"I took that picture," Glory said bitterly. "It was in a frame on the piano in my sister's house. Some vulture must have gotten in the door and stolen it. Unless the kids gave it out, but they wouldn't be that stupid." There was also a picture that flashed from time to time of Alex and Lisa, smiling and holding wineglasses at some charity event. In it, Lisa is hugely pregnant.

The television in the bar area off the lounge, which usually played silently when there was a game on, was tuned to Fox News with the sound up. Every seat in the room was taken. Glory sat in the corner with Margaux

Kleinkramer, drinking coffee. From time to time a man from the Major Crimes Unit would come down and summon someone to the bedroom where they were conducting interviews.

"I'm so sorry for your loss," Maggie said, finding a spot near Glory after her own interrogation. "How is your sister?"

"She's sleeping now, finally," said Glory. "Margaux gave her some Valium."

"Does she know what happened to her husband?"

Glory nodded. "I gave her enough oxycodone to knock out a horse last night, so she was pretty out of it when the fire started. But she was in a terrible state this morning. Her memories of the night before were all crazy, but she understood. I don't know what she'll do. They were married for twenty-six years."

Shep Gordon, lead detective of the State Police Major Crimes Unit North, working out of Ainsley, didn't like people from Away. He'd been in the navy. He'd been MP on a mammoth ship he used to patrol riding a brass bicycle (normal bikes rusted at sea). He'd served with all sorts, and he thought they were fine in their places, but not in his. He'd come back from his tour of duty and gone straight into the state police, like his dad. Shep Gordon was enormous. Off duty he rode a Harley and at all times kept his head shaved because if he didn't he had a fluffy little peak of hair on the top of his skull that he thought gave the wrong impression. Back when he was a rookie he used to moonlight as a security guard out at the paper mill. Never had a lick of trouble; bad people did *not* like it when they saw 310 pounds in uniform coming at them. He'd raised six children and an unknown number of mongrel dogs and his policy with all of them, whether they pissed on the floor or used bad language in front of their mother, was "Hit 'em with a newspaper, throw 'em out the door." Only one of the children had turned out very well, and the dogs wouldn't hunt, but he saw no reason to rethink. His girl Marilyn was a corrections officer down in Warren. She was tough and mean and he was proud of her.

Before he rose to his present heights, Shep had been a crime scene technician, having graduated from the Maine Criminal Justice Academy, and had special forensic training at the Royal Canadian Mounted Police College in Ottawa. No one outside the fire marshal's office knew more about arson than he did, so when he got the word that the fire at Oquossoc Inn might be suspicious, and there was at least one body, he let Bangor know that this one was his.

The half circle of driveway at the main entrance to the Inn was clogged with response vehicles. The crime scene van was stopped half-blocking the road, and the deputy sheriff's car, and a half dozen other police cars, plus the private cars of some of the fire-fighters, had pulled in and been left wherever they stopped. Shep clocked the scene, then drove his 4X4 around to the side of the building and into the park-ing lot from which he could see the blown-out window and charred surface of the upper-story room where the fire had burned hottest. It was blackened and wet and no longer smoking. He got out and stood in the bleak early sunlight of what promised to be another heart stopper of a day, and stood studying the patterns of smoke and damage on the outside walls.

Within seconds he was swarmed by a crowd of re-porters from god knows where, asking unbelievably stupid questions. Assholes with flashbulbs, what were they *doing* here? They had a weekly paper in this part of the county that told you who got married, who had died, what went on at the selectmen's meeting, and gave people a place to write in to complain about the road commissioner or to advertise yard sales, and he thought that was about enough in terms of minding other people's beeswax. Once when he had just been promoted he gave an interview to some bimbo from the Bangor Fishwrap. Came out sounding like Jed fucking Clampett. Wasn't ever making that mistake again.

He bulled his way through the swarm of assholes all stretching microphones toward him, yammering. What was the *matter* with these people, couldn't they see he just got here? The two words he kept hearing were *arson* and *Artemis*. What Roman gods had to do with it, he didn't know and didn't care. He wanted to talk to Denny Robertson, big-time.

The Special Response team from the fire marshal's office was working carefully through their list of procedures in Mr. Antippas's charred bedroom when Shep got there. It was a large room, with what had once been pale blue wallpaper. What was left of the paper was now grimed with smoke and peeling in wet strips off the walls. The carpet, once plush navy wall-to-wall he judged, was sodden and mostly melted, especially in the area from the king-size bed to the blown-out glass slider leading to a narrow balcony overlooking the parking lot. The floor-to-ceiling curtains, what was left of them, dangled in wet black tatters from the hooks along the left side of the balcony wall. There had been an enormous old-fashioned TV sitting on the dresser opposite the bed, with built-in DVD and VCR players. The cathode tube had exploded. The rest of the furnishings in the room were a desk and chair by the window, an upholstered chair and a floor lamp, and a bench at the foot of the bed. The deceased's suitcase was in the closet along with his hanging clothes. The floor of the closet was being used as a laundry basket, judging from the socks and enormous wrinkled undershorts tossed there. Farthest from the source of the fire, the contents of the closet were mostly intact. There was a stack of drawers, one containing clean underwear, one with fresh shirts still in their laundry packaging. Nice stuff. Shep checked for labels in the gigantic undershorts to see where they came from but there weren't any. Must be custom-made. Damn.

He went through to the sitting room next to the bedroom, which also overlooked the parking lot and the mountains beyond. The damage here was mostly from water, as someone had left a terrace door open. There was a laptop open on the desk, pretty well soaked. An ice bucket sat on the coffee table full of water, and beside it a coffee cup the victim had been using as an ashtray had a disintegrating cigar butt in it. On the arm of the chair, open and facedown, was a hardcover book. Shep peered at it. *Brothers Karamazov*. That surprised him. Guy was a self-improver, either that or his wife made him join a book club. A coat closet near what served as the front hall of the suite held a hotel safe, locked, and a minibar. Shep opened the minibar and peered in. Expensive nuts, chips, and cookies, all were gone. Other stuff too, probably. The tech guys would have a list.

The electricity was out in this wing of the hotel, so the team had had to set up lights and run extension cords out from the old part of the building. Photographs of the rooms were taken from every angle. There were fingerprints beside the light switch and on the door-knobs. The fingerprint tech had carefully lifted them, after treating them with superglue fumes to heighten their definition. Sketches were being made, measure-ments taken, everything duly noted. Shep went back to the bedroom.

The body on the bed was enormous, even larger than Shep's. It was on its back, lying peacefully on the side of the bed nearest the slider, charred and roasted. If it had been wearing any nightclothes, they were gone now. The facial features were blackened gristle; the lips were burned off so the expression seemed to be all teeth. Padding and upholstery of the headboard was mostly burned away, and the bedcovers were a combination of ash and melted synthetics, stiff and shiny. The crime scene tech was gingerly sampling materials into jars and labeling with precise notes the locations they came from.

Lem Perkins, the local coroner, was lounging in the corner of the room with Buster Babbin, watching.

"Lem," said Shep.

"Shep," said Lem.

"Morning, sir," said Buster. Shep gave him a minuscule tip of the head.

"What've we got here?" he asked Lem.

"White male, about three hundred and forty-five pounds, sixty-one years old, name Alexander Antippas. That's according to Gabe Gurrell. I can't tell much of anything as things are. Don't dare turn him over for fear he'd come all apart. We're waiting for the hearse from Morrison's to come bag him up." Morrison's was the funeral home in Bergen Falls. They would take the corpse to the medical examiner's office in Augusta.

"Cause of death?"

"That's the sixty-four-dollar question. I'm guessing he was dead before the fire started, otherwise why is he just laying there?"

Shep grunted. "What's Denny say? Arson?" He was going to wait for the tech team to finish, but he wanted to have a closer look at the way the fire had moved, where it had been hottest.

"Guy was a smoker," said one of the techs. "Cigars. He might have fallen asleep with one in the bed. Wouldn't be inconsistent with what we've found so far."

"Know if the lights were on or off?"

"Can't tell. You can turn them on or off from either the switch at the door or the ones beside the bed. The position doesn't tell us anything."

"Bathroom been dusted and photographed?"

It had. Shep went to have a look.

The bathroom door had been closed when the fire broke out. There wasn't much left of the door, beyond hinges and the doorknob, but it had minimized the damage to the room. The toilet seat was up. There was a cashmere dressing gown on the hook on the back of the door. Chapstick and Kleenex in the pocket. Towels were neatly stacked on the vanity; clearly the room had been cleaned since the guy last took a shower here. A toilet kit was open beside the sink. Mouthwash, shaving gear, surprisingly grotty manicure kit, toothpicks, dental floss, earplugs, sleep mask. Either the room was dark enough for him as it was, or he hadn't gone to sleep yet. There were a clutch of amber prescription vials, no surprise for someone in the kind of shape the deceased was in. The evidence techs would bag the meds and log them in.

The toothbrush and toothpaste were lying on the counter. Not standing in a glass. He opened the mirrored cabinet above the sink. No glass in there either. He went to the door.

"You guys notice there's no glasses in here?"

"Yeah, Buster did. No wastebasket either."

Shep looked. He opened the cabinet under the sink. No wastebasket. He went out again.

"You find them out here?"

"We found parts of a glass, was probably on the bedside table. Must have broken in the heat; the lab will tell us what was in it."

"Wastebasket?"

"No trace. The manager said they're made of raffia, the ones they use in the bathrooms. Lacquered."

"What is that, raffia?"

"Like straw or something. Totally flammable."

"Huh," said Shep.

The day dragged on. Martin Maynard made no secret of his belief that the local talent were in way over their heads on this one, if indeed there had been a crime. Personally he didn't think there had been. He was restless and deeply resentful that they wouldn't let him go for his run. They were treating him like a suspect instead of an ally. Officious clowns. He spent a lot of time on the phone to the Bureau and already knew that in fact the police had no power to keep any of them where they were, unless they were prepared to arrest them, but his bosses thought he should stay and cooperate, at least until morning.

Gabriel had given up trying to follow regulations where Colette the dog was concerned. She couldn't be left in the room with Mrs. Antippas. She howled and cried when she was carried past the hallway to Mr. Antippas's room. Glory had her in the bar on her lap.

Hope came into the bar and told Margaux Kleinkramer she was wanted in room 3B. One by one they were being called to present their bona fides and be fingerprinted.

"Even me!" said Hope, amazed. "I'm the deputy sheriff's mother!" She watched as Margaux left the bar with none of her usual ebullience.

"I have to wash my hands," Hope said to Maggie. "Come with me."

When they were sequestered in the powder room, with the water running, having checked to see no one was in the stalls, Hope said, "I know you think this is a joke, but I have to tell you, there is no way on God's green earth that Margaux Kleinkramer is an Aquarius. I really think I should tell Buster."

Maggie could picture *that* scene.

"Do you suspect her of something?"

"I suspect her of not being who she says she is. I'll bet you lunch at the Four Seasons; she's a Capricorn, probably with Leo rising. Aquarians hate liars, and we already know her name isn't really Margaux. What kind of person lies about her sun sign?"

"Running her prints should be interesting."

"I think the whole thing is going to be interesting."

Maggie suddenly asked, "You know Jorge Carrera, my security guy at school? Who took us to the Rangers game?"

"He was fun."

"He *is* fun. He was chief of detectives in the NYPD before he came to us."

"I had a feeling he was a big deal."

"His retirement gig was to bodyguard a boy whose mother was prosecuting terrorists. She had fatwas and death threats all the time. When the boy graduated, Jorge stayed. He has the most depressing view of human nature."

"I knew there was a reason I liked him so much," said Hope. "I wish he were here."

"Buster is going to do fine."

Hope didn't look convinced, and Maggie understood that that was what made her think of Jorge. She too wished he were here.

Buster was still with the Major Crimes guys when the van from Morrison's Funeral Home arrived. The day had turned a glorious blue and gold, which gave him a needed lift. He'd been up since two-thirty in the morning and had had nothing to eat except a handful of fancy cookies at the meeting in the hotel dining room that morning.

No one had said he was expected to stay, but no one had said he couldn't. He was the first responding officer in the case, and he'd had some training, mostly in Nevada before he came back east. Even though school, even criminal justice school, was never going to be his long suit, he had hopes of making detective, and if he wanted to marry Brianna, which he was pretty sure he did, he'd need the pay raise.

Hartley Morrison, third-generation funeral director and rhythm guitarist for Buster's favorite local rock band, Burn Permit, arrived at the door of the charred bedroom, having been led through the dank wet corridors by one of the crime techs. Hartley was a short man in his thirties with a broad muscular torso and very little neck, so that his head appeared to grow directly out of his shoulders. He was wearing corduroys and a flannel shirt, rather than the black suit he would have donned to greet the family of the deceased.

"Buster," said Hartley. "Shep." Then, "Whoa, that's a big sucker," as he looked at the body on the bed. "I hope the double-wide gurney is big enough." He turned to help his assistant lift the gurney over the power cords and debris in the hallway. The crime techs and Shep and Buster watched as the two of them maneuvered it into position by the bed as close to the corpse as they could get, and lowered it to match the height of the mattress. No one was quite sure how they were going to handle a corpse this size and in this condition.

Talking in shorthand to each other, Hartley and the assistant agreed to position the open body bag over the corpse, roll him bag and all onto the gurney, and then zip him in facedown, rather than risk turning him more than once. Nobody questioned the wisdom of this. No one wanted to see the flesh coming off the bone like overcooked barbecue.

"In 'Nam, they called these 'crispy critters,'" said Hartley. "My dad said."

Buster suddenly felt he might be sick.

Two of the crime techs moved into position to help.

"All right, me hearties," said Hartley. "Heave ho."

With surprising smoothness, the four men rolled the body off the bed and onto the gurney. The crunchy noise as the charred flesh of the front of the deceased was suddenly compressed under the full weight of the rest of him made Buster's gorge rise again, but it was nothing compared to the sight that greeted them next.

After a beat, Detective Gordon spoke for all when he said: "What the *fuck* is that?"

Crushed into the mottled flesh on the dead man's backside was the flattened, partly coiled body of a good-size gleaming black snake.

"I'd say it was a timber rattler," Buster said. "Some kind of pit viper anyway."

Shep turned to stare at him. "What are you, a fucking herpetologist?"

Buster shrugged. "I had a thing for snakes at one time," he said. Obsession was more like it, as his mother could have told them all, and no doubt soon would. His boyhood bedroom had been lined with poster-size pinups of photogenic reptiles from *National Geographic* and the like, and his bookshelves were filled with books on snakes of the world collected from used bookstores and library sales with what was left of his paltry allowance, after it had been docked because he couldn't sit still or hadn't done his homework. The most upsetting set-to Buster ever had with his mother had occurred when he turned ten and she refused to consider getting him a boa constrictor for his birthday. "They're really not dangerous until they get to ten feet long!" he'd insisted tearfully, unable to understand how anyone could resist this argument.

After staring at him for a beat longer, Shep said "We don't have any fucking rattlesnakes in Maine."

"Yeah, we do, sir. Or we did. They're supposed to be extinct in the state, but nobody knows for sure."

One of the crime techs said, "I'd say that was a less interesting question than how the hell did this one get into the guy's bed."

There was no way to keep a thing like a three-foot rattlesnake embedded in a dead man secret for long, so they'd have to move on this quickly. Standing in the sodden, blackened bedroom after the corpse was removed, Detective Gordon had listened to Deputy Babbin on the subject of *Crotalus horridus* long enough to decide to cede all snake-related investigating to Buster for fear that otherwise he'd still be standing here at dinnertime, and Buster would still be talking. Buster thought a necropsy on the snake would be interesting, and urged them to preserve it in the same conditions as they kept human bodies awaiting autopsy. Shep thought it wouldn't but in self-defense he agreed to convey that request to the M.E.'s office.

Freed at last from Buster's viper disquisition, Shep went out to his car to tell the M.E.'s office what they had found, and to point out that they needed to know which of the exciting possibilities, multiplying by the minute, it seemed, would prove to be the cause of death. Buster was to help keep the civilians in the inn out of the way as Morrison and the others maneuvered the gurney with its overflowing cargo through darkened hallways to the undamaged part of the hotel and into the back elevator. There was no way they could safely carry a load that heavy and fragile down the stairs, and there would be hell to pay if they dropped it.

The press swarmed Shep when he stepped into the Mountain Inn parking lot. Was the autopsy finished? Did he have a statement? What was the cause of death? Was the victim alive when the fire started? Did they have a suspect? Had he heard that the funeral for Artemis had been postponed in light of the second tragedy? Had he been in touch with the victim's children?

"No comment," said Shep as he waded through the throng. Had he been in touch with the victim's children? What? How the hell would he know how to be in touch with the victim's children?

Meanwhile, downstairs at the front of the Inn, Buster found various kinds of chaos erupting. In the dining room, the tables had been moved to the walls and a woman called Bonnie was leading an aerobics class. In the lounge, people were playing cards, cribbage, or Boggle. On the glassed-in porch overlooking the mountains and the parking lot, Mrs. Detweiler and his mother had laid out a two-thousand-piece jigsaw puzzle they had found in the bench of a window seat.

Mrs. Detweiler looked up from where she was pecking through the underbrush looking for edge pieces and said happily, "I love puzzles."

"What's it going to be a picture of?" Buster asked in spite of himself, although he was looking for Mr. Gurrell and determined not to be distracted.

"*Ship of Fools,*" said Maggie. "Hieronymus Bosch. Fantastically appropriate, we thought." Buster had an idea who Bosch was because his mother was always dragging him and Lauren to the museum on the weekends, when he wanted to go to the zoo and visit the snake house. He always got Bosch confused with Breughel, however you spelled that other one, but he thought that Bosch was the one most likely to give center stage to various serpents.

"Buster, could I just tell you something?"

"I'm kind of busy, Mom," said Buster. "Arson? Murder? Ring a bell?"

"Please don't be fresh. I really think you should know that Margaux Kleinkramer is not who she says she is."

In spite of himself, he said "How do you know?"

"Because she claims she's an Aquarius and she couldn't be."

Buster groaned, "Oh Jeez, Ma . . ."

"Was Mr. Antippas murdered?" Maggie asked, briefly suspending her search for straight edges.

"I'm not at liberty to say," said Buster, which Maggie took for a yes. In spite of herself, she felt an unseemly thrill. Now she *really* wished Jorge were here.

Buster found Gabriel Gurrell in his office drinking a large glass of something that looked like pond slime. "Sorry," he said, looking embarrassed. "Lunch. Would you like . . . ?"

"That's all right. Really," said Buster. "What *is* that?"

"Chef makes it for me. Mostly kale, I think. I'm trying to reduce," he added, gesturing briefly at the pear-shaped girth that curved out over his belt buckle. "Can I order something for you? A sandwich? Coffee?"

Buster thought a sandwich and coffee sounded wonderful, but he didn't think he should take free food from someone he might be investigating. A slap of his backside told him that when he'd pulled on his pants in the dark in the middle of the night, he'd omitted to put his wallet back in his pocket. He could see it in his mind's eye, lying on top of the dresser they'd ordered from IKEA when Brianna moved in. He'd spent a day and a half trying to put that frigging thing together and finally had to ask Brianna's father to come over and do it. That was humiliating, but really, the directions made no sense. Roy Weaver was one of those guys who can build or fix anything without looking at directions. Had Roy responded to the fire this morning? He must have, he almost never missed, but Buster hadn't seen him.

"How can I help you," Gabe Gurrell was asking him, possibly for the second time. Oh, right. Timber snake. He noticed he was jiggling his legs and stopped that, then reported what they'd found when they turned the deceased over.

He expected amazement. He expected denial. After all, as anyone knew, a timber rattlesnake was practically unheard of in the state and if in the wild would be at the end of its normal cycle of activity anyway, preparing to hibernate, not slinking into inhabited buildings. And besides timbers preferred the deep woods, being naturally shy of people, although not of other snakes. In fact they often hibernated in dens with other species, copperheads in warmer climates and in Vermont . . . or Maine . . . oops. Legs jiggling again.

But Mr. Gurrell had his head in his hands and he wasn't peppering Buster with expressions of shock or denial. He wasn't claiming the thing must have come in through the pipes, or anything else a person who knew nothing about snakes might say.

"Gabe," said Buster. "You know something about this?"

Gabe raised his head and looked at him. His naturally rather droopy features now looked deeply sad. "I hope I don't, but I might." He stood, putting aside his glass. Which is what Buster would have done with it too, if someone gave him a kale milk shake. "I think we better go have a talk with Earl."

Buster knew he was having trouble staying on track. This happened to him all the time, but it was worse when he was tired.

"Earl," he said.

"Earl Niner. He lives here, he came with the place."

"The Niners who farm over in West Bergen?"

"That's his brother. Earl had a landscape business outside town until his accident. His people wouldn't take him in after what happened, as I understand it, so Howard LaBoutillier, who had the inn before me, gave him a room here. He takes care of the horses and works in the garden. He earns his keep."

Buster had not thought to suggest that Earl did not, but Gabe seemed intent on making this point. He was following Gabe down the stairs and outside, this being the quickest way at present to get around the burn site and reach the wing where Earl lived.

"The children at the Consolidated School once dedicated their yearbook to Earl. They all called him Ertsy-Dirts," Gabe rattled on defensively as they walked. "I'm told he used to grow huge pumpkins for them to carve at Halloween. Dozens of them. And he ran a sort of petting zoo, too. The kids took field trips to his place every spring to see the baby lambs, and piglets and some stranger things. I heard he had a capybara."

They reentered the inn by a side door and climbed the stairs to the second floor. You could smell smoke here more strongly. Gabe led the way to the end of the corridor.

"Earl," he called as he rapped on a door. "Earl!"

After a silence, a surly voice said, "Who is it?"

"It's Gabe Gurrell, Earl. Could you open the door? I need to talk to you."

After another silence, Buster heard footfalls approaching the door, then a chain lock being slid back. The door opened. The man within was so bent over that he had to crane his neck up at a painful-looking angle to look into the eyes of a person standing upright.

"Earl, this is Deputy Babbin. Buster, this is Earl Niner. May we come in?"

Earl looked from one to the other with a stony expression, then opened the door wide enough for them to enter.

The room was unlike anything Buster had seen outside a zoo. More an avian habitat than a man's bedroom, there was a jungle gym of tree limbs in a huge cage in the corner with different kinds of pegs and rope perches from shoulder height to ceiling. As they entered the room a large—in this room it looked very large—green parrot began shrieking and flapping until Earl walked over and opened the cage door so it could hop onto his shoulder.

The floor of the room was lined with newspaper, extremely clean, and littered with toys of various kinds. Pictures of the singer Artemis looked up at Buster from several panels of newsprint near what he took to be the door to the bathroom. The bird too looked clean and glossy, but there were patches where he'd been picking at himself, Buster saw, and some fluffy underfeathers drifted near the narrow camp bed where Earl apparently slept. A small chest of drawers against the room's inside wall completed the human equipment.

"Walter's upset," Earl said. "Yapping scares him." As if on cue, the parrot began to howl in exactly the pitch and timbre of the Antippas's poodle, a sound all inhabitants of the inn had come to know. Buster had to admit, this did not look like a happy bird. But that was not his prime area of interest at the moment. What had riveted his attention, from the moment he entered the room, was a very large glass terrarium, you might say, nearly five feet high, built against the wall beside the little chest of drawers. Like the larger space of the room, it held a tree branch. Its floor was carpeted in rocks and leaves. There was a lamp, infrared Buster guessed, for heat, though the lamp was off at present. A framed piece of heavy mesh was fitted to the top of the case, hinged to the frame and fastened with metal hooks and eyes.

"This cage is not for Walter," Buster said to Earl. Walter, looking now at the cage, began to make the noise of a smoke alarm, a horrible piercing whine.

"Say 'Hello,' Walter," said Earl to him soothingly.

"hahaha," said the bird, which stopped the smoke alarm. He shook himself as a dog does after being in the water.

"Earl?" said Gabe.

"This is a snake habitat," said Buster.

"Yes," said Earl.

"And it's empty," said Buster.

Earl didn't speak. He reached up to stroke Walter, who cuddled against his head.

"What kind of a snake, Mr. Niner?"

Earl didn't answer.

"Mr. Niner?"

"His name is Grommet," said Earl. His old eyes were pink-edged and sad.

"And he is a timber rattler?" Buster asked gently, and Earl nodded.

Gabe was staring at the floor. Buster studied the cage with the eye of an aficionado.

"You're aware that the timber snake is a protected species?"

After a pause, Earl nodded briefly.

"And it's illegal to keep a protected animal as a pet?"

"He was a rescue snake," said Earl.

After a pause, Buster echoed him. "A rescue snake."

"Fellow down in Ellsworth had a tourist trap on the road to Bar Harbor. He had wolves in cages, and a buffalo. A bobcat. When the ASPCA shut 'im down, no one wanted Grommet."

"Why didn't you just let him go?"

"Wasn't right," said Earl. "He'd never lived in the wild. He's real sweet."

Buster looked at Gabe, who was now looking out the window.

"And do you know where he is now, Mr. Niner?"

Earl shook his head. "Came up to my room after supper, and his cage was empty."

"When was this?"

"Last night."

"So he was there at . . . ?"

"Six-thirty. Thereabouts."

"And you came back to your room at what time?"

Earl looked at Gabe but found no help there.

"Don't wear a watch," he said, showing Buster his wrist.

"Approximately."

"Maybe . . . seven-thirty. Seven-forty, something in there."

"And were you going to mention this to me? Or the other officers? You're aware there's an investigation going on?"

"Nothing to do with you. I hoped I'd find him." When Buster didn't say anything, Earl said, apparently addressing the floor, "You found him, ain't you?"

"We have," said Buster, hoping it was all right to divulge this.

"Don't suppose he's all right?" Earl asked.

"No, he isn't."

Earl sat down heavily on his cot.

Guests at the inn who had been fingerprinted and questioned were permitted after lunch to leave the building, though they were strongly requested not to leave the village and to be back by sundown. Martin Maynard immediately took off for a twelve-mile run, but most others headed for Just Barb's, or the Bergen Library, where there was wi-fi. This caused a crisis in the press corps, which didn't know whether to follow them and hound them with questions or to stay and await a statement from the police.

Maggie and Hope settled themselves in the corner booth at Barb's, and Sandra brought them coffee and a plate of her mother-in-law's famous ginger cookies. "On the house," she said. Both women thanked her warmly before sinking back into their computers. Maggie was wading through e-mails from friends and acquaintances who wanted to know what was going on, was she all right, were they all under arrest, and so forth. These were sparsely interleaved with dry notes and queries from the school evaluation team she was leading in Buffalo in two weeks, god willing. Hope meanwhile was diligently downloading astrological information and pondering the charts of her new friends.

"Here's a note from Jorge," Maggie reported.

"What's he say?"

"He sounds jealous. He promised to come help if they arrest either of us. Are you finding interesting things in the stars?"

"Oh you have no idea," said Hope. "It's indecent, really, it's so interesting."

"Why didn't you ever tell me that you do this?"

"I knew you'd think it was silly."

"I didn't know I was so intolerant."

"Oh you're not, you're just a Libra."

"What does that mean?"

"You believe in what works for you."

"Doesn't everybody?"

"Yes and no."

"Thanks."

"Look," said Hope, "it's a tool. If you're good at using it, you'll see the point of it. If not, not."

Maggie was about to answer when something caught her attention. After a pause, she said to Hope, "That young woman talking to Sandra. She's Buster's girl-friend."

"Buster doesn't have a girlfriend," said Hope. She angled herself sideways in the booth so she could see the front counter.

"Yeah, he does," said Maggie. The young woman was plump and strongly built. She had long dark hair caught in a knot at the back of her head, and a tattoo on her neck that disappeared into her collar. She was wearing a pink uniform dress and white sneakers. Sandra noticed them both looking their way, so Maggie gestured with her hand, as if they wanted something, and Hope turned around so as not to stare at the girl.

"You ladies need something else?" Sandra asked cheerfully.

"I'd love more coffee," said Maggie, "and I have a question. Who is that pretty girl you were talking with?"

"That's Brianna, Buster's girlfriend," said Sandra.

"I thought so," said Maggie. "We'd love to meet her, if she isn't in a rush."

"All rightie, I'll see if she's got a minute."

"How the hell did you do that," Hope said as Sandra whisked away. "You couldn't hear what they were saying."

"Of course not. I'm much deafer than you even think I am. I read lips."

"Now you're being competitive," said Hope.

"Yes, I probably am. Sorry."

"I forgive you because I know from your chart you can't help it."

The Oquossoc cocktail hour came early that evening. Taking a leaf from the airlines' playbook for what to do when enraged passengers have been stranded on a runway for entirely too long, Gabe decided to open the bar and declare all spirits and the house wine were on him. Teddy Bledsoe announced that in that case, he would donate his talents as mixologist. Maggie and Hope were sampling his Negronis and enjoying the last of the evening sun on the glassed-in porch, where Maggie had made surprising progress with the frame of her puzzle, when Hope said, "Hello? What's this?"

A sleek silver Mercedes drove into the parking lot, led and followed by state trooper cruisers. Maggie turned to see what Hope was seeing.

"That's the Kleinkramers' car," said Hope.

They watched as the press crew woke up, turned in a pack, and began running toward the cars, like hounds on a treed fox. To no avail, though. The Kleinkramers emerged from their car, and flanked by four troopers, they were whisked into the building by a side door, leaving the press corps baying and more or less flinging themselves against the closed door in frustration.

Maggie looked at Hope, who said, "You are going to owe me such a lunch."

"I think we better see what's going on." They abandoned their cocktails and joined the other guests in the lounge. Even Glory and Lisa were downstairs. All watched as Homer and Margaux were escorted to the elevator. When the doors closed behind them, the room started to buzz.

One of the troopers let slip to Bonnie McCue, who had plied him with cookies, that the license numbers of all the guests were on a watch list, which had seemed to the state police like overkill until this couple were stopped trying to cross the border into Quebec. Several minutes later they saw Buster beetling into the inn and up the stairs.

"That does it," said Hope. "We're not leaving this room until Buster comes back. We're going to make him tell us everything."

It took an hour. Around them, the room hummed with speculation and gossip. Lisa began to cry, and Glory and Bonnie surrounded her, and after a while she consented to a Bloody Mary and a dish of Cajun pecans, and looked as if she felt better. Gabe had brought her the Polo Lounge phone and left it permanently at her table as she talked with her children, her lawyer, her step-daughter's PR rep, and her children again. When the phone rang, Glory answered, screening calls to protect her sister from the press and from Artemis's manager, who wanted to plan a double funeral and needed to know when Alexander's body would be released.

Buster came down the stairs at about seven and was mentally halfway home to bed, when he saw his mother beckoning. He paused and exchanged a look with the uniformed officer who was now stationed at the front door. Then he turned back and went to stand, hat in hand, before his mother and Mrs. Detweiler.

"I have to go," he said. "I've been up since two this morning."

"You mean you haven't even had a nap?"

"Mom—I'm working. What is it you wanted?"

"Let's go back to the puzzle," said Maggie.

Buster followed them, feeling once again that he was being called to the principal's office. He was so tired he felt drunk.

The remains of their cocktails were still there, watered down and sweating on their coasters.

"Here, have a Negroni," said Hope.

"I'm driving," said Buster, wondering why he wasn't in his car at this minute.

"Oh take it, you'll feel better," said his mother. He took her glass and polished it off.

"Now. What happened with the Kleinkramers?"

"I can't tell you."

"Of course you can."

"We won't tell anyone else," said Maggie.

"We have a big bet riding on it," said Hope, as if this trumped all.

And Buster thought he was going to weep if he didn't get home and get some sleep, so he told them.

In Berkeley, California, in 1970, a college student named Melanie Gray was murdered in her off-campus apartment. The killing appeared to be part of a ritual of some kind. The face and hands had been marked with red paint, and candles burned down to stubs encircled the corpse. The body was almost completely desanguinated owing to a slash wound in the throat so deep her head was nearly off. Hope was impressed that Buster had said "desanguinated" and even pronounced it right.

"I remember that case," Maggie said. "I was in college in the East but I had friends at Berkeley."

"I remember too," said Hope. "There were footprints in the blood . . . ?"

"Two footprints in the blood, and the murder weapon was never found. Nothing had been stolen. The assumption was that she knew her killer, or killers, and may even have participated willingly. Am I remembering this right?" Maggie asked.

"There was some theory about bad LSD, and a boyfriend . . . no, wait, it was peyote buttons and the boyfriend was an anthropologist. Very involved with Stone Age religious rites."

"No one was ever charged."

"Yes, the boyfriend was charged and so was Melanie's roommate, but they were never tried."

"Buster?"

Buster was drumming his fingers on the table to keep himself awake.

"What was the roommate's name?" Hope asked.

Maggie offered, "Eileen Bachman? Bookman? Beekman?"

"Bachman," said Buster.

"And when they ran all our prints, they hit a match with Eileen," said Hope.

"Margaux Kleinkramer," said Maggie.

"Can I go now?"

"Drive carefully. Thank you, honeybunch."

Buster was so annoyed at being addressed as honeybunch while he was in uniform, that he forgot he was stepping outside into a swarm of news bugs, god they were like deerflies or chiggers or something, buzzing and biting. Carnivorous insects, there was a concept.

Hope and Maggie told no one what they had learned, but there was small chance that the press corps would fail to worm it out of someone, and indeed, by the end of dinner, the news was on the airwaves.

Eileen Bachman, one-time suspect in the still-unsolved Berkeley murder that the press at the time had called the Druid Slaying, was staying at the Oquossoc Mountain Inn under an assumed name at the time that Artemis's father was killed there. Local police were not yet saying that Antippas's death was suspicious, but the press wasn't in a mood to split hairs about that. *Esquire* magazine had published a long feature on the Berkeley murder at the time, with pictures of Melanie Gray, her then boyfriend, her grieving parents, her roommate Eileen, and the murder scene. Fifteen years after the murder, *Vanity Fair* had revived the whole story when it was learned that the other suspect, the victim's boyfriend, had killed himself. Both articles, with pictures, were getting substantial play again in online news and gossip sites and spilling onto the TV news, in spite of the fact that no one had suggested that Margaux had motive or opportunity or was in any way involved in what happened to Alexander Antippas.

The Kleinkramers had kept to their room and dinner had been sent up to them, but around nine o'clock, the elevator doors opened and there they were. Margaux was carefully made up, and Homer was composed and wearing a cheerful smile.

In the lounge, all heads had turned; all eyes were on them. A preview of what Margaux would face everywhere she went for the rest of her life.

"Hello, everybody," said Margaux brightly. She scanned the room, hesitated a moment, then headed for Hope and Maggie's table by the window where they were playing honeymoon bridge.

"May we join you?"

"By all means," said Hope. "What are you drinking?" One of the waiters from the dining room had zipped to their sides as the Kleinkramers settled themselves.

"Gin martini with a twist," said Homer.

"I believe I'll have sparkling water with a dash of bitters," said Margaux. Maggie saw that she was already stoned to the gills. Pills? Marijuana? Whatever it was, it was getting the job done. Her eyes were glassy and she exuded a beatific calm.

"Canasta?" said Hope.

"Lovely," said the Kleinkramers.

Buster was asleep with his boots on when Brianna got home from her shift at the nursing home. He was facedown on their bed in the tiny bedroom with the lights on. She knew that if he was wakened suddenly he might come up fighting or dive for his gun, so she rattled around in the kitchen, put the kettle on, and then washed the dishes left in the sink while she waited for the water to boil.

Buster wandered out of the bedroom, looking dazed. Half of his hair was standing straight up.

"Hey, sweet thing," said Brianna. She went into the bedroom, took off her pink uniform, and came back out in the fancy terry cloth robe Hope had sent to Buster for Christmas the year before. As if he ever put on anything after his shower besides his boxers and a wife beater. The kettle whistled.

"Want some tea?"

Buster shook his head. He was still coming back from whatever dream he'd been in.

"Did you have any dinner?"

Buster shook his head again. "I was going to heat a can of chili, but I never got to it."

Brianna took a frozen pizza out of their tiny freezer and popped it into the toaster oven. This was pretty much the sum of her culinary repertoire, but it was fine with Buster. He loved pizza.

"Sandra down at Barb's told me what happened at the inn last night."

"How'd she know about it?"

Brianna gave him a look that meant, is that a serious question? "So how's it going?"

Buster sighed. He looked at the telephone, and saw that the answering machine was blinking. He must have missed some calls when he was sleeping.

"The vic was a huge fat guy, bigger than Shep Gordon. Pretty badly burnt. You know when you leave hot dogs on the grill too long and the skin starts to—"

"Yes," said Brianna, cutting him off.

"Not a pretty sight." Involuntarily he recalled the face with the lips burned away and the teeth grinning.

"So the fire killed him? Was it arson?"

"I guess Sandra didn't hear about what we found stuck on the guy's back." He told her, and she screamed. Brianna had seen a lot and she was hard to shock, but she really hated snakes. He started to tell her about the particular traits of the timber rattler, but she said, "Buster, stop." He did, or switched tracks.

"We still don't know what killed him. If he was alive when the fire got going, why did he just lie there? So we're waiting on the M.E."

"I had a surprise today too," said Brianna.

"Rumble at the bingo game?"

Brianna was working in the Memory Neighborhood this month, with the dementia patients. Many were sweet, even if they kept asking the same question over and over, but a few were angry or unpredictable. She had a couple of big strong patients who took some handling.

"No, I met your mother."

She popped the pizza out of the toaster, slid it onto a plate, and set it down in front of Buster. He was eating before she had time to hand him a knife and fork. After tearing into most of a wedge, chewing the way you do when your mouth is too full and the food is too hot, he said, "I thought you just said you met my mother."

"I did. She was at Barb's with her friend Maggie. They asked me over to their table and we all had pie. I thought she was very nice."

Buster stared at her. "Wrinkly old number about this tall? About a hundred and thirty pounds, blond hair that looks like a wig?"

"She is not wrinkly and I thought she was very pretty and very nice. She asked about my job, and all about how we met, and she said they hoped they'd see me again. I thought we might meet them in town for supper before they go."

Buster was nonplussed. His plan for how to let his mother know he had a girlfriend was to send her an announcement when their first child was born.

The phone rang. They both startled at the sound; a call this late had to be bad news of some kind. Brianna lost the game of chicken they were silently playing as to who was going to answer.

Buster could hear the speaker talking loud and fast and then Brianna screamed. There was some confused howling then, from both Brianna and the caller. Brianna hung up the phone and shouted at Buster,

"Shep Gordon just came to the house and took Cherry away! He took her away to Ainsley!"

Shep Gordon had been on the phone with the M.E.'s office, trying to get some hard information about cause of death. The M.E. wanted to do the autopsy herself, this being a high-profile case and a complex one, but had eaten a bad tuna sandwich for lunch and gone home with food poisoning. The assistant M.E. had looked over the body and reported that the front half of the vic was cooked pretty good and it was disgusting to watch, how the flesh fell away from the bones if you fooled with it. They had to wait for the toxicology report to know for sure about drugs and poisons in his system, but it looked as if the snake had struck at least twice before meeting its own end. There were puncture holes on the upper back and on the back of one huge thigh. The way they reconstructed it, the snake must have been deep under the covers at the foot of the bed when Antippas got into it. It must have rattled, or tried to, but would that have been heard? Deprived of its chance to scare an enemy off, the snake had struck. The thigh first, they figured, then it slithered up, maybe trying to find the way out of the bed. Whatever happened next—the vic sat up? Threw back the covers? Rolled over looking for what had stuck him? The snake had gotten its fangs in again, deep, and wound up under the body when the guy felt the effect of the first bite and fell back. While they waited for the M.E. to come back, the office was doing research on what kind of venom this snake was packing and how it would affect a guy this enormous. They'd get back to them on this. But just spitballing, it looked like what Alexander Antippas died of was smoke and carbon monoxide from the fire. The airways, what was left of the nose, looked to them as if he'd been breathing as the fire heated up and engulfed the room.

Not a nice way to go. Not at all. The guy must have been fucking terrified, knowing what was happening, and unable to help himself.

Shep drove back to Ainsley in a contemplative mood. He thought he'd take his stepson shooting at the rifle range on Sunday. Kid drove him nuts, but Shep could be nicer to him; a little bit went a long way with this kid, who hadn't had much luck in the father department. It would please the wife too, which might work out well for Shep also. Nothing like the thought of finding a big poisonous snake in your bed to make a guy appreciate the homely pleasures.

Back at the barracks, Shep had talked to the fire marshal's office. He asked to see all the photos from fire scenes in the area in the last two years. There hadn't been that many, and few of them had been at all suspicious. One guy in West Bergen had tried to burn his barn down to collect the insurance, and he'd done a piss-poor job of it. Mostly it was wiring, chewed through by squirrels or just overloaded, that started things. A lot of times, especially in old farmhouses, there weren't many outlets because there wasn't that much to plug in when the electricity had come in. Now though, you had your computers and hair dryers and a bunch of other hair things he didn't understand, his wife had this thing that heated her curlers. And TVs and toasters and microwaves and then, oh god, Christmas lights and all that. People would get extension cords and have all this stuff running from one plug and then be surprised when the house burned down.

What he was interested in now was what he could see in the background of the fire pictures. Who was there watching. People liked to watch fires; you couldn't blame them. He liked to have a bonfire at New Year's himself. If there was snow, and it was safe. He and his buds would pile up old tires, and trash wood you couldn't burn in the woodstove without gumming up the flue, and they'd have this huge pyre going all day, with people standing around drinking coffee and hot chocolate, the kids with marshmallows and the grown-ups with rum in theirs, cooking hot dogs on sticks and just enjoying the color and the life in the flames, the sparks going up into the blue dome above them.

But people who set fires, they enjoyed fires in a different way. For some it was sexual. You looked for guys wearing big loose overcoats, having at themselves insides their clothes. God, some people. If the fire broke out at night, you looked for people who were fully dressed, instead of rousted out in their jammies, like they knew ahead of time what was going to happen.

He went carefully through the pictures Deputy Babbin had taken. He'd been first on the scene at Oquossoc. There was Gabe Gurrell looking panicked, with a coat on over his nightshirt, and his skinny shanks stuck into puffy sheepskin slippers. Like bunny slippers. Nightshirt? He supposed that made it easier to clear the decks for action than pajama pants. Was Gabe getting any action? Where'd you get a thing like that, a nightshirt, he wondered. Shep bought most of his clothes at Manganero's, where you could also get gas for your car or diesel for your truck, buy a head of lettuce, get your work clothes and boots, your fishing and hunting gear including a good selection of rifles and shotguns, or rent a wedding dress.

Once the fire trucks arrived, the pictures were busier. Some of the guests from the inn were in the parking lot, gaping upward at the fire as the men did their work, putting up ladders, hauling hoses, attacking the flames. The guests were all half dressed or in nightclothes, wrapped in blankets or bathrobes. Buster had done a good job, shooting away from the fire, recording the background. Who was there who shouldn't be? Whose cars were those? He enlarged the pictures on his screen as much as he could without losing detail; made a list of license plates, including partials; took note of the watchers. In addition to the firefighters, there were only two people completely dressed. One was a skinny bent-over guy, wearing a barn jacket and dungarees. Shep couldn't see the face. He'd seen people bent over like that with rheumatoid arthritis. Mrs. Carter, who went to his wife's church, when you talked to her she seemed to be talking to her shoes, but she was an old sweetheart, sharp too, and she bore the pain wonderful. He couldn't see the face on this guy, but he had a hunch it was that fellow Niner, who'd had the accident that time. Shep had been a deputy patrol officer back then, and he remembered talking to men who responded to the scene. A wonder the guy could walk at all, a wonder he was still breathing.

Out among the cars, it looked as if there was another figure, shoulders hunched, hands in pockets, wearing a sweatshirt with the hood up. Skinny and small, could even be a woman. Shep couldn't get any detail at all on the face. He was out in the dark of the parking lot, well away from the rest of the people. Or she.

Shep went to the photos taken by the real photographer, the crime scene guy. You could tell by the light from the flames and the number of cars and people in the shots that this was later, closer to morning. In a lot of them, police vehicles were lighting the scene with their headlights. There was the bent-over guy, facing the fire. His face was in bright light and Shep was now sure it was Niner. Now where was Mr. Hoodie?

There he was. He'd come in closer to the scene, and was standing near one of the fire trucks. He was keeping in the shadows, but there was one shot that showed the face clearly. The hood was pulled tight so just the features showed, no hair, no neck. He still couldn't tell if it was a man or a woman but it was small and young. Youngish, anyway. He looked carefully at the cars in the parking lot, making note of which ones had been there from the beginning and were still there, this late in the scene.

He went out to the bullpen and asked, "Anyone here from the Bergen area? Bergen, West Bergen?"

"Dorothy. She's from Bergen Falls. I think her mom still lives there."

"Get her, will you?"

Dorothy lumbered into Shep's office. Shep gave her a seat, and pulled up the pictures of the fire that included Mr. Hoodie. She looked carefully at the pictures as he scrolled through them. When he got to the one with the face showing, he stopped. Dorothy leaned into the screen.

"Can you make it bigger?"

He did his best, and Dorothy said suddenly, "Oh sure, I got her now. That's Cherry Weaver. I know her mom. Cherry used to work at the Upper Cuts shop here in Ainsley. She did my perm once."

Shep leaned in and studied the intent little face peering out of the closed circle of the hood. It looked like something medieval.

"Roy Weaver's kid? What's she doing at the inn, you have any idea?"

"I think I heard she was working there, but don't take my word for it."

"No I won't. Thanks much."

Dorothy went back to her desk, and Shep printed the pictures that showed his two persons of interest, then went back to the bullpen.

"Harris? Wheatly? Will you guys get back over to the inn and talk to Gabe Gurrell? Find out what Earl Niner has to do with the inn, why he's here in these pictures with all his clothes on. Then find out everything you

can about this girl, Cherry Weaver. What was she
doing there last night. And find out if either of them
knew Antippas, had any reason to harm him."

His detectives took off, back to Oquossoc, and Shep
settled in to look at the rest of his pictures of local fire
scenes.

Day Six, Friday, October 11

It was three-thirty in the morning when Brianna was allowed to see Cherry. It might have gone faster if Buster had come with her, but Brianna didn't think so and wouldn't let him. A local deputy sheriff didn't swing much weight in these leagues and besides he'd been up for like twenty-two hours straight and needed the sleep. Plus, she sort of didn't like picturing Buster telling his mother that he'd spent the night getting Brianna's sister out of jail.

Cherry was not under arrest, but no one would tell Brianna if she was there as a witness or a suspect. Brianna sat in the unhealthy fluorescence of the police barracks waiting room, watching peace officers go in and out with purposeful demeanors. Now and then she would try to ask someone a question, and always she'd be told to wait for Shep.

When Cherry came out at last she was alone; she took one look at her sister and burst into tears. Cherry's mouth went into a strange oblong shape when she cried. Brianna clamped an arm around her and marched her out of the station, while with the other hand she called her mother to say she was taking Cherry home with her. The call went to the answering machine, of course. Beryl wasn't one to lose a lot of sleep over other people's messes.

Cherry had had about an hour of sleep in Buster's Barcalounger before her sister woke her that morning, though she was trying to be quiet about getting Buster's breakfast. Brianna had a double shift at the nursing home that day, filling in for a colleague called to jury duty. She'd taken it on because she wanted the money; she hadn't counted on getting zero sleep between midnight and eight, but she had to go, and there was the question of what to do with Cherry. Cherry was a mess; they couldn't leave her alone. She might talk to people she shouldn't; she might panic and take off.

"I'll take her up to the inn to stay with your mother," said Buster.

"I don't want to go to the fucking inn," said Cherry. "I wish the whole thing had burned to the ground."

"Hey!" Brianna said sharply. "Don't you say that! Don't say anything like that, ever again. To anybody!"

"Don't have a cow, man. They hate me and I hate them. I can say that if I want to."

"No you can't! Jesus, Cherry, don't you know what's going on here?"

"Yes. Everyone always blames me. I didn't *do* anything! I was just standing there!"

Brianna had heard this litany in the car last night. It was as if the shock of being suspected had caused Cherry to revert to the strategy of a much younger person, insisting that she never went near the birthday cake even though she had chocolate icing in her hair. As if no one could prove a thing if you just kept denying it. *Had* she done something?

"You have to talk to Mom, and get yourself a lawyer and until you do that, you can't talk to anyone. You have to be with people who can look out for you."

"Can I go to Dad's?"

Brianna was scrambling eggs. She hadn't thought of that as an option. No one would, really, think of Roy Weaver as a port in a storm, except, apparently, Cherry. "If you can find him," she said.

Cherry dug in her pockets for her ancient clamshell phone, and punched in her father's number. Brianna watched her. Cherry's face was defiant as she clapped the clamshell shut.

"Probably still asleep," she said. "You can just drop me there, I'll be fine."

"Listen. You have to make decisions. You need good advice and you need help. You need to talk to Mom."

"She always blames me."

"That's because you're such a fuck-up!"

"Thanks, a lot!" She began to cry tears of self-pity.

"Jesus. Stop it. I know you didn't do anything, and so does Buster, but you . . . Oh, hell, I have to go." She kissed Buster on the cheek, took a piece of dry toast from the toaster, went to get her coat from a peg and her purse and her car keys. She got the toast stuck in the sleeve of her coat as she put it on, then she was out the door, which slammed behind her.

Cherry looked up miserably at Buster, who put half the scrambled eggs on a plate and handed it to Cherry with a fork. She stared at it as if she wasn't sure what to do with it. Then she asked, in a small voice, "Is there any ketchup?"

Buster found the bottle in a cupboard and gave it to her. They ate in silence, Buster at the table and Cherry in the Barcalounger, still in the sweat clothes she'd been wearing when Shep Gordon carried her off so many hours before.

Judge Hennebery was no longer young, and since his wife had died, was not often completely sober. His daughter was after him to retire and move to Florida to a death camp; she never had had any sense, Ellen. What kind of grown-up woman would sign her name Elli, with a circle over the *i*?

He liked coming to work. He liked having a place to go, and the courthouse in Ainsley was a little ant-hill, humming with gossip and activity. He liked going out to lunch every day to the Chowder Bowl across State Street, where they knew exactly how he took his coffee and saved him the end pieces on meat loaf day. He liked watching boys he'd known when they were in Little League all grown up, in office, in uniform, taking themselves so seriously.

When Shep Gordon came in first thing on Friday the judge couldn't resist having a little fun with him.

"You back again, Shep? You look like a yard of chewed string, doesn't your wife let you get any sleep? Must be nice, she's a good-looking woman."

"We're working on a homicide, Your Honor," said Shep, politely. He wasn't sure if the judge remembered or not. Was he as dotty as he sometimes seemed, or did he just enjoy rattling people?

"Homicide now, is it?" said the judge. This was news. Hadn't had one of those lately. Yesterday it was a suspicious fire of unknown origin. "And what is it you want from me this morning?" Hennebery asked him.

"Arrest warrant, sir."

"That was quick. You got your paperwork?"

Shep handed up the affidavit he had prepared, and Judge Hennebery read it slowly, humming. Then he slid his reading glasses down his nose and looked over the rims at Shep.

"You want me to sign this and risk getting mowed down flat by Beryl Weaver? I been crosswise with her before. It's quite an experience. That's a lot of pressure on a man not in the first blush of youth."

"I'm sorry about that, but—"

"Oh I'm just joshing you, Shep. I'll sign it. But you better have done your homework."

"Understood, sir. Thank you."

The day had dawned sullen, with gray light that didn't seem to be half-trying, and dense, blue-gray cloud cover hanging over the lake, which the inmates of the Oquossoc Mountain Inn watched glumly from the dining room as they ate their breakfasts. Everyone knew the rain was coming, and when it began, moments after a crack of thunder that sounded like a cannon being fired on the roof, it rained down in straight sheets like the downpour created by machines on movie sets. Buster hustled Cherry from the parking lot in through the kitchen door and to the staff locker room. She was soaked and shivering, and thoroughly pissed when she went to hang up her sweatshirt and found her locker padlocked. She followed Buster into the kitchen, wet as she was, and stood for inspection by her mother, who had turned from the sink to look at her. Buster was hoping against hope that Beryl would stop what she was doing and come to wrap her arms around Cherry, who had, let's be honest, had a shitty night and was about to have a shittier day.

But Buster should have known better. "Look what the cat dragged in," Beryl said to her younger daughter. To Buster she said, "Am I babysitting?"

"She needs to be with someone who can give her good advice. I don't know, but I think she's about to be arrested. Do you know a lawyer you can recommend?"

"I know a lawyer, but I can't recommend him," said Beryl.

Buster saw Chef Sarah spot them from where she was supervising the hot line. Sarah wiped her hands on the dish towel she carried in her apron tie, and came to them.

"Cherry. Are you all right? Do you need some breakfast?"

Cherry shook her head. "I ate."

"I'm sorry to hear what happened last night. Can I help in any way?"

Cherry shook her head dumbly, her eyes suddenly wet. Softness undid her.

"I'll tell you what. We're finishing the breakfast rush here, and then I'm teaching a butchering class. But when I'm done I'll find you and we'll go talk to Mr. Gurrell. I'm sure you didn't do anything wrong, Cherry. We'll figure this out. Try not to worry."

Cherry took a moment to think about this unexpected kindness, but then looked up and met Sarah's gentle gaze. She nodded. Her mother, who had been watching from the sink, advanced on Cherry, holding a paper towel, and said, "Blow your nose." Then Beryl went back to washing up.

By the time Shep got back to the barracks, Carson Bailey, assistant state attorney general, was waiting for him.

"How's it going, guy?" he asked, shaking Shep's hand. Carson was from inland, son of a chicken farmer who'd tried to compete with out-of-state agribusiness and failed dramatically. The huge chicken barn where once he'd presided over the opposite of whatever is meant by "free range," in chicken husbandry, was now a vast indoor antiques and flea market, and Archie Bailey had died young in a "hunting accident." He hadn't lived to see Carson graduate from law school and move to Augusta, the first in his family to work at a white-collar job. No one knew how Archie would have felt about it. Carson, named for Johnny (his mother was a fan of *The Tonight Show*), looked like a doofus, with his doughy face and puffy hair, but he was good in the courtroom.

Carson followed Shep to his office, where they closed the door so Shep could fill him in. "Fill me in," was what he always said, as if a case were a page in a coloring book. First he got the outlines, then he went to work with the crayons.

"We had the girl here for a couple of hours last night—"

"You didn't charge her?" Carson interrupted. He had told Shep not to charge her until they could dot every *i* and cross every *t*. He wanted his cases to stick tight when he threw them at the wall. And he never met a metaphor he couldn't mix.

"And we made good progress," said Shep, ignoring him.

"But you Mirandized her?"

The card with the Miranda warning on it that Cherry had signed was passed to Carson.

"She had plenty of grudge against the deceased, I'll tell you that. She is one very angry little item. Whole family is trash."

"And she didn't ask for a lawyer?"

"No."

"Okay. Well, fill me in."

"She'd had a run-in with Antippas when he first arrived at the hotel. Antippas was rude, it wasn't her fault, yada yada, everyone hated him, it wasn't just her, but Antippas complained to Gabe Gurrell about her. Gurrell gave her her notice the next day. Gurrell swears it wasn't just about Antippas, but Cherry didn't believe it."

"Make any threats against him? Antippas?"

"No, but she had a roaring blowup with Gurrell in the lobby the afternoon of the fire. Plenty of witnesses. Took off her uniform and threw it at him and marched out in her underpants."

Carson whistled.

"So we've got motive. Revenge on Antippas *and* Gurrell. Opportunity?"

"Plenty. Her mother, Beryl Weaver, works in the kitchen. Got her the job. Cherry knows the layout, and has access to anywhere in the building."

"Tell me about this firebug thing."

Shep showed him the pictures of the night of the Oquossoc fire, then pictures from four other fires in the area in the last two years. In all of them, Cherry Weaver could be seen in the background, hanging around watching, always in her sweatshirt with the hood pulled up except for one taken against snow in which she wore a red-and-black-plaid peaked cap, with ear flaps. Carson whistled again.

"Any priors?"

"The usual. Twice swept up with some older kids who broke into camps off-season to party. Her older sister sowed some wild oats, and if their mother was working and Brianna was watching Cherry, she'd just take her along. Listen, I've got something else for you. When Cherry was fifteen, she was arrested for shoplifting at Renys in Ellsworth. First offense, suspended sentence, and of course, her juvenile record is sealed."

"But you know a guy."

"I do. Guess what she was trying to knick."

"Fill me in."

"A can of lighter fluid."

Carson's doughy face split into a smile. "Was she really," he said, as if he'd just learned Cherry had baked him a cake.

The two set to work. They wanted to search Beryl Weaver's house, Cherry's car, her locker in the staff room at the inn, and anything else they might think of. Even though Cherry had shrugged and said "Sure, I don't care," when asked if it was all right with her if they looked around her room, they didn't want a bit of this questioned in court once their case was made.

Buster needed to get to work, and he still needed a place to park Cherry, since it didn't look as if her mother was going to pitch in. She couldn't stay with him; she couldn't be anywhere near an investigation when she was its prime suspect. He knew how this worked. The moment the police believed they had their man, or woman, the investigation went into a funnel. Prosecutors were no longer striving to find out what had happened, they were only looking for evidence that supported what they already believed. Other possibilities, other suspects, any evidence that pointed another way, was ignored. Shep and Carson Bailey were now building their case against Cherry. Buster wanted to be there, to know what arrows were pointing in directions they were ignoring now, or suppressing.

He found Hope and Maggie on the glassed-in porch, drinking tea and working on their jigsaw puzzle.

"Good morning, dear," said Hope fondly. "And Cherry! How nice to see you."

Buster hadn't spent so much time under a roof with his mother in decades. It was disorienting to find her helpful. He ventured, "Cherry needs to settle somewhere until we can . . ." He didn't know how he should finish the sentence.

"Yes of course," Hope said, turning to Cherry. They had heard what had happened to her in the night, as had everyone else in the inn. The word had radiated from the kitchen staff outward from the moment Beryl had come in to work. "We'd love to have you join us, Cherry. Chef Sarah is going to give a manly lesson in knives and butchery this morning, and we don't think we need to learn about that."

"Makes me sick," said Cherry. With a look of gratitude toward his mother, Buster slipped out.

"Me too," said Maggie. "I remember in biology when they made us dissect a cow's eyeball. You had to hold it still with a fork. I still can't even think about it."

Cherry looked suddenly so ill that they dropped the subject. She really was under terrible strain, poor little thing.

"Are you good at jigsaw puzzles?" Maggie asked.

"Don't know," said Cherry.

"Of course you don't, you haven't been wasting your life the way I have. Well come sit, and I'll explain my methodology."

"And if you don't like it, you can sit with me and knit. Do you know how to knit?"

Cherry shook her head. She'd never in her life encountered grown-ups like these, except to wait on them, one way or another. Grown-ups with indoor pastimes other than drinking beer or watching the tube.

"Well look at you!" said Maggie, approvingly. Cherry had methodically collected all the variegated greenish-black pieces, and had succeeded in putting two together.

"Oh I hate you," said Hope. "I've been at this for hours and I haven't fit a single thing in. This puzzle is too big. I'm going to look at the picture."

She turned over the box the puzzle came in, which Maggie had turned upside down to defeat temptation, and showed Cherry the picture they were trying to form.

"You mean you had that all along?" Cherry asked. What *was* it with these people? It was already, like, impossible, all these millions of pieces, and they were making it *harder*?

"Maggie is a purist but I'm not," said Hope. "Let's stage a rebellion. See, here's where your pieces are going to go." She pointed to the leaves at the top of the mast of the *Ship of Fools,* and Cherry bent over to peer closely at the image. It was unlike anything she'd ever seen. There were a lot of, like, medieval people in a little sort of round boat that only an idiot would go to sea in, and a skinny nun and an ugly guy with a shaved head were trying to bite some round bread or something that was hanging between them even though there was food on the table (table? In a rowboat?) while these other people, naked, were in the water trying to get in or get the food.

"That's the picture we're making?" was the politest thing she could think of to say.

"Yes," said Maggie. "It's Art. Don't you like it?"

Cherry hated it.

"Good girl," said Maggie. "We don't like it either, but it looked as if it would be fun to work on."

"When it's done will you frame it?" Cherry asked.

"We hope we won't be here long enough to find out. But no, we'll take it apart and leave it for the next people."

Cherry thought she better not say how stupid this struck her to be, but in the meantime, she was quite liking the sorting and fitting. She spotted another piece of "her" part across the table and went back to scanning for more.

"We met your nice sister yesterday," said Hope.

Cherry was surprised. "Brianna?"

"Are there more of you?"

"Oh. No, just me and Brianna. There was a brother before I was born, but he died."

"I'm sorry," said Maggie. "But your parents must have been very happy when you were born," said Maggie.

"I don't think so. They got divorced when I was two or something."

"Oh. I'm sorry," said Maggie again.

"Yeah, it sucked," said Cherry, and there was a silence, during which Cherry found another match among her leaf pieces.

"Buster and Brianna are close, I understand," said Hope.

Cherry looked up. "You know Buster?" She had heard this lady call Buster "dear," but she thought that was just like Sandra at Just Barb's, or the cashiers at Walmart, who called everybody "dear."

"He's my son," said Hope.

Cherry didn't mean to show her astonishment, but she did. This was Buster's *mother*? Buster, who was a cop and lived in a trailer with her sister?

"So, we're concerned about you," said Hope. "And I hope you'll let us know if we can be any aid or comfort."

Cherry's mouth went oblong and she began to cry.

Hope instinctively moved to Cherry's side and put a hand on her shoulder. Cherry flinched.

"I'm scared," she said. There followed a storm of crying, great gouty sobs, as if her insides were trying to get out. This child hadn't found a lot of sympathy in her life, Maggie thought. She'd seen people cry like this and be lying through their teeth, but still.

"Of course you are," Hope murmured. "Who wouldn't be?"

Cherry went on being buffeted by the storm of her own tears.

"Do you know why they took you last night?" Hope asked. "Did they tell you?"

Cherry managed to say, "They just kept asking me why I was there, watching the fire that night."

"You were there?"

The girl nodded and wept.

"You'd gone home, but then you came back?" Hope asked.

Cherry nodded again. "My dad's a fireman. So."

Hope and Maggie's eyes met briefly.

"Whenever there's a fire, you go?"

"If I'm home, and I hear the call go out."

There was a silence. Hope handed Cherry a packet of tissues from her knitting bag, as the sobs were finally subsiding. Being listened to instead of badgered was having a calming effect. Cherry mopped at what was left of last night's mascara, mostly on her cheeks, and blew her nose.

"How do you hear the call?"

Cherry looked puzzled by the question.

"On the scanner."

"You have a police scanner?"

"My mom does. In the kitchen." As if to say, don't you?

"Is she connected to the police in some way, your mother?"

"No. You just have them to, you know. Know what's going on."

"Does your mother go to fires too?"

"Not unless it's someone she knows. I go to see my dad. To see he's all right. And, like, to *see* him."

"Ah," said Hope. "I hope you explained that to the police last night."

Cherry shook her head dismissively. "They weren't listening to me. They were just like 'Why did you do it?' Over and over."

Both women knew this wasn't good. Everyone in the inn knew she'd resented Mr. Antippas, and had a blowup with Mr. Gurrell. Still, the police couldn't really think that this scattered little thing could have . . . did they? Could she have?

"Does your father know? That you come to watch him fight fires?"

Cherry shrugged.

"You never talked about it?" Hope asked.

Cherry shook her head. "He's real busy."

"Has anyone called him? Does he know what's happened to you?"

"He wasn't home."

There was another silence. Cherry said resentfully, "They kept going, 'You like fires, don't you?' and I'd go like '*yeah*, in *fireplaces* . . .'"

"Dearie," said Maggie, "have you ever been in trouble before?"

Cherry looked at the puzzle. She said, "No," crossly, as if this should be as obvious as having a police scanner in the kitchen, but Maggie knew instantly she wasn't telling the truth. You get good at seeing the tells after forty years of dealing with schoolchildren. She wondered what was on Cherry's record, and whether it would hurt her.

Abruptly Shep Gordon was in the room, followed by two large square men in uniform from the state police. The quiet space, full of sunlight, was confusingly and all at once full of men and noise. Someone yanked Cherry to her feet and barked, "Hands behind your back!" Handcuffs were clicked into place. Shep Gordon blared, "Cherry Weaver, you are under arrest on suspicion of criminal arson, and homicide. You have the right to remain silent . . ."

Hope and Maggie watched, stunned, as Cherry was marched out of the room, with a burly uniform on each side holding her shackled arms. In a moment, they were all out in the parking lot, surrounded by shouting, flashing, clamoring reporters. Cherry had her chin tucked down to her chest and her eyes shut as she was dragged through to the waiting sheriff's car.

Buster had appeared beside his mother.

"They wouldn't let me warn you," he said. He could see that both his mother and call-me-Maggie looked disoriented, as if a television show had suddenly come to life in the middle of their living room.

"But was that necessary? Three big men? Handcuffs? She's scared to death and as big as a minute!"

"I guess that's the way they do it," said Buster. Clearly, he wasn't happy. Shep was a big deal in his world. But there was Brianna. And the terrifying Beryl. And his own instincts. Cherry was a screwup, no question, but she wouldn't do something like this. She wouldn't know how.

"What's going to happen now?" asked his mother. "Does she have a lawyer?"

Does she have a lawyer. What twenty-three-year-old has a lawyer? Oh, wait, yes, there were quite a few who did, probably. He'd had one himself, that time in Tucson when he was about Cherry's age. But no, Cherry didn't.

"No."

"She better get one, fast. Don't you think? Does the family have any friends who practice?"

In Hope's world, everyone had a family lawyer, if only for drafting wills and trusts. Really, half the people you met at dinner were lawyers it seemed. Her son-in-law was a lawyer.

"I don't know how she can pay one," said Buster. "I think her mom's house is under water, since the crash, and anyway . . ." Buster saw a look pass between Maggie and his mother.

Maggie said, "Will the court appoint someone?"

"They will. I guess." He didn't look as if he thought this was going to be much of a bulwark between Cherry and the shit slide thundering toward her.

"What's the evidence against her?" Maggie asked him.

"I don't really know," said Buster.

"Well, can you find out?" asked Hope. They both looked at him with identical gazes, the looks of adults in authority waiting out a child who just claimed that his homework was torn from his hand by a mighty wind.

He thought of Brianna. Brianna might have things to say about her family when she was alone with Buster, but faced with any threat from the outside world, you didn't want to mess with her. She was the one who had really raised Cherry after their dad left. And let's face it, if Shep Gordon and Carson Bailey thought they had enough to indict, Cherry was fucked, and so was he. He was going to have to risk pissing off *somebody*.

Hope and Maggie had taken a table for two in a corner of the dining room for lunch. They had a lot to talk about.

"You know I could pay for a lawyer," Hope said. "She deserves a decent defense, no matter what she's done."

"She hasn't done anything criminal," Maggie said."Unless she's a sociopath, and I don't think she is."

"I read they're more common than you think. One person in twenty-five, I think it was."

"I don't actually doubt that, I just don't think Cherry Weaver is one of them."

"But you don't think I can offer to get her a lawyer?"

"I do not. Brianna is Buster's girlfriend, not his wife. If you treat her like a daughter-in-law, you're getting between them in ways that won't be good. You can't offer. If they ask, that's different."

They fell silent and looked up politely as their server put bowls of wild mushroom bisque before them.

"But I don't want to stand by and see her railroaded."

"Neither do I."

"Because it isn't nice and it isn't fair, and if they do that, we'll never find out what really happened."

"*There* you go," said Maggie. "We'll wait for Buster to get back to us, and until then, I'm going to call Jorge."

"And I'm going to call my old friend at the *Boston Globe*."

"I didn't know you had a friend at the *Globe*."

"Before I knew you. Investigative reporter. He always said he could find out anything he needed to know with three phone calls."

The Memory Neighborhood at Ainsley Nursing was built, according to the most modern ideas, in the shape of a doughnut. The hole in the middle was an outdoor patio where the inmates could smoke and feel the sun on their faces when there was sun. The rest was a soothing circular loop, carpeted in a cheerful royal blue, designed to give comfort to the "wanderers," patients who felt a restless need to be going somewhere else, who would however be lost and terrified if they actually succeeded. Along this circle route, everything was familiar, all furniture and colors the same, with just enough variety to give a sense of process or progress if you were on your way along it. Here on the left was a space with seating and a television. Now on the left was a nook with a piano. Followed on the left by a crafts area, where confused people could pass the time by sticking buttons onto cards, or doing little projects with glue and sparkles, and here, on the left, was a door to the outside, except the outside was in the middle and not a route to somewhere else. You could go out this door, and cross the outdoors and go in that door on the other side, identical to this one, and be in a place very much like the place you just departed from. Along the outside of the doughnut were the patients' bedrooms, and the necessary service areas, a little kitchen, the meds closet, the shift supervisor's office. Also, of course, a door to the actual outside of the building that could only be opened with a code punched onto a keypad. The code was beyond the residents. It was 1234.

The day nurse-supervisor at Ainsley Nursing, Hazel Littlehawk, had heard the news about Cherry's arrest from her husband who worked with the K-9 unit for the state police. Cherry Weaver was being photographed and fingerprinted over at the Ainsley Jail, but Hazel kept the news to herself until Brianna Weaver finished giving lunch to the new resident, who had bitten the aide who tried to feed her oatmeal this morning. Brianna had discovered that the new resident liked to sing although she couldn't talk, and was doing better with her. They were doing "You Are My Sunshine" for the eleventh time around spoonfuls of applesauce.

When Mrs. Harker had been fed, washed, and toileted, and was quietly settled in the dayroom watching a *Hollywood Squares* rerun, Hazel took Brianna into the little closet that served her for an office.

Brianna hadn't realized how much she had hoped that somehow Cherry was going to be scolded for being a flake and a potty mouth and sent home, until she learned that any such possibility was extinguished. This was really happening; her sister would be indicted for criminal arson and homicide. She could be down at Windham for the rest of her life. She was probably in a cell somewhere right this minute, without her phone, or her own clothes or . . .

"What am I going to do?" she asked Hazel.

"You're going to get her a lawyer, and you're going to keep her spirits up," said Hazel.

Brianna didn't know Hazel very well, but knew her reputation as a hard-ass, fierce about the time clock and a stickler for regulations. She looked at the woman's broad flat face, her dark impassive eyes, and considered for the first time that Hazel's path to her present position had probably not been strewn with rose petals.

"How do I get a lawyer?"

"Can anyone pay? Your mom? Your dad?"

Brianna didn't really have to answer. Hazel knew what Brianna got paid, and had a pretty good idea that no one in the background had won the lottery.

"Your church?" Hazel asked. Brianna just shook her head. The only time they ever went was when they were little and all the children in the village got presents from the Baptists on Christmas eve if they could recite a Bible verse. Her mother had been raised Methodist, but the congregation had dwindled to such a tiny number that they couldn't pay a minister or keep up their pretty nineteenth-century meetinghouse. The building had been sold to rich Episcopalians out on the coast and moved down there, with its steeple following the sanctuary on a flatbed truck. There was nothing left now but the graveyard with her grandmother in it, all by itself at the side of the road. It had an iron railing, and a tall pointy monument to the veterans of some war, but she didn't know which one. Once in a long while one of the farmers with relatives there would trailer his mower over and cut the grass.

"My sister-in-law just graduated law school," said Hazel. "She passed the bar last month. She wants to do family law, but while she's getting started, she has some time. Might take the case pro bono."

Brianna, still in her uniform, parked her Subaru in the parking lot of the Rite Aid, and found her way to the back door of a long, low concrete building across an alley that housed a pet supply store. Precious Paws fronted on the High Street. The room at the rear, with no proper address and no parking space, had not been designed to be rented out, but most likely was intended for a manager's office for the front of the store. Evidently the dog raincoat and fish food business wasn't booming, any more than anything else in this economy except liquor and lottery tickets. The only indication that Brianna was in the right place as she walked over the patch of weeds outside the steps was a cheaply printed business card that read CELIA LITTLE, ATTORNEY AT LAW, taped on the inside of the glass of the storm door that had been left in place since last winter. Or forever.

Was this a good idea? With so much at stake?

Standing on the concrete step, trying to make up her mind, Brianna finally decided that at the least, Celia

Littlehawk had seen the inside of a criminal law text-
book way more recently than the only other attorney she
knew, the eldercare lawyer who served some of the clients at the nursing home. He was brash and creepy and
had a broad Massachusetts accent. She could of course
let the court appoint somebody, but she distrusted this
notion instinctively. What would you get, some lazy hack
who couldn't get a better job in Portland or Augusta?
She didn't have a lot of faith in public servants.

She knocked.

Celia Little was expecting her. She was shorter,
broader, and a good deal younger than Hazel, and
her straight black hair was cut in a no-nonsense bob.
The room was spare and paneled in the kind of fake
wood wallboard you could buy at Home Depot by the
sheet. Ms. Little had a metal desk with a laptop open
on it, a rolling office chair, a wastebasket, a chipped
wooden bookcase holding legal textbooks, and a small
blue upholstered love seat that was all too clearly de-
accessioned from the Memory Neighborhood of Ainsley Nursing. Brianna knew why, when she accepted
Celia's invitation to sit, and the foam of the seat greeted
her weight by emitting a faint exhalation of urine. Brianna wished that before she had opened the door, Celia
had exed out the screen on her laptop that was still dis-
playing an ongoing game of solitaire.

Celia took out a fresh legal pad and a ballpoint, and began taking down information. She was brisk and businesslike, and Brianna found herself wishing her well; it seemed to her that Celia was performing a role-playing exercise from her Business Practices course. She didn't ask any of the questions Brianna expected, like how she was going to get paid. After a while, she took out her cell phone and called Shep Gordon's office. She introduced herself as Cherry Weaver's attorney, and said that she would like to see her client. There was some waiting, then some uh-huhs on Celia's end, then she turned to Brianna and gave her a smile and a thumbs-up.

"I don't want her questioned without me there," she said confidently into the phone, and hung up. "They'll let us see her in half an hour," she said to Brianna. "Why don't you go buy her a toothbrush and anything else she might need before tomorrow, and I'll meet you at the jail. You know where it is?"

Brianna did.

The Ainsley Jail was a relatively new structure serving the whole of Webster County. It had a large parking lot, fairly empty at the moment as these were not regular visiting hours. The building was wide and low, made of institutional yellow brick, generally designed to depress. Inside, the ceilings were low and covered in acoustic tile, the floors a nasty brown linoleum, and the walls were lined with putty-colored ceramic tiles. Brianna was told to hand over the toiletries she had brought and sit in the waiting area, while Celia was taken through a locked door to meet her client.

Cherry looked like a whipped dog when she was brought out. She was wearing an olive-drab jumpsuit, and every line of her face and posture of her body conveyed fear and misery. The guard showed her to a small table with two chairs in a hallway. Nonplussed to be given no more privacy than this, Celia stared at the guard, still standing beside Cherry, until he walked to the end of the corridor and disappeared around the corner.

Celia explained that Cherry should hold nothing back, that everything she told her lawyer was held in confidence, and that she would do her best for her.

"Do you have any questions?"

Cherry was staring around her, at the grim tiles on the walls, the streaky linoleum of the floor, and at her own bare goose-bumped arms. This wasn't at all like TV. She asked, "Are you a real lawyer?"

Celia said she was, and asked Cherry to explain the facts of the case. As Cherry talked, a halting, back-and-forth stream of details, self-justification, and outrage, Celia took notes in a fluent Palmer script that Cherry found impressive. In her school they didn't learn cursive. The richer kids had computers and typed; the rest printed. When she had run out of questions, Celia asked, "Would you take a lie detector test?"

Cherry looked up from her bitten nails, seeming startled. For a long moment, she didn't say anything.

"Are those like . . . legal?"

"Legal, yes. They can be very helpful, although they are not usually admissible in court. Never mind, though. If you'd rather not, it's better not to."

"No, it's fine. I'll take it."

"You don't have to. It was just a question. Let's leave it for now." She put her legal pad back into her briefcase and rose. Cherry got up too, and immediately, the deputy reappeared from around the hall corner.

"Stay here," said Celia. "I'll send your sister in." Cherry sat back down, and watched Celia walk away down the hall, free as air.

Day Seven, Saturday, October 12

The Citation the Poole sisters booked for their return flight to Los Angeles was a bigger plane than they needed, but it was fast, and they didn't want to wait for the Embraer Lisa usually asked for. Mr. Gurrell had driven them to the private aviation terminal at the Bangor Airport, where the pilots, clear-eyed young men in crisp uniforms, greeted them kindly, took their luggage from Gabe's car, and loaded it into the cargo bay. Glory's clothes were packed in a Black Watch plaid canvas suitcase some guest had abandoned at the inn sometime in the 1970s. Mr. Gurrell stood on the tarmac at the foot of the steps onto the plane and shook first Lisa's hand, then Glory's. He couldn't say, one more time, how sorry he was for their losses, so he didn't. They said whatever they said to him from behind their large sunglasses, then turned and climbed aboard, Lisa moving painfully but carrying her dog, and Glory behind her with their hand luggage. As Gabe drove out of the terminal parking lot, he passed the hearse from Morrison's arriving with Mr. Antippas's casket. He didn't wait to watch it being loaded into the cargo hold with the suitcases.

For the Poole sisters, the flight across the country had never seemed longer. Lisa sat with Colette in her lap and her huge sunglasses on, looking out the window, as the plane lifted smoothly off the airstrip and banked south. Below, the state of Maine seemed a wilderness of greenish-black evergreens, as if it had barely been settled at all. When she'd arrived six days ago, she'd had a husband and four children. Today she had a dead step-daughter, a broken nose, and an ankle that would never be right, and what was left of her husband was traveling with the luggage.

She was still on oxycodone, because she hated pain, but she didn't like the way it made her feel. It was constipating and it wasn't right to be less than completely present at such a moment in her life. She didn't like the way her thoughts seemed liquid, flowing into one another, as if all time was present and always had been. She knew that there had been times, really important ones, when she'd let life happen to her. She'd somehow found herself married to a man she had meant only to enter a few rooms with because they made a beautiful couple. She thought he was going to be eye candy, but he turned out to be more like a mangle, powerful and determined to a degree she hadn't experienced before. She hadn't really thought of herself as a mother; she had thought she would be someone herself, do something, turn heads and cause talk, maybe start a fashion business or write a best seller. She had meant to marry a rich American with a trust fund and a degree from the Harvard Business School, not whatever Alex had turned out to be.

But Alex didn't just *think* his life was going to be a certain way, he *knew,* and when she found she was part of his certainty and tried to wiggle loose, he slept with her sister. Why that had led to her marrying him instead of . . . that piece seemed to be gone. But she didn't want this one to be. She was a widow. Widow. A sleek, golden-tanned widow, with a suitcase full of silk and suede clothing and her husband right next to it, all his big American dreams in the dark, in a double-wide box. Beautiful, lithe, powerful young Alex—he had wanted to be called Alec, one of the few things he wanted that never happened. Immigrant on the hustle, and such a marvel to watch, how quickly he learned, how he impressed men with ten times his privilege and education, got them to invest in him, and proved them right. The way women watched him when he crossed a room, even after he'd started to balloon, he moved like a dancer and made you think about what he'd be like in bed.

She knew that the dead come to you in dreams, especially when they've been wrenched from life unprepared. She didn't want to miss that. She didn't want Jenny to try to get to her and find a scrim of drugs keeping her out, as so much had kept her out in life. Wasn't that just Jenny exactly, a soul so full of want, right outside, able to see what she was trying to get to, but always behind glass, kept out by something invisible but obdurate. Crying. She was like a spirit, banging at the windows, crying but not making a sound. She felt that Jenny was crying, and she wanted to be open to her if, finally, she could help.

Colette began to wiggle on Lisa's lap. Glory, who had taken one of Lisa's oxycodones, she was a nervous traveler, was her excuse, didn't notice at first. Usually she was more attuned to what the dog needed than her sister was. More attuned to what Alex Antippas needed too, for that matter, though her interest in that was long behind them. Behind them, beneath them, literally at the moment beneath their feet, but beneath them in all ways. She shouldn't have crossed that line with him, but then if she hadn't, she'd never have known for sure that she shouldn't. She, Gloria, had always been a tuning fork, vibrating in response to what emanated from other beings, and something in Alex had been calling to her, unmistakably. It was her problem with men, insofar as she had a problem with them, that she knew exactly what they were thinking, what they wanted, when they were lying, when they were coming on. They *didn't* like it, as a rule. They didn't like being known. Women did, usually. Men thought it was a trick, rather than her strength as a woman. She wondered, if she'd had children of her own, if they would have adored her for her ability to really see them, or resented it, as men did. Most men. Not Alex, but he had been unusual. Very unusual. Not necessarily in good ways, but they had recognized something in each other. And now, he was a charred lump.

She had not infrequently wanted him dead. Didn't like how he treated people, especially her sister, and also minded that he'd chosen Lisa and not her, even though he admitted Glory was better in bed. And now he *was* dead, and something unexpected and unpleasant had happened: she remembered she had once been in love with him.

Why was Lisa trying to get up? Oh the dog.

Glory said, "Stay, I'll get her." She rooted around in the dog bag for a Wee-Wee Pad, and put it down in the aisle between them. Colette jumped down from Lisa's lap, squatted, and emitted a puddle of a size to indicate that Glory had intervened at the last possible minute.

Colette hopped back to Lisa's lap while Glory took the sopping pad into the bathroom and put it in the trash. She washed her hands, while checking her makeup in the mirror. She looked like hell. She had run out of her own shampoo, and the stuff the hotel gave you left her hair looking like something you'd scour a pan with. And her roots were showing. She'd brought her color formula with her in case she had to get a touch-up before she got home, but obviously *that* hadn't happened. The light in these airplane bathrooms was horrible; it looked as if she had two black eyes. God it would be good to sleep in her own bed.

But there was much to go through before that happened. The press would be at the airport. The people from Forest Lawn would be there to take Alex away. He would be buried beside Jenny; he had barely outlived her. *If* the lawyer had managed to buy the plot they wanted. Had that happened? She couldn't remember. It was good that at least her sister wouldn't have to get off the plane soaked with dog piss.

She slept a little. She woke and wondered if, when they stopped in Denver to refuel, she would have time to pop into the airport and have her nails done. But no, they'd be out at the private terminal, where there weren't any services. She'd just have to remember to keep her hands away from her face when they got to L.A., if the photographers were there, and she was sure they would be. Jenny's press agent would never be able to resist tipping them off.

One thing she could say, this terrible week had been great for her career. She was booked on morning talk shows three days this week, and the producer of her old cable show had been calling to talk about a special on grieving. Her stylist was collecting wardrobe for her, and her hair person would come to the house tomorrow evening. She was planning to stay with her sister for the next few days, or until she was sure Lisa could cope. Jenny's manager, the scumbag, had arranged for a star-studded "Celebration of Artemis's Life" at the Staples Center for Monday, Columbus Day, when the whole world would be home from school and work and able to tune in. Taylor Swift was coming. Lady Gaga was in Europe but had sent a tribute video.

Cissy Houston would sing a gospel hymn, and read a prayer for Artemis and Whitney. Maybe she could spin the grief special into a series. She could do a couple of shows on addiction and recovery, and at least one on the perils of child stardom. She knew somebody who knew somebody who knew Britbrit's press rep. Brit would be a great get, if she could pull it off.

And when were they going to bury Alex? They'd been ordered not to have him cremated, as if he weren't half-cremated already, until the toxicology reports were definitive. They still didn't know what had killed him. Maybe they never would, it wasn't exactly NCIS up there. That deputy sheriff, Bubbah or whatever he was called, she'd known kids like that. Poster child for ADHD, hadn't anyone up there heard of psychopharmacology? He couldn't sit still, he was always tapping or jiggling something, he was always in the wrong place, looking the wrong way. Cue the Ritalin fairy. How many times had he asked her if she was sure her sister hadn't left their room the night of the fire. Left their room? Lisa could barely leave her bed. Glory had been afraid she was going to have to call housekeeping for a bedpan for her, as if anyone had one of those in the linen closet anymore. Except actually, a place like that inn, a great monument to life in 1885, probably did. They probably had hot water bottles.

Someday, if it was ever all right to laugh about any of this, she could do a very funny imitation of the great detective, solemnly asking, "When were you born? Do you know what time? Can you find out?" It would make a marvelous skit. She was good at imitations too, a great mimic.

Gabriel Gurrell, who hadn't been off the grounds of the inn since a brief trip to the drugstore in Bergen Falls Wednesday morning, was not rushing his trip back from Bangor. He'd been in crisis mode since the smoke alarm went off early Thursday morning, and he needed the silence. For some reason a song from his youth kept playing on the jukebox in his head: "Mama said there'd be days like this, there'd be days like this, my mama said . . ."

Except Mama had not remotely told him there would be days like this, let alone a week like this. He felt as if he would start gibbering and making obscene gestures if he didn't get some quiet, a hot shower, and a proper night's sleep. What had made him imagine that running a country inn in some rural backwater was going to be a peaceful life?

His insurance agent wasn't calling him back. "Family emergency," his girl said. The guy was quick enough to pick up the phone when he was selling.

No. No. No, he wasn't going to think about his fire insurance, or rebuilding, or whether he could keep the rest of the hotel open during the construction, and if so how? Welcome to peaceful Oquossoc, where the shrieking of power saws and the crashing of hammers start at seven in the morning and don't stop until three? Welcome to historic Oquossoc, where every guest receives a construction-grade set of ear protectors at check-in?

What were the chances he could get a contractor to wait until nine in the morning to make noise?

None. No chance. The workday started here at seven whether you had cows to milk or not. Electricity might as well not have been invented, the workday was the same as it had been when it was rise with the sun and go to bed when it gets dark.

Stop. If he couldn't stop running around this hamster wheel, trying to answer questions that had no answers, he would go mental.

He'd danced to "Mama Said" one summer at Rehoboth Beach when he was . . . fifteen? Mid-1960s? With that girl with the Jean Seberg haircut, whose father raised chinchillas. His sister Jean had a huge collection of girl-group 45s that she kept in their pristine paper sleeves, in a little square sort of suitcase for carrying records to parties. They were filed in there like legal briefs. *C* for the Crystals, *D* for the Dixie Cups, *S* for the Shirelles. His sister had a battery-driven record player too, and one night he had liberated them from her room in the little screened cottage they rented for two weeks in the summer, and been the hero of the beach party. Mama said there'd be days like this. Will you still love me tomorrow? "Rockin' Robin." Tweedleytweedleydee. Tweedleydeedleydee. Robin was the girl's name. She showed him which star was Betelgeuse. Sand between his toes and in the cuffs of his blue jeans. Firelight. Rolling Rock beer.

What his mother actually said, when his sister found that the needle on her record player was ruined and there was sand in most of her tenderly-cared-for record sleeves, was, "Oh Jean, he didn't mean to. Pour me another one, will you, hon?"

To her two fatherless children, the two weeks at Rehoboth was a beach vacation. They could do everything they wanted to do on foot or on bikes. To Doris Gurrell, it was two weeks in a gin bottle. Gabe had never, before or since, known a person who took such deep pleasure in getting blotto, day after day, starting with beer for breakfast. The rest of the year she worked two jobs, made sure the children had clean clothes and a hot meal at night, and only took a drink or two on weekends. When he was growing up, he had dreaded the thought of his mother retiring. What would there be to keep her from drinking all day every day until she died? But she had surprised them. When she retired, she gave up drinking altogether, took lessons in dancing the tango, and married one of her elderly dance partners. He took her on tango cruises to Nassau and the Bahamas every winter and left her very well provided for when he hung up his last pair of dancing shoes.

Gabe was working at the Biltmore in Santa Barbara by that time, and he was so relieved to know that he didn't have to worry about taking care of his mother any more that he impulsively married a girl he didn't know nearly well enough, as it turned out. The marriage ended abruptly, two years in, when he learned she had had an abortion without telling him and had no intention of having children. How had he happened not to have discussed this topic before that euphoric week when rushing down to City Hall with this beautiful creature had seemed like such a good idea? Youth was a condition defined by the fact that you don't know what you don't know until it's too late.

He'd assumed for years that he'd marry again and have children sooner or later, but whether because that early mistake had made him overcautious, or for some other reason, it never happened. Women were so irate about all that it cost them to be the child bearers during those bra-burning, hairy armpit years, the mess of their periods, cramps and headaches, childbirth itself . . . but how about the fact that if they wanted to have babies, they could?

When he first met Sarah, he was managing the Clift in San Francisco, a small gem of a hotel off Union Square that catered to the old line, well-born, well-heeled traveler. She had had a small restaurant of her own back east, she said, dinner service only, but running her own place had been too much for her, and like so many people who want a fresh start, she decided to try California. She had taken the only job that was open at the Clift kitchen where she had friends, doing food prep and other lowly tasks. It was a little puzzling, since the nature of the job didn't sync with her résumé, but she said she wanted the experience of a big kitchen. And she needed the health insurance. The executive chef had liked her and moved her up quickly; her cooking skills were real. What was clear to Gabe, though, was that she'd had some kind of very hard time. Romantic, financial, some kind of breakdown. He didn't know what, and she wasn't talking, but certain things made him think she'd been living very close to the edge. She was much too thin, and she had the health problems of a person who couldn't or wouldn't take care of herself. At first, given his own experience with his mother, he suspected substance abuse, but he knew the signs very well, and she didn't have them. She wasn't impulsive, or compulsive. She didn't lie, there were no unexplained absences. She could take a glass of wine, no problem, and not reach for another.

He'd been attracted to her from the start. They were of similar ages, and her diction and manners told a different story from her battered appearance. He liked a woman with a bit of mystery, and he paid attention to her. She was having a problem with her neck when they first met, and he sent her to a celebrity chiropractor. The chiropractor discovered she was missing two teeth in the back of her lower jaw and said Oh, well, no wonder. He couldn't fix her until she had the teeth replaced. Gabe lent her money to have the work done, since even the hotel's fancy health plan didn't cover it. She accepted his friendship, at first warily, but eventually, warmly. The teeth were fixed, her neck pain went away, her skin and hair looked better, healthy, and she gradually filled out and began to smile and laugh more. For a brief, to Gabe heavenly, interlude they were lovers. Then a restaurant out in the avenues offered Sarah her own kitchen, and she was gone. Eventually the Clift was sold to one of those "groups" that believe that a hotel lobby should be so dim that you need a flashlight to sign the guest register, and attracted young hipsters from Europe or the movie business wearing black and sporting name brand luggage, watches, and strollers. Even their babies wore black. Gabe decided it was time to go back east. They didn't see each other again for years, until he bought the inn and asked her to come with him, and she came.

As he drove into Bergen, he had a sudden thought of the lunch tray that would be sent up to him as soon as he was back in his office. A big tumbler full of green slime that Sarah made for him, two rye crisp crackers, and a pot of green tea. Every once in a while he called down to the kitchen and asked for a club sandwich or a bacon cheeseburger, and Sarah laughed, and sent green slime. He was allowed to eat whatever he wanted for dinner, that was something. And of course, there was always the chance that if he got down to fighting trim she would marry him, though his belief in that was, he recognized, a triumph of hope over experience.

Just Barb's. A plate of fried shrimp with tartar sauce, coleslaw, and French fries. A real Coke, with caffeine and sugar in it. He passed the restaurant, regretted it, stopped at the corner, and parked the car.

Shep Gordon and Carson Bailey were sitting in a booth, drinking coffee. Shep gave Gabe a wave, beckoning him over. "Take a pew," Shep said expansively, and Carson scooted over to make room.

"You look like you're just finishing up."

"We've got most of the problems of the world solved," said Shep. Evidently they were in the mood for company. Or an audience. Gabe sat down. Sandra appeared, and took his order.

"You got anybody left up at the inn?" Shep asked.

"Mrs. Babbin and her friend. They're staying on for a few more days. Mr. Clark was still there when I left this morning, but I think he leaves tonight."

"There's a lot of nervous chat in the county about what you're going to do," said Carson.

"How do you mean?"

"Whether you'll rebuild, or. You know. Shut it down."

The bluntness of the question, given his state of fatigue and muddle, struck Gabe dumb for a moment.

"The inn means a lot to Bergen," said Carson. "Town's biggest employer." As if Gabe didn't know that.

Sandra arrived with a knife and fork for Gabe, and a glass of water.

"There's a lot of bad feeling toward Cherry Weaver, I'll tell you that," said Shep. "A lot of people saying she as good as killed this town, if the inn goes."

Gabe's food arrived. He looked at it and suddenly saw it as a big mound of grease with a calorie count in the four figures, and thought of Sarah. Shep reached over and took a shrimp from Gabe's plate with his fingers and ate it. Okay, fuck it. If I end up as big as Shep, I'll join the police force and scare people for a living, Gabe thought.

"Poor Cherry," he said, chewing. He shook salt onto his mound of shrimp, and added ketchup.

Carson Bailey gave a bark of laughter. "Poor Cherry!" He shook his head. "Poor Cherry is going to have a good long stay at the taxpayers' resort in Windham. 'Poor Cherry.' After what she did to you?"

Gabe swallowed. "You guys are that sure she did it? Antippas smoked in his room all the time, you know. Housekeeping was in a swivet about it. The curtains, the bed clothes, all stank of smoke. I didn't know how I was ever going to rent it out again, unless I redid the whole room."

"Won't have to worry about *that* now, anyway," said Carson.

No, thought Gabe glumly, and his rage at Alexander Antippas drained away. Again.

"Her own lawyer thinks she's guilty, you know," said Shep. "Little Miss Weaver."

Gabe stopped chewing and looked at him.

"Really?"

Carson's and Shep's eyes met. They were feeling extremely pleased with themselves.

"Her lawyer *told* you that Cherry did it? Is that even legal?"

"She's pretty green. The lawyer. Might be her first criminal case."

"But how could she do a thing like that?"

Shep and Carson began to chuckle, Shep's noise a deepish huh, huh, huh, and Carson's more of a giggle.

"I guess you get what you pay for," said Carson.

Shep said, "She was having a cigarette in front of the jail, and a corrections officer we know was standing right there, smoking a cigarette. He asked her how the case was going and she said, it wasn't the case she'd hoped for. Said Cherry didn't want to take a lie detector test, and in Crim Law they teach you it's not a good sign."

"Oh," said Gabe. "Well that's not exactly a confession."

"No, but if her own lawyer thinks she did it, it tells us a lot."

The assistant AG for the great state of Maine caught Sandra's eye and pointed to his coffee cup and his pie plate. He was reupping on both.

The Antippas house was in the hills, near enough to the Hotel Bel-Air that the family could order food as if they were calling room service and send one of the kids to pick it up. It wasn't the house they'd lived in when Jenny was small and the babies were born; that had been a more modest affair in Studio City. The new house was a gift from Jenny. She'd commissioned it when her first album went triple platinum. The architect was a famous devotee of Frank Lloyd Wright, and his creation was dug into the hillside, with bedrooms cantilevered out over the drop below, and an infinity pool that seemed to float above the cityscape, so when you were in it, especially at night, it was like swimming in sky.

What had been called a living room when Lisa was growing up in Ontario was called by the architect the "great room," as if it were winter quarters for medieval Norsemen with the family and servants and animals all cooking and eating and sleeping around the same hearth to survive the winter. The great room had walls of glass, and when Lisa and Glory walked in at the end of their journey, it was so filled with flowers that they were walloped by the mass of colors and smells obscuring the fact that once a family had lived here. Some of the "floral tributes" had been in place since Tuesday and a swampy odor rose from the vases, but Lisa's children had no idea about changing the water or removing dead stems. More arrangements covered the dining room table, most still wrapped in cellophane, with cards attached.

"Condolences," "Deepest Sympathy," "Our thoughts are with you at this *difficult* time," from Jenny's agent, her manager, her record label, her stylist, the stars of the morning talk shows, her publicist, and the publicists of half the recording artists in Hollywood. The children had just left them wherever they found room, and waited for their parents to come home. Then a fresh wave had arrived when news of Alexander's death hit the papers, from all the same people and some new ones. "At this difficult time." Why did they even try?

Sophie and Ada were sitting in the great room, waiting. They burst into tears as they heard, at last, the sound of the dog's scrabbling toes on the slate floor of the hall. As Colette rushed toward them they were rushing the other way, into the two women's arms. They shook and sobbed there. Then they switched, and embraced and sobbed in the arms of the other. Jeremy was downstairs in the family gym. Someone sent for him, and he appeared, wearing shorts and a sweaty T-shirt with a picture of Artemis on it, a relic from her "Break Me" tour. His earphones were around his neck, and as he moved close to them, they could hear Jenny singing from the tiny iPod strapped to Jeremy's arm. He too began to cry, as he hugged first his mother, then his aunt. Colette pranced among them, upset, overjoyed, annoyed, and confused, barking.

The housekeeper, Manuela, came out of the kitchen and she too was embraced, as she murmured in Spanish with tears in her eyes. She was a plump woman in a pale blue uniform with wire-rimmed glasses and her glossy black hair in a bun. She gestured at the jungle of flora in the great room, then led the way into the dining room.

"The children wanted you to see them," said Manuela.

"I understand."

"You want me to fix them?" She meant change the water, trim the stems, save what could be saved. Lisa reached for the card attached to an enormous bunch of white roses. "Our thoughts are with you in your sorrow." From the law firm Alex used when someone sued him.

"No. Please. Please get rid of them. Keep the cards."

Manuela's husband, Freddy, came in from the car with the luggage, and carried it through to the bedrooms. Lisa followed him, limping. She had been longing to be at home for the last five days, but now that she was here she felt trapped. It was too much sensation, too much intensity, too much horror. The intrusion of all the curiosity and false sentiment was more of a burden than she'd expected, and added to it now was the grief of her children, all looking to her to make it better somehow, to help, to cope. They said God never sent you more than you could handle. Who were They, and what the hell did They know about it?

She walked into the bedroom she had shared with Alex for so many years. She'd just had it redone in the spring. The walls were covered in French hand-blocked paper, patterned in gold vines on a cream-colored background. The gold vines caught the evening sun and flared, as if they were burning without being consumed. The headboard of the enormous bed was covered with sand-colored shantung silk, matching the curtains and the carpet. There was an oily stain on the silk on Alex's side of the bed where his head had rested when he watched the enormous TV embedded in the wall above built-in pear wood dressers.

She watched Freddy put the suitcases on the silk-upholstered bench at the end of the bed, Alex's covered with Ls and Vs. Alex had liked logos that let the world know how much he had paid for everything. She could get rid of those now. No more Louis Vuitton luggage, no more scarves with linked Chanel Cs on them, that Alex gave her at every birthday. If she wanted to get rid of them. Did she? She couldn't tell. She'd been Alex's creature for so long.

Alex's suitcase. The police had brought his suit-case and the clothes, whatever they didn't think was evidence, to the room she and Glory shared, and Glory had packed it for her. Glory had really tried, this week. The suitcase stank of smoke and wet, although things that had been in the closet had survived the hosing surprisingly well. The maid must have closed the closet doors. Alex never did.

And now. Should she unpack it? Why? Should she send his beautiful custom-made shirts to the laundry, so they could hang in the closet for no one to wear, ever again?

His clothes? His sock drawer? His desk, his computer? Did she really want to know what was in them?

What if it had been she who had died? What would be found in *her* drawers? The sex toys from Babeland in her bedside table? Maybe she should tape notes to them right now: these were presents and I never used them. And I never threw them out because I was planning to give them to the poor. What a good idea.

Maybe she should just throw the suitcase out without unpacking it. Or give it to Freddy. Maybe someone at his church weighed 350 pounds. You could put two of Freddy in one of Alex's suits; maybe they could figure out a way for two people to wear the clothes at the same time.

When her son's school sent the eighth-graders to Ecuador to see the cloud forests and the Galápagos, they always had a clothing drive so they could take suitcases full of castoffs to donate when they got there. All over Quito you could see children playing in the street wearing blazers with school crests, and on their way to the mountains Jeremy had caught sight of a farmer plowing on his tractor, wearing a tuxedo. But what was the chance they could use clothes as big as this?

The funeral people, with their ritual pomp, made death seem so dignified. She realized that she should have told Manuela that she and Freddy could take the truck and carry all those flowers to their church, where armies of ladies would pull out all the living blooms and reassemble them for the altar, or to take to shut-ins.

She roused herself and hobbled back to the kitchen, but it was too late. Manuela had already obediently carried the masses of bouquets out the back door and left them in piles beside trash barrels. And up on the road, outside the gates, photographers with long lenses were taking pictures of them.

Day Eight, Sunday, October 13

On Sunday morning Earl Niner found Gloria Poole's suitcase. He put his pitchfork into the pile out behind the stables where he dumped the dirty straw and horse apples after he mucked out the stalls, and deep in the middle of it, he hit something solid. He dug it out and carried it, still smeared with dung and a few tendrils of rotting salad, to the basement door of the hotel and left it in the dank room where the gardening tools were kept. Then he went to tell Mr. Gurrell. Gabe called Shep Gordon at the barracks and was patched through to him at home. Shep was off-duty and just about to take his stepson to the shooting range. He told Gabe to call Buster, since he was right down the road.

Buster arrived with all speed, blue light silently revolving. He had forgone the siren. Gabe Gurrell met him at the front steps.

Gabe said, "I thought it was best to keep him in my office, on his own, before everyone in the back of the house has a chance to ask him things and tell him their theories." Buster agreed that that had been a good plan, and followed Gabe upstairs.

Earl was sitting rigid in an overstuffed armchair covered in mint brocade, staring at his mucky boots and dirty fingernails, and fidgeting. Buster had planned to question him in Gabe's office, but he felt a visceral sympathy when he saw how itchy Earl looked. He'd get nothing but monosyllables from him in here.

"Why don't you show me where you found it," he said. Earl got out of his chair more crisply than Buster would have thought possible and bolted for the door.

Earl led the way down a staircase that let them out on the side of the building. He scuttled along with more freedom of movement than he ever displayed in the public parts of the hotel. Buster knew the feeling. This was a man at home with solitude and animals and with judging the weather by smelling the wind, not with carpets and fancy upholstery. Buster wondered why he lived inside instead of out in the barns and sheds somewhere; surely there was a stableman's apartment. But he realized he knew the answer. His animals needed constant temperatures, especially the parrot, and protection from drafts. Nineteenth-century workman's quarters probably didn't have the latest in creature comforts.

They trudged silently out past the kitchen garden, across the stable yard with its well-worn mounting block, and entered the big stone stable. The front entrance was an immense sliding door, big enough to admit a truck with a fully stacked hayrick. Earl had to hold the handle with both hands and hurl his weight sideways to get the door rolling.

Inside, in the fragrant dimness, Buster saw rows of box stalls, now mostly empty. There were brass plates on the doors with the names of long-dead occupants. FROLIC. BLUE RIDGE. SAFETY. Safety was a good name for a saddle horse. There were five animals left, two ponies, two sleepy old geldings, and a mare. The dim air was full of dust motes from the hay and straw stored in the lofts above, and smelled of the loamy sweat of the horses. They stood, heads down, drowsing through the morning, except for the mare, a pretty chestnut named Kitty, who stretched her neck over the top of her stall door, and watched them come through. Buster stopped to stroke her velvety nose and she nuzzled at his pockets to see if he had any treats for her. Earl had to stop and wait for the deputy to remember where they were supposed to be going.

They clattered across the bay where the horses would be cross-tied to be washed down and groomed after exercise. Earl had his brushes and curry combs and hoof picks all carefully cleaned and hung on a Peg-Board. The concrete floor slanted toward a central drain, and a bucket and sponges stood by the tap. Buster's attention snagged here too; he loved special equipment, especially when it had to do with animals. He looked at the lunge lines coiled and hung on hooks. The halters, the leather supple and glossy. The lead lines, for beginning riders. Earl almost lost him again at the tack room, with its rows of English saddles on triangle-shaped brackets that projected from the dark wainscot wall, the stirrups neatly tucked up at the top of their leathers, and rows of bridles on hooks, with all kinds of bits. Snaffles, curbs, and one draconian one of a type Buster had never seen before. He would have liked to nip in and have a better look at it, but Earl was rolling back the door that led outside behind the barn. The broad slant of sunlight cutting a sudden path across the floor recalled him, and he followed Earl out into the weak autumn warmth.

There was a paddock out here, for letting the horses out in the fresh air. In the distance Buster saw a riding ring, well made, if in need of a coat of paint.

"Do you give riding lessons?" Buster asked.

"Not me," said Earl. "Girl from Bergen Falls boards her horses here. She gives lessons and takes the guests on trail rides. This is where I found her." He gestured at a wide square compost heap, held in place by a low wall of logs. "I turn the pile a couple or three times a week. Stuck my pitchfork in and hit something. Cleared a hole and there she was."

By the end of this speech, Buster had understood that "she" referred to the suitcase, which was a relief. He took out his pad and pencil.

"What time was this?"

"Don't wear a watch."

"Do your best."

Earl thought about it. "Must have been about nine-fifteen, nine-thirty. Mr. Rexroth was just going out on his way to church, and he has to drive a ways." Earl gestured in the direction of the front driveway, where you could just see the inn's big stone gateposts from where they stood.

"And this is the compost heap for the whole operation?"

"Yuh."

"Garden waste, kitchen scraps, the whole nine yards?"

"Yuh. We dump it all right here."

"I thought you had to have some kind of closed-up bin to get it to cook right."

"You see the steam coming off it?" Earl asked.

"I do."

"She just cooks away no matter what we do to her. We got all the right things, going in. Even earthworms. When this pile gets up over the rails, we start a new one, and in a couple of weeks, this one is ready for the gardens."

Buster scribbled. "So the kitchen dumps out here, and the garden crew?"

"Yuh. Housekeeping too. They all got their own wheelbarrows. Have to, otherwise, someone's always complaining that someone else took their wheelbarrow and never brought it back."

"Housekeeping? What do they put in?"

"Shredded paper. Ash from the fireplaces."

Buster was losing the thread a little, thinking of the compost bin he had built for Brianna, with instructions from the Internet. They were doing something wrong; the stuff they put in there didn't so much cook as it rotted. And not very fast at that. He wondered if fireplace ashes would help. Maybe Earl would come over and give him some advice. Unconsciously, as he did when he was trying to sort something out, he had started to pace. Earl sat down on a straw bale and watched him with interest. The silence stretched.

"I've been trying to work out when was the last time I turned it," he offered helpfully.

Buster remembered what he was supposed to be doing.

"That would be important to know," he said, turning to a new sheet in his notebook.

"I think it must have been Wednesday morning."

"You haven't turned it since the fire?"

"Been busy. That's what makes me think Wednesday morning. Unless it was Tuesday."

Buster made notes.

"And when you found the suitcase, what did you do?"

"I took it in to the tool room and went to find Mr. Gurrell."

"You didn't try to open it?"

"It's not *my* suitcase."

"You must have been curious."

"Curious about a lot of things. Doesn't make 'em my business."

"And were you wearing gloves at the time?"

Earl pulled out and waved the work gloves that had been stuffed into his back pocket. "You don't want to pitch manure without your gloves. Give ya blisters."

Buster started back to his vehicle for an evidence bag, by which he meant a trash bag in this case, in which to put Earl's interesting discovery. (Most country people had trash bags in their cars in case of roadkill, unexpected dump runs, or needing somewhere to put wet bathing suits.) As he passed the door to the kitchen he stopped to note the wheelbarrow standing by the steps. He took in the scene. Technically, he should have taken a picture or made a sketch of it, standing right there, but he didn't need to. For all the things he couldn't do that were easy for other people, he had his own unusual skills. One of them was that he could take in a huge amount of visual data and map it later, to scale.

The kitchen door opened, and Mrs. Weaver came out with a large bucket full of vegetable trimmings, fruit peels and cores, and what looked like dozens of egg shells and a couple of pounds of coffee grounds. He watched her empty them into the wheelbarrow. She straightened, turned, and gave him a long look. Reading faces was one of the things he wasn't so good at; was that disgust, or sorrow, or accusation? Whatever it was, she gave him a good dose of it, then turned and climbed the steps.

He was the police. Her daughter was in jail. Why should she be happy? On the other hand, Brianna . . .

Buster was about to move on toward the parking lot, when he heard a tap on the kitchen window. Chef Sarah was there. She smiled and held up a finger to him, meaning "wait a minute."

He waited.

Sarah emerged with a sweater thrown on over her apron, and her bare feet stuffed into chef's clogs. She was carrying a paper bag.

"Sorry, I had to find something to put these in. I made chocolate croissants this morning and nobody ate them. They're no good the second day. Take them with you."

Buster wasn't sure what to do. They weren't supposed to take presents, especially not at crime scenes. "I shouldn't," he said, beginning to back away. He could smell them now. Chocolate and butter.

"Of course you should," she said kindly. "You're missing your lunch." She tucked the bag under his elbow. Embarrassed, he thanked her. She was hurrying back to the kitchen, which he was glad of, because that made it too late to give the bag back.

Hope and Maggie had been to church and enjoyed the service very much. The church itself was picture-postcard beautiful, a nineteenth-century monument to simplicity, white clapboard with a square sanctuary, and a short but shapely steeple. The windows were leaded, with ripply old hand-blown glass, but clear instead of stained, which made the interior particularly stark and peaceful. The hymns, played on a piano by a short round lady with a head a little too small for her body, were tub-thumpers, clearly played by ear. Maggie found that if you tried to sight-read the harmonies in the hymnal, you soon found yourself in conflict with the accompanist. That left the tiny choir a little at a loss, since they *were* reading the music, but the congregation joined in lustily. The preacher, an erect spindly man wearing ancient black robes, gave a simple homily for the children in the front rows, who afterward were led down to the Sunday school in the basement. Then he delivered a gentle sermon for the rest of the sinners. Maggie had the impression that everyone in the room had heard it before, but she felt that everyone enjoyed a lesson drawn from the wisdom of the *Peanuts* comic strip. At the close of the service they were urged to join the fellowship hour in the parish hall, where the preacher happened to know there would be some of Mrs. Missirlian's good banana bread. Hope and Maggie didn't have to be asked twice.

The parish hall underneath the sanctuary was lit with fluorescent fixtures that looked like overturned ice trays. There was green linoleum on the floor, and blackboards on wheels stood in the corner where Sunday school had been conducted. The children, now freed from Sunday strictures, were running in and out of the throng playing tag, their hands full of cookies. Maggie and Hope surveyed the scene, then chose their marks. Maggie headed for the piano lady, while Hope homed in on a beefy young man with a soul patch and a cross tattooed on his neck.

"Good morning," Maggie said, offering her hand. "I just wanted to thank you, you played with such spirit. Maggie Detweiler."

"Peg Nuttle," said the piano lady, beaming. She had plump soft arms with dimples at the elbows, and a very sweet smile. "So nice of you to say that. I'm self-taught, I'm afraid. We had an organist, a beautiful musician, but he died. Is this your first Sunday with us?"

"It is, and we thought it was lovely. So you're not a professional?"

"Oh, no. We're pretty much all volunteers, here. I'm a kindergarten teacher."

Maggie felt a little click of satisfaction. She had a kind of radar for school people and had a small bet with herself that this was one. "Well, how lucky I am to meet you. I'm a teacher too, or I was, and wherever I go I always want to know about the local school. Is it that pretty brick building up the street, with the big elm in front?"

"That's it. And I just live around the corner. Makes for a short commute. Not that we exactly have a rush hour here."

"K through eight? K through twelve?" asked Maggie.

"Oh no, we only go up to six here in the village. It used to be that that's all the schooling the country children got, sixth grade and then they went to work. Nowadays they go in the bus over to Bergen Falls to the junior high. They got a real nice new building there now."

"I'd love to see it."

"Are you in town for a while? I think Mrs. Pell is in California visiting her daughter, she's the principal."

"We're staying at the inn."

"Oh. My," said Peg. "The inn, they've had such goings-on. Were you there for the fire?"

"We've been here since last Sunday. My friend"—she indicated Hope across the room, deep in conversation with the soul patch man—"has family here."

"Now who would that be?" asked Peg, her interest refocused.

"Do you know Deputy Babbin?"

"Buster! Such a sweetheart! I've taught boys like that."

"We've all taught boys like that," Maggie said, smiling. "You know, we're awfully sorry about Cherry Weaver being arrested."

"Oh, it's a terrible thing. I was saying to my sister, I really don't know what to make of it. I wouldn't have thought . . ."

"Well that's what I wanted to ask you. You knew her when she was little?"

"She was in one of my first classes."

"We always remember our first ones, don't we?"

Peg agreed, pleased to be talking with someone who knew the territory.

"She wasn't bright like her sister, of course," said Peg.

"Did you teach Brianna too?"

"No, but it's a small school. Brianna always won the spelling bee. Everyone thought she'd go to college. She'd come in at lunchtime to see Cherry, and that little girl just lit up every time. Nice children."

"Tell me about Cherry."

"She was one of those ones who see words backward?"

"Dyslexic?"

"I think so. We only did prereading in kindergarten at that time, and she could handle that, but she struggled later. She was a sweet child. She made me a May basket. She . . ." Peg caught herself and stopped.

"What?"

"Oh, I was just going to . . ."

Maggie said, "Go on. I've heard it all."

Peg said, "Well. When I thanked her for the basket and told her what a dear little girl she was, she said she liked me better than she liked her mother."

"Ah," said Maggie. She had indeed heard this story before, and it was a very tricky moment for a teacher, especially in a small town. You're pleased to be loved, but you also know that something is wrong in one of your families, and what if anything should you do about it? She nodded sympathetically.

"Of course I said I was sure she didn't really and she seemed stung. Disappointed in me. I still remember that. She was shy of me for a while, but she got over it. A very sunny nature she had then. I was always sorry about how it changed her, later. She'd come back to visit me when she was in fifth and sixth. Just drop in during recess and sit in my classroom, on one of those little chairs, and play with the guinea pig. When she was in my class, I had chosen her to take the guinea pig home over Christmas. She was so proud of that."

"I love it when they come back," said Maggie. Though in fact it gave her pause when a kid would rather hang around with grown-ups than with her own age group.

When Maggie related this conversation at Barb's, where they had repaired for an early lunch to compare notes, Hope said, "I think Cherry's mother must be a Capricorn."

"Because?"

"She's such a hard-ass."

"Apparently. Does your soul patch man know the Weavers?"

"Intimately. He ran with Brianna and her friends in high school, and half the time Cherry was with them, because Beryl Weaver was working nights. He said Cherry didn't like her mother, and when I asked him what made him say so, he said 'have you met her?' When she drove the school bus she threatened to tape their mouths shut if they weren't quiet. She kept a roll of duct tape on the dashboard. Actually used it a time or two."

"Did he mention the father?"

"He did. He worked for a tree surgeon summers and weekends when he was in school, and Roy Weaver was part of the crew, when he felt like earning a buck. Roy used to taunt the high school kids. His way of greeting them was to grab them hard by the crotch and say, 'Just wanted to see if you'd grown a pair.' Then he'd laugh. My guy said it really hurt."

"Lovely. Did he know anything about Cherry being in trouble?"

"Yep. You were right. And he's the one who drove her to the mall."

"Back up."

"Here's the story. A lot of tree work is winter work. Did you know this? You get ice and snow coating the tree limbs, the limbs fall down and take down the power lines—in the worst weather, the tree men are out in bucket trucks eighteen hours a day, clearing away the deadfall so the power guys can fix the lines. He says your hands and feet are so cold when you get home that you soak them in cold water and it feels as if it's boiling. I told him I knew the feeling.

"So some of the linemen had these hand warmers that you carried in your pockets. They burn for hours. They work like cigarette lighters, but enclosed some-how—I just took his word for it."

Maggie had her phone out and was Googling "hand warmers."

"Well, look at that," Hope said, when Maggie showed her the screen. "I had no idea. I should have them in every pocket. Anyway, my guy showed one to Cherry and she got excited and wanted to get one for her father for Christmas. He didn't know she was planning to steal it."

"And she was how old?"

"Fifteen. But unfortunately, it wasn't the gizmo she stole first. It was . . ."

"Don't tell me."

"Yes. The lighter fluid it runs on. If you get the fanciest kind, something Zippo makes, it doesn't give off as much smell and that's important if you're hunting. Her dad's a gun nut. You don't want your prey to . . ."

"Got it," said Maggie. "So she was arrested at fifteen for stealing a fire accelerant, and now they've got her for arson and felony murder."

"Exactly. She must have been pretty poor at stealing. She also lied about it, which doesn't help. She told the police she wanted it for her boyfriend. They wanted to talk to the boyfriend so she made up a name. When they couldn't find him she said he'd just joined the navy . . ."

"Oh the poor booby."

"And all because she was embarrassed that she was trying to be a hero to her dad."

"I assume Detective Gordon knows about the arrest, even though it shouldn't be on her record?"

"Of course he does."

"What made your church friend tell you all this?"

"I think he'd been dying for someone to ask him. He's got a little sneaker for Cherry would be my guess. And he hates the dad. Also, he might have spent just a little bit of time in the slammer himself. He suggested that he didn't think it was the right place for Cherry."

"I thought that looked like a prison tattoo."

Detective Gordon was waiting when Buster carried his bulky treasure into the barracks in Ainsley. He said, "What happened to you, you run into a bakery truck?" Buster looked down and brushed at his uniform shirt, showering croissant flakes onto the floor.

Shep took the bagged suitcase into the evidence room, where he and Buster and a crime tech donned plastic gloves. "Let's see what we got here." He took the suitcase from the trash bag and set it on the table. The crime tech took out a pair of tweezers and began fussily picking up bits of horse plop and vegetable matter and dropping them into plastic bags.

Shep took the suitcase.

"Detective," said the tech, "I was going to dust for prints first."

"After will do fine," said Shep. He popped the clasps and opened it.

It was almost empty. There was a plastic bag with the Oquossoc Mountain Inn name and logo on it, and on the other side, "laundry" printed in moss green script. There was also a pair of heavy leather gloves, a thing like a weird butterfly net, and an apparatus that looked like the kind of grabber you use to pick up your socks from the floor when you've had a hip operation and can't bend over. Shep's mother had to use one of those for months after she broke her pelvis.

Shep picked up the laundry bag and looked in.

"What's in it?" Buster asked.

"Underpants," said Shep. He used to say "panties," but his wife had broken him of it by calling his underwear panties and shirties and socksies until he got the point. He picked up the butterfly net thing and held it up. It didn't look new, and it didn't look random; it was a four-foot-long double bag made of slippery material, and had a triangular frame at the top attached to a telescoping handle. "Now what the hell do you make of this?" he asked. "You ever seen a thing like this before?"

"Nope," said the crime tech.

"Sure," said Buster.

The other men looked at him. "It's a snake bag," he said. "You pick up the snake with those tongs, and pop him into the bag, then you whip it closed with these." There were ties attached at the top. Shep stared.

"Well, aren't you a fountain of wisdom today," he said.

"How does the snake like it?" asked the tech.

"Depends on how used he is to people, and what kind of a mood he's in. They don't mind the bag once they're in it. It's like a den in there. Don't usually like the tongs so much though, unless you're real good at using them."

They all contemplated the equipment.

"This stuff belong to that Niner guy?"

"I guess it must," said Buster, "but I didn't see it in his room. All he had, that I saw, was a hook and a pair of handler's gloves. And not these gloves. His are a different color."

"A hook."

"A snake hook." Buster got out his notebook and drew a picture of a pole with a curved metal hook on the end. Then he added a snake, suspended in loops from the hook about a third of the way along its body. "You got to practice some to learn to slip it under without hurting him, and you have to get him in the right spot, third or halfway along, so he doesn't slip off, or strike."

There was a silence.

"I got to tell you," Shep said, "this is seriously creeping me out."

Buster shrugged.

"I guess we better see if little Cherry has a thing for snakes," Shep added. "And go over this whole rig for prints, inside and out." He patted along the inside of the suitcase, then unzipped one of the side pockets. Out came a little sewing packet, a tube of stain remover, a couple of packets of nail polish remover wipes, a corkscrew, and a fat amber vial of pills. The prescription was for Lisa Antippas, oxycodone, take every 4 to 6 hours as need for pain. Quantity 90.

"Ninety?" asked the crime tech. "What was she going to do, open her own drugstore?"

Day Nine, Monday, October 14

Monday morning, the Antippas household had been buzzing since 6:00 A.M. Sophie and Ada had done their own hair and makeup, but Artemis's stylist was with them with a rack of dresses that had been lent by eager designers.

Sophie had announced she was wearing her own clothes, but when she saw how her sister looked in a black silk Calvin Klein sheath, she too began trying things on. In the master bedroom, their mother was having her makeup redone, because she'd started to cry and had ruined it the first time. The makeup artist was dyeing her eyelashes black, so she wouldn't end up with mascara all over her face.

In the guest suite, Glory's hair was being blown out by the guy who used to style her for her talk show. She had spent the previous afternoon with twists of foil all over her head having her highlights done and the room still smelled of peroxide. Behind her, the bed was covered with dresses and suits, and a seamstress sat patiently watching the blow-out, waiting to do a last-minute fitting as soon as Glory decided for sure what she wanted to wear.

Jeremy, in the suit his father had bought him for his college graduation, was sitting outside by the pool under a shade umbrella. It was a bright day, perfect California weather. His mother could see him out the window, and knew by the way he was moving his shoulders and head, that he was lost in whatever music was streaming into his ears through wires too tiny for her to see from this distance. Artemis was in his head and singing to him.

In the living room, Manuela and Freddy sat stiffly in their best church clothes. Outside, two long limousines sent by Forest Lawn sat ready to take them all to the Staples Center.

Shep Gordon was off duty on Monday, at the Columbus Day parade in Ainsley with his wife. His stepson was playing the drums in his high school marching band and his wife's sister and her children were with them, standing in the drizzle, the kids poking each other and failing to pay attention or keep still as they waited for Donnie to pace proudly by. There was only a skeleton staff back at the state police barracks that morning, so it was Detective Flax who took the call from the crime lab. They had had no trouble finding a match for the prints all over the snake handling gear in Ms. Poole's suitcase. They belonged to Henry Rexroth.

Flax hated to interrupt Shep on his day off, but he knew he'd want to know. The only reason either one of them thought to tell Buster was that Buster was in uniform, working the parade. Things rarely got out of hand at eleven in the morning on a fall Monday in Ainsley, but the Harley club would be riding. They were mostly retired guys with their wives riding pillion or in sidecars, but a lot of them were veterans as well, flying American flags, and if you got a handful of crunchy granolas dressed like Indians chanting something like "Columbus was an Imperialist Tool," there could be trouble. Buster stood beside his cruiser, which was parked across one of the side streets to prevent anyone from inadvertently driving onto the parade route, wearing his shades in spite of the drizzle, popping one fist against his open palm, trying to look menacing.

Gabe Gurrell was at a loose end. His hotel was virtually empty. Mrs. Babbin and Mrs. Detweiler had driven off to do some sightseeing and have lunch with a friend in Bar Harbor. Normally this would be a busy weekend, but the news about the fire had caused a rash of cancellations in spite of how cheerfully the website announced that fall color was at its peak and the inn was ready to welcome and cosset guests.

The new girl on the desk seemed to have things under control, so Gabe went to the kitchen, looking for Sarah. He found that Oliver Brooks was running the lunch service, which consisted of a handful of walk-ins. He should have known Sarah wasn't there when the kitchen sent him the BLT he had asked for instead of green slime.

Gabe went up the back stairs to Sarah's apartment. If there was silence he wouldn't knock, afraid she'd had another migraine and was napping, but when he reached her door, he could hear the sound of the television.

She answered the door. She was wearing jeans and a sweatshirt, which startled him; he rarely saw her out of her chef whites these days.

"Sorry," he said.

"That's all right. I was just . . ." She trailed off and opened the door wider, which he took as an invitation to see for himself. He stepped in, and she closed the door behind him and went back to her chair.

"I came to see . . . Could I take you out to dinner tonight?"

She looked up, distracted.

"Where?"

Not the answer he was expecting.

"What would please you?"

Another pause. Her eyes kept cutting back to the television. She picked up the remote and muted the sound from the broadcast.

"Little Savannah Roseff, who trained with me here, is cooking in a new place on the other side of the lake. I heard she was doing my coffee soufflés and I hope it's not true." The dessert soufflés were a signature dish of Sarah's.

"Let's check it out," said Gabe.

Sarah was watching the screen. He had to move to her side to see what was on it.

The Antippases' funeral thing for the daughter. On the screen was a static shot of a mountain of balloons, stuffed animals, posters, and bouquets stacked against a barrier outside the Staples Center. On the pavement at the foot of the mound was a row of current magazine covers, all with pictures of Artemis. Artemis smiling, a publicity still from the Disney days. Artemis with her head thrown back and eyes closed, a mic in her hand, while beyond the stage a sea of people waved cell phones over their heads, the screens glowing like candles in the dark. Artemis in a sequined cobalt mermaid gown, grinning and holding up a Grammy award. Artemis in sweats with her head down, her lawyer clutching her elbow, doing a perp walk after one of her many DUIs. They cut to a live shot of teenage girls, one white and one black, weeping and holding a homemade poster that read *gone to soon*. Then a shot of limousines, with motorcycle escort, proceeding gravely through the crowds that were waiting to see the celebrities arriving.

"What's the place called?" Gabe asked.

Sarah clicked the television off. "The Firepond," she said. "It used to be a blacksmith's shop. On a stream. Very pretty."

"I'll see if they're open," said Gabe.

No response.

"I'll let you know," he added.

She was looking out the window at the gray sky, a moody contrast to the unreal brilliance of the California day the rest of the world was watching.

Gabe Gurrell had been kinder to Sarah than any man had ever been. Her father had been nearly fifty when she was born, and he was an old-fashioned man given to unpredictable angers, and never completely comfortable around women or children. Gabe was a completely new experience. He was patient and forgiving and despite being in a seemingly perpetual state of harassment, had a blessedly even temper. Which was probably exactly why Sarah felt no pressure to accept his proposals. He never rattled his saber or suggested there would be any consequence if she kept him dangling too long. But lately she had felt a certain longing, and wondered if she'd left it too late to try to share a life with a good man.

When Sarah was a girl, there were things she wanted the way only lonely children can want things, without any understanding of how unreachable or unreasonable they might be. She had wanted to be a veterinarian and have six children and live in a house full of animals, like Doctor Doolittle. Also, she wanted to be a famous singer, which would mean everyone would love her. The music teacher at her elementary school thought she had perfect pitch. In third grade she sang "I Dream of Jeannie with the Light Brown Hair" in an assembly on Stephen Foster, and Mrs. Lee went into transports. Her parents even found the money for her to study voice for several years. Come to think of it, the happy family dream and the rich and famous dream were the same dream, because when she was famous and everyone loved her, she would marry a man who looked like

Harrison Ford and have six children and live in a house full of animals like Doctor Doolittle. That had been her plan.

The other thing she had wanted desperately was a little bay pony named Cinders. Cinders belonged to the boy on a nearby farm who got polio because his parents didn't believe in vaccinations. Sarah's parents couldn't afford both the upkeep on a pony and voice lessons. The pony, Sarah reflected, would have been dead in the ground these past thirty years by now. But there were ponies here, and Clarence and Walter, and often there were children. She would go to dinner with Gabe, and then they'd see.

Gone to soon. Gabe went back to his office, shut the door, and turned on the television in the corner. He was slightly embarrassed that he wanted to watch this, and he told himself that he wasn't merely drawn to the spectacle, or to the pleasures of witnessing painful and intimate feelings that are none of his business. He wanted to see Mrs. Antippas and her sister. They were known to him, they were real to him. He was part of this story but it was weird to be part of something on the same screen that brought you *American Idol* or *Survivor.*

And then he couldn't seem to turn it off. He watched the stream of music gods and movie stars climbing out of their limousines and walking between the walls of people. Alicia Keys. Mariah Carey. The governor of California. Justin Timberlake. Rihanna. Two regulars from *Saturday Night Live,* where Artemis, irreverent and transgressive, had been a favorite, according to the reporter murmuring into her microphone. A feed from inside the auditorium, where a gold-plated casket was covered in white flowers. Orchids and roses. A gigantic screen on the stage showed a video of Artemis in performance, while the crowd filling the hall stared as if frozen, wiped their eyes suggestively, or in some cases fell to sobbing.

Here came Lisa Antippas limping slowly down the aisle to the reserved seats in the front row. She was leaning on a young man the reporter identified as her son, Jeremy. Next came Glory on the arm of a large unidentified man with the look of a bodyguard, and then the twins, Sophie and Ada, on too-high heels, holding on to each other. The reporter intoned, "This is our first glimpse of the family since the death of the troubled superstar. They are grieving a double tragedy today, first the death of a daughter and sister, followed by the bizarre death of the singer's father, Alexander Antippas, in a hotel fire on Thursday in the state of Maine. After the service here at the Staples Center, there will be a procession to Forest Lawn, where Artemis will be laid to rest. We're told that later this afternoon, the family will have a second service in a chapel at Forest Lawn, a private farewell to her father, who will be buried beside the daughter he outlived by only two days. You wonder what this family can be going through . . ."

The shot switched to outside again, where another motorcycle escort accompanied yet another limousine. The network reporter, in dark suit and dark glasses, said softly into his microphone, "Well that's right, Allie. There's been a rumor here for several hours that the First Lady and her two daughters, who reportedly are heartbroken Artemis fans, would be attending the service here today, and that was their limousine that just moved through security here on their way into the center. Security is extremely tight as you can imagine . . ."

The coverage moved back inside to where the video onstage was of Artemis, backlit on a night stage, singing the soaring anthem that had become her hallmark, her supple voice rippling the grace notes with a power and control that seemed preternatural. To hear her was to yearn yourself to say one more thing to someone loved and lost long ago, and simultaneously to seem to see this gifted girl-woman emotionally naked. You couldn't listen to her sing this song without wanting to rescue her yourself, Gabe thought.

When the shot switched to an image of the sodden and blackened hole in the new wing of his own hotel, he felt a sudden burst of rage against Alexander Antippas. Imagine being the father of this glorious, damaged girl, and not bothering to go to her, to honor and say good-bye to her in spite of the way the story had ended.

Well, Antippas was with her after all. Gabe hoped he was down on his big fat incorporeal knees begging her forgiveness.

Oh, man. This week had really been hell on all of them.

Shep had Buster with him when he arrived at the inn to question Henry Rexroth, since the visit was snake-related. The new girl on the desk telephoned up to Mr. Rexroth's room for them.

"Mr. Rexroth, you have some visitors. Should I send them up?"

In his bare room, with its one armchair and all his writing materials out on the small desk, Henry Rexroth rolled his eyes to the ceiling. Send them up? Here?

He emerged into the lobby, thinking possibly it would be that nice couple he had met at the Congo church in Ainsley on Sunday, but it was not. He hesitated only slightly before crossing the room to Shep and Buster. There was a large trash bag standing beside

Shep's foot, with a yellow tape across it on which was printed the word EVIDENCE.

"Good afternoon, gentlemen," he said. "Sorry I'm not dressed for company, I was just finishing up a sermon." He was wearing flannel trousers, and a dress shirt with the sleeves rolled up.

Shep said, "We'd like to ask you a few questions, Mr. Rexroth. Would you like to do it here, or at the station?"

Henry Rexroth thought this unnecessarily bullying in tone.

"Here would be fine," he said calmly. "Let's go to the library." He led the way, and Shep stayed right on his heel. Buster brought up the rear, carrying the trash bag.

Mr. Rexroth and Shep took high-backed wing chairs on opposite sides of the cold fireplace. Buster pulled the broad sliding glass-paneled pocket door closed behind them, shutting them off from the lobby, and put the bag down on the floor between Shep and Rexroth. At a signal from Shep, Buster pulled on plastic gloves and took the suitcase out of the bag. He set it on the floor at Rexroth's feet. Rexroth's face was completely still. He didn't even blink. Shep nodded, and Buster opened the suitcase.

They watched Rexroth's face carefully as he saw what was within. His eyes flicked toward the door once. Then he looked up and met Shep's gaze. He looked frightened and resentful.

"Have you seen those things before, Mr. Rexroth?" Shep asked. Buster took out his notebook.

With all the dignity he could muster, Rexroth said, "I have. That is my snake handling equipment."

"And can you explain to us how you happen to be in possession of snake handling equipment?"

"It was my father's before me."

"What was he, a zoo guy? Or animal control?" Everyone in the room knew that Shep was asking questions to which he already knew the answers.

"He was pastor to a Christian congregation in Ohio. Those tools were part of his ministry, and then mine."

"You worshipped snakes?"

Rexroth was offended and showed it. Just for a moment they saw they were dealing with a very angry man. Then the mask was back, unreadable and patient. "No, of course not. I said it was a Christian congregation. We believed that the Lord would protect us from venom. The Bible says in Mark sixteen—"

"What kind of snakes?" asked Buster. Shep shot Buster a look which he missed.

"Well, domestic vipers of all kinds," said Mr. Rexroth. "But some exotics too, when we could get them."

Buster was about to pursue this line when Shep cut him off.

"And you led this congregation . . . when?"

"From the early nineties until four years ago."

"And what happened four years ago?"

Mr. Rexroth's eyes flicked to the door again.

"Mr. Rexroth?"

"My wife was bitten by a water moccasin. She didn't often handle the snakes but it was a moment of . . . She was filled with the spirit. She came up the aisle to me and held out her arms, with her eyes shining. And I gave the snake to her."

The room fell silent.

"And then what happened, Mr. Rexroth?"

"It bit her. She died."

Mr. Rexroth was struggling with emotion, and they gave him time to master it, though Buster wanted to know much more about exactly what the symptoms had been and how long it took for the death. He didn't know much about water moccasins.

"And then what happened?" Shep asked, surprisingly gently.

"I was arrested. The serpents were seized. There was talk of criminal charges but none were brought, in the end. The whole congregation was witness to the fact that she took the snake voluntarily. Asked for it."

"What happened to the snakes?" asked Buster. Shep turned in his chair to look at Buster, a look he finally noticed and understood to mean Will You Shut the Fuck Up?

Mr. Rexroth, seeming dazed, didn't find the question odd. "I believe they were destroyed." He seemed to feel as guilty about that as about the fate of his wife.

"So you came to Maine?"

"Not immediately. My congregation was disbanded, though I believe some of my people now worship in Kentucky. I traveled east. I tried congregations here and there, but nothing felt right."

"You were looking for a job as a preacher?"

"Oh no. Just for a church home. But something was always missing."

"So how do you make your living, Mr. Rexroth?"

Rexroth looked embarrassed. "There was some insurance. From my wife's death. And my . . . uh . . . mother sends me a stipend."

Shep and Buster looked at each other.

"Your mother can't be young," said Shep.

"No," Rexroth said glumly. "She seems eternal."

"Lucky she's generous," said Shep.

"Yes. No. Well it's not that, exactly."

"What is it, exactly?"

Suddenly Rexroth seemed to remember where he was and what was going on. "Is this necessary? What's my mother got to do with it?"

"We don't know. You tell us," said Shep.

After a pause, Rexroth said, "She remarried after my father died. Her husband isn't a believer."

"She pays you to stay away," said Buster. Shep looked surprised.

Rexroth turned to him resentfully and said nothing.

"So you drove around looking for a church home," said Buster kindly.

Rexroth said, "I love animals. I used to stop at shelters and volunteer. I'd walk the dogs and pet the cats. I like to be useful."

"You didn't like Mrs. Antippas's dog," said Shep.

Rexroth stiffened. He said defensively, "It was a horrible little thing, but I didn't wish it harm."

Shep let the silence stretch after this remark. Finally he said, "Go on. Animal shelters."

"In one place over in Orono they had this bloodhound whose owner had died. Housebroken, nice temperament. It's hard to place a big dog. I went back into the room where they keep the dogs in wire crates, shelves of them. Clarence seemed to recognize me. He saw me coming. He looked at me with those eyes, as if he'd been waiting for me, and when I put my hand up to the cage, he leaned the top of his head against the wires. I could feel him saying 'What took you so long?' The shelter people said they were going to put him down if they couldn't find a home for him.

"But then I discovered that none of the motor courts and such where I tended to stay allowed pets. I went back to the shelter and said I had to give Clarence back, and they told me about Oquossoc. Mr. Gurrell took me in."

"How long ago was this?"

"I'm sure Mr. Gurrell has told you."

"You tell us, Henry."

"Three years. And three months, it was the beginning of the summer."

"You must have been pleased to find a snake right in the next room," said Buster.

"I was not," said Rexroth forcefully. "I foreswore the handling of serpents when Beverly died. Clearly I had misunderstood the scriptures, though I don't yet understand how. But I believe the Lord put that snake next door as a sign to me."

"Sign of what?" Shep asked, seeming really interested.

"That I still need to be tested before He will take me back," Rexroth answered with irritation. "What would *you* think? I mean, how often do *you* check into a hotel and find there's a snake in the next room?"

"Gotta point," said Shep. "Let's talk about the night the snake disappeared."

"Fine," said Rexroth. He uncrossed his legs, then crossed them the other way. He looked like an irritated bird, with his chest feathers ruffled.

"Where did you keep your snake rig?"

"In the closet."

"In a bag, or a case or something?"

"No, just up on the shelf."

"And who knew it was there?"

Rexroth paused, thinking. "Gabe Gurrell, of course."

"Why 'of course'?"

"I felt he deserved to know the truth about me. He was offering me a home."

"All right. Who else?"

"Earl Niner."

"You are friendly with Mr. Niner?"

"I wouldn't say that. We are neighbors," said Rexroth stiffly. "But I wanted him to know the equipment was there, in case he ever had need of it."

"He didn't have his own?"

"He just used a hook. Grommet was very tame."

Shep looked at Buster, as if to say, you can explain this to me later.

"Housekeeping knew. They'd come in to clean when I took Clarence for his walk. I mean, I'm sure that they saw the equipment. You'll have to ask them if they knew what it was for."

"All right. Now, do you know when the equipment disappeared from your room?"

"No. I discovered it was gone when Earl told me the snake had disappeared. I went to look for my equipment, so I could help him to get him back."

"Wednesday evening, this was?"

"Yes. He spoke to me in the hall when I came upstairs after dinner. He was hoping—well I believe he was hoping that I had the snake for some reason, since he knew . . ."

He stopped.

"What, Henry?" Shep pushed.

"Nothing. Earl told me the snake was missing, and I went to my closet and found the equipment gone."

"And you hadn't in fact taken the snake yourself?"

"Of course I hadn't!" Rexroth snapped. "I knew you were going to think that! I already told you, I will not handle a serpent ever again. I swore an oath!"

"But you were willing to use the equipment to help recapture the missing snake."

"I was going to *lend* the equipment, I wasn't going to . . . oh forget it. Are we done?"

"Not quite yet. The equipment was gone by Wednesday evening but you don't know when it disappeared? When was the last time you saw it?"

Rexroth was now looking sullen. Finally he said, "Last Sunday morning."

"Sunday morning. You're sure?"

Rexroth nodded.

"What was special about Sunday morning?"

"Nothing."

Another silence, until Shep said, "Henry, would you rather finish this conversation in Ainsley?"

Rexroth looked at his watch and muttered, "It's time for me to walk the dog."

"Sunday," said Shep.

Finally Rexroth said, "I see it every Sunday. Before I go to church, I get it down, and I say a prayer for my wife and ask her forgiveness. Then I pray for understanding for myself, and put it away again."

"Like your hair shirt, or something," said Buster.

"If it makes you happy to think so. If I don't walk my dog there's going to be a mess to clean up. Is one of you going to do it?"

"One more question," Shep said. "In the days before the fire, did you see anyone in your part of the hotel, on your hallway, who didn't belong there?"

"Yes."

"Well?"

"Wednesday afternoon. I went up to my room by the back stairs, and ran into Cherry Weaver in the hall outside my room."

There might as well have been a giant thud in the room.

"Did you speak?"

"I said good afternoon. She seemed nervous, and she said Mrs. Antippas had sent her up with a bowl of scraps for her horrible dog."

"Did she have a bowl of scraps in her hand?"

"No."

"So she had delivered the bowl?"

"Ask her."

"But how would she get into the room?"

"I have no idea! Maybe she cut herself a key."

"We will ask her."

"Can I go now?"

"For the moment. But don't leave town, Henry."

Rexroth was up and pulling the sliding door. "If Clarence has messed in my room, I'm going to put it into a bag and leave it in your car."

Maggie and Hope passed Shep on his way out as they were driving into the hotel parking lot.

"You know what bothers me?" Maggie asked.

"No."

"The way everyone uses *grieve* as a transitive verb. You can *mourn* a loss, or grieve *for* a loss, but nowadays—"

"Oh darling, shut up," said Hope. "I don't even remember what 'transitive' means. I'm just sorry we had to watch the whole thing on the radio. Look, Buster's car is here. I wonder what's going on." As if on cue, Buster emerged from the side door, carrying the big black evidence bag. They were on him before he got to the end of the path.

"What are you doing here?"

"Just checking a witness's story with Mr. Gurrell," said Buster.

"What have you got in the bag?"

"I bet it's Glory's suitcase!"

"Where did they find it?"

"Who took it?"

Buster thought about telling them he couldn't discuss it, but into his head flashed the image of a torture he'd read about when he was ten in which bushmen bury you in sand all the way up to your neck, then pour honey on your head and watch ants swarm into your hair and eyes and ears and nose until you go straight out of your mind. He decided to give up without a fight. They hustled him into the sunroom, which had become their own personal headquarters. He told them about Earl and the compost pile, and the snake gear and Mr. Rexroth.

"Show us," they demanded as one.

"The snake stuff?"

"Of course. Come on, open up."

He put on gloves and opened the suitcase and they contemplated the bag, the gloves, and the snake tongs. Maggie was about to reach for the tongs, when Buster gave a cry of distress. He fished out the ball of latex gloves he had in his pocket and handed each of them a pair. Both women seemed rather thrilled at this development. Once gloved, Maggie took the tongs and extended the telescoped handle. She tried the weight of it and opened and closed the snake-grabbing jaw with great interest. She offered it to Hope, who made a face, as if she'd accidentally bitten into mold. Ignoring the snake gear, she turned to the rest of the contents of the suitcase.

"La Perla undies," she reported, after examining everything.

"Oo la la," said Maggie.

Buster told them what Henry Rexroth had said about seeing Cherry outside his room the day of the fire. They grew instantly serious.

"Will someone ask Mrs. Antippas whether she really sent Cherry there?"

"Shep will have someone from LAPD go talk to her. Not today, though."

No. The family was otherwise occupied today.

"Have you talked to housekeeping yet?"

"No, that's up to Detective Gordon."

"Where is he?"

"I think he went home."

"That's right, we passed him on his way out," said Maggie.

"Let's go see if Mrs. Eaton is still here," said Hope.

The housekeeper's domain was in the basement, in a big clean room adjacent to the laundry. Mrs. Eaton herself was taking the evening shift tonight, not wanting to pay her girls for working on the holiday. The three of them found her just arranging her cart, piled high with cleaning equipment, boxes of little wrapped soap bars, two-ounce bottles of shampoo, body lotion, and mouthwash, and a carton of foil-wrapped chocolates for the guests' pillows. Hope had been stockpiling hers for her granddaughters, whom she planned to see on her way home.

"Could we have a minute, Mrs. Eaton?" Hope asked. She felt they were old friends, since she had waylaid Mrs. Eaton several times to explain with perfect politeness why duvets were an invention of the devil and no sensitive person could sleep under them. A properly made bed had sheets, blankets, a pretty blanket cover (Hope's were monogrammed) and a bedspread. You could choose or discard any of these layers yourself as conditions demanded. With a one-size-fits-none duvet, how could you adjust for changes in temperature during the night, your own or the thermometer's? Surely this was a simple proposition.

The hotel *had* blankets, Mrs. Eaton conceded. Hope was so glad; she confided with a cheerful laugh that she'd stayed in more than one upscale hostelry that had gotten rid of every blanket in the place in celebration of this new trend in bedding. Really, whose idea was this? It might or might not make sense in Sweden, but what about a summer in, say, Pittsburgh? Or San Diego?

Mrs. Eaton had let it wash over her, privately thinking that if a hotel threw out its bedding there had probably been bugs involved. It had been years since anyone had asked her for blankets. She had spent more than she should to give her newly married daughter and son-in-law a duvet for Christmas, and they just loved it. She had ordered it on the Internet. Her daughter used her old blankets to line the dog's bed.

The Oquossoc blankets were neither new nor fresh, and Mrs. Eaton had had to cycle them through the dryer with sheets of Bounce to get rid of the aroma of ancient closet that clung to them, before she made up

Mrs. Babbin's bed. And then the next night she had to do it again because the new girl had taken Mrs. Babbin's blankets back to the basement and given her a nice duvet again.

The other one seemed to be relatively sane, and Mrs. Eaton had admired her nightgown, which had ribbons laced into the hem. It was the other one who spoke to her now.

"When the upstairs girls go into the rooms to make them up, how do they open the doors?" Maggie asked. Like most hotels, the inn had installed electronic readers instead of old-fashioned locks, and the "keys" were thin plastic wafers the size of a credit card.

Mrs. Eaton took a card from her pocket and held it up. It looked exactly like the key card Maggie had in her own pocket at the time.

"I take it that's a master key? What does it open?"

"All the bedrooms," said Mrs. Eaton. "And the linen closets on each of the corridors."

"But not the doors to, say, Mr. Gurrell's office?"

"That too. Someone's got to run the vacuum in there."

"What doesn't it open?"

"The kitchen. The pantries. The food and liquor storerooms. Kitchen staff keep those clean themselves."

"I see. And where are the master keys kept?"

Mrs. Eaton gestured toward a battered metal desk against the wall, where she kept her record books. There was a phone on it and a wheeled desk chair, and several clipboards on which requests from the guests were tracked. "That top drawer locks."

Maggie walked over to the desk and tried the drawer. It opened easily, and in the left-hand corner among the tangle of ballpoint pens, rubber bands, and paper clips that always fill such drawers, she saw a neat stack of apparently identical room keys.

"I don't keep it locked when I'm the only one here," said Mrs. Eaton, as if she'd been criticized. "Obviously."

"And when you do lock it, where is the key?"

Mrs. Eaton fished a small metal key out of her pocket. It was on a ring at the end of a chain with a tiny wooden lobster buoy attached. She saw Maggie notice it. "Grandson," said Mrs. Eaton. "Christmas present."

"So you keep the master key cards here, and when your girls clock in, you give them keys, and they give them back when they leave?"

"That's about the size of it."

"And where do the master keys come from?" Hope asked.

Mrs. Eaton didn't seem to follow the question.

"If you needed more master keys, what would you do?"

"Ask Mr. Gurrell and he'd make them, or have the front desk make them."

"So," said Buster, stating the obvious, "anyone who worked the front desk could have access to any guest room."

"That's about the size of it," Mrs. Eaton repeated. There was a cold note of disgust under the flat sentence, and Maggie thought again of how many people in this hotel feared they were going to lose their livelihoods because of Cherry Weaver.

They thanked her for her time. As they were at the door, Maggie asked, "Do you keep this door locked, Mrs. Eaton?"

"Of course," said Mrs. Eaton.

"Just when you leave for the day, or whenever you leave the room?"

"When I leave for the day, or when I'm on duty alone and have to go upstairs. When we're busy, the girls are in and out of here all day, but someone in charge is always here to answer the phone."

Maggie and Hope had persuaded Buster to stay at the hotel for dinner. He had called Brianna to see if she was home, but Brianna was having supper with Beryl Weaver, which he very much did not wish to join, so he accepted his mother's invitation. They were sitting in the sunroom, and Hope and Maggie had returned to the jig-saw puzzle. They had the boat and the fools in it filled in, but the background sea and sky were going slowly.

"What about a cocktail?" Hope asked.

Buster jumped to his feet and said, "I'll go. What'll you have?"

Maggie had just put together two pink pieces of the banner that floated from the boat's mast, and was intently scanning what looked like acres of little bits, looking for other shards of the same color. She looked up at Hope, and was just in time to see over Hope's shoulder Gabe Gurrell drive out of the parking lot with Chef Sarah in the passenger seat.

"Cook's night out," she said. "Don't order anything complicated for dinner."

"I was thinking of thin gruel anyway," Hope said. "That was a big lunch."

"It was. I'll tell you what I was thinking. Isn't that beast of Mr. Rexroth's a bloodhound? A tracking dog?"

"You know, I think it is," said Hope.

"Yes, it is," said Buster, still hoping he was on the way to the bar to order drinks for them. He considered himself officially off duty, as of about four hours ago.

"I was wondering if the dog could tell us anything about who took the snake gear. He was probably in the room at the time."

Buster sat back down. He wanted to dismiss this suggestion as something a professional would disdain, but frankly he wondered why he hadn't thought of it.

Hope asked, "Would there be any harm in trying?"

"He might lead us straight to Cherry's locker," said Maggie.

"Oh. Yes. I don't suppose we can suppress it if we don't like what happens?"

"No," said Maggie. "But nobody listens to us anyway."

"That's true," said Hope. "Buster?"

Buster wanted to say "I'd like a quart of Budweiser, please" but instead agreed that it was worth a try. Big slobbery Clarence was practically the definition of an underdog, and Buster was always in favor of surprising people who underestimate underdogs. They might solve this thing themselves, right now, while the Great Detective was off having his dinner. He went out to his car to retrieve the evidence bag from where it was locked in the trunk.

Mr. Rexroth was in the library. He looked smaller than a week ago, Maggie thought, as she paused in the doorway. He looked up, startled, as they came in, as if they were a herd of bison thundering into his sanctuary. Maggie apologized, and explained what they wanted.

"Clarence is not really a working dog," he objected. "I don't know if he's had any training. He's not used to strangers."

"Do you know that he *hasn't*?" Maggie had interrupted because she could see that he would keep piling on excuses out of sheer anxiety.

"No, I don't, but . . ."

"Every dog needs a job," said Hope. "They like to be useful. I think he'd enjoy the opportunity."

"Let's go see," said Maggie. And Mr. Rexroth, apparently unable to think his way around this fast enough to stop it, stood to be swept along in their wake, and Buster knew exactly how he felt.

Clarence was glad to see them. He'd been asleep on the bed, which caused Mr. Rexroth to act cross and make excuses, but Hope and Maggie fussed over the dog and told him what a brilliant handsome boy he was. Clarence faithlessly gave them his full and slobbery attention. Mr. Rexroth crossed the room and sat down on the oak chair at the tiny desk where he usually did his writing.

"Now Clarence," said Hope, "we have a job for you. Get down now, and sit." Before the men could tell her this was a ridiculous way to talk to an animal, Clarence scrambled off the bed and sat at her feet, looking up at her, as if he'd been waiting for someone to recognize his gifts for years.

"Buster," said Hope, "give us the snake bag."

Buster passed out gloves again, then put the suitcase on the bed, opened it, and handed the snake bag out to his mother. Hope put it to Clarence, who was instantly passionately interested.

"Here now. Good boy. That's right, sniff," she said as Clarence worked the thing over with his large wet nose. "Now Clarence," said Hope reasonably, "we need to know who came in here and took it. Understand?" She withdrew the bag from the dog and said, "Clarence, work."

"Mom, that's not how the handlers do it," said Buster.

But Clarence wasn't standing on ceremony. He went straight to Mr. Rexroth and sat down, staring at him.

"Good boy!" said Hope. "Clever boy! Now come here. Here, Clarence."

Clarence abandoned Mr. Rexroth and went back to sit at Hope's feet again with a happy expression that said "What's next, boss?"

"Now. That was very very smart of you, but not what we needed. Now smell this again."

She presented the bag again, moving it so he'd smell the handle as well, then gave him the tongs. Clarence studied them assiduously with his large mobile snout.

"Good Clarence! Now Clarence, work! No, no no," she added, as Clarence made for Mr. Rexroth again. "No. Not Mr. Rexroth. Buster, open the door."

Clarence sat near Mr. Rexroth, but facing Hope, with his ears pricked.

"Find the other person, Clarence. There's another scent and you know whose it is. Show us, boy!"

Buster was feeling that his mother had watched entirely too many episodes of *Lassie*. Clarence, find little Timmy!!

But Clarence was on his feet, nose to the ground, heading for the door. His head moved back and forth in a pendulum pattern, vacuuming for scent.

"Mrs. Babbin, he must be on leash when he leaves the room!" cried Mr. Rexroth.

"We can't interrupt him now, he's working," she answered, following Clarence out the door, with Maggie right behind her and the men bringing up the rear.

"Isn't this amazing?" Hope asked Maggie. "It's like the first time you use a Ouija board and you don't believe it's going to work at all, and then the pointer starts moving."

"I wish you hadn't said that," said Maggie. "I was just getting into this."

The dog stopped outside Earl Niner's door and sat down with authority.

Hope turned and gave Buster a questioning look. Mr. Niner? Now what?

Buster stepped up and tapped on the door. "Earl? It's Buster. Are you in there?"

They all stood holding their breaths, listening for sounds on the other side. Then the knob turned and the door opened. Earl was in his usual painful posture, in dungarees, a T-shirt, and bare feet, with a parrot on his shoulder.

Walter the parrot took one look at the dog and with a scream, dug his claws into Earl's shoulder and flapped his useless wings. Clarence rushed into the room past man and bird and went to the empty snake habitat. He sat down and stared fixedly at it, as he had at Mr. Rexroth.

Earl, torn between distress for Walter and anger that these people would bring a dog into his room, retreated to the far corner, where Walter hopped desperately onto his hand to be ferried back into his cage, uttering terrified cries. Earl closed the door, and Walter began picking at his breast feathers while Earl tried to soothe him.

"Brilliant, Clarence!" Hope cried. "Just brilliant! Good dog!"

"Earl, I'm sorry," said Buster. "I didn't know it would upset him."

"Don't know much, do you?" Earl answered angrily.

Maggie said, "He's not tracking a person, he's tracking the snake!"

"Exactly!" cried Hope.

"That ought to work. Well done, Clarence! Mr. Niner, could we have something that belonged to Grommet?"

"Will you get out of my room and never come back?"

Maggie swore that they would.

Earl went to the terrarium and broke off a bit of branch that Grommet had slithered over in happier days.

When Earl had closed the door on the little hunting party and they were in the hall, Clarence was given the bit of branch to peruse with his nose. He seemed thoroughly gratified.

"All right! Clarence, work!" Hope commanded, and the dog set off at a good clip toward the rear of the hotel. Nose to the floor, he swung his head like a Geiger counter across his path as he moved with assurance to the back stairs and started down. Hope and Maggie looked at each other, triumphant, and clattered after him. Buster was right behind them and Mr. Rexroth followed, not wanting to be blamed if the dog did something to disgrace him.

Maggie and Hope had not been down these stairs before and were full of interest. This was the staff's domain. Clarence stopped at the landing for the second floor, sniffed thoroughly at the crack of the door that led into the guest rooms, then turned and returned to the stairs, continuing his descent to the ground floor.

"He's going to the staff lockers," Hope said to Maggie. These, they knew, were down another flight, in a room next to the laundry.

But Clarence was not. He sat down firmly, staring at the heavy metal door that led out of the stairwell. Buster stepped up to push it open, and they found themselves outside the kitchen in the large pantry where the plates and glassware were washed and stored. It was empty at the moment, as the staff was in the kitchen having family meal before dinner service began. There were two more doors in this room, one a swinging door with a glass pane that led into the kitchen, the other a blank door on the opposite side of the sinks. Clarence, scrubbing the air for scent, moved to this second door and sat again, staring at it as if he could open it with thought waves. Maggie and Hope looked at each other. Buster opened the door.

The door led into a second small room, narrow and not quite plumb, that had the feel of a space created accidentally by some ill-thought-out addition or remodeling. More a larder than a workroom, the shelves above the counters were stocked with large containers of flours, canned goods, imported nut and olive oils, bottles of homemade vinegars, and jars of preserved lemons. There were drawers and cupboards beneath the counters. The drawers, Maggie found, were filled with dish towels and other kitchen linens. Clarence, all-business, went straight to a cupboard to the left of the door, and sat down to stare at it.

Before they could open it, the door from the kitchen swung open and Oliver came in. He stopped, looking surprised.

"Hello," he said. "Looking for ketchup? Sriracha sauce?"

"I know he shouldn't be in here, it's not my fault," said Mr. Rexroth piously. But Oliver said, "Hello, Clarence! You usually get room service, don't you, big guy? But you found where we keep your stash." He opened the door to the cupboard Clarence was fixed upon. On the lower shelf were stockpots and large saucepans, and a large plastic tub that had once held dishwasher powder. Oliver took it up and peeled the top off, and Clarence, his nose twitching with joy, began to wiggle and drool, his eyes fixed on Oliver and on the tub in his hand.

"Let's see, what have we got for you? This looks like curried chicken salad." He held a chunk of something covered in sauce the color of turmeric, and before Mr. Rexroth's squeaks of objection could become verbal, Clarence had seized it and swallowed, seemingly without chewing.

"He shouldn't have spicy food!" cried Mr. Rexroth, although it was he himself who didn't do well with spicy food; Clarence seemed particularly to relish it.

Hope and Maggie were looking deflated.

"So he comes in for treats that are kept in that cupboard?" Maggie asked.

"Well, Sarah usually takes them up to him. You can't put meat into the compost, so we all save the scraps that would go to waste, and Clarence gets some and Mrs. Weaver feeds the rest to her pig."

Clarence was staring fixedly at the tub, his eyes yearning and a thread of drool intact from his dribbly jaws to the floor. His tail began to thump the floor as Oliver pulled out another chunk of chicken and he whisked it into his gullet without ever touching Oliver.

"Hot Lips Houlihan," said Oliver.

Day Ten, Tuesday, October 15

Tuesday morning, Cherry Weaver was brought before Judge Hennebery for presentment. Brianna was there, but neither of Cherry's parents had bothered to come. Carson Bailey handed the judge a copy of the charges they were bringing, and dropped another copy on the defense table in front of Celia Little. He asked the judge to set bail at $20,000.

Celia Little, instantly on her feet, cried, "Your Honor, you might as well set it at a hundred thousand dollars!"

The judge said, "Very well, I'll set it at a hundred thousand dollars."

Celia, Cherry, and Brianna shrieked in surprise, which apparently amused the judge greatly. He looked down at Celia over his glasses and said, "Isn't that what you wanted me to do?"

"No, sir, I want you to release her on her own recognizance! She's got no money, her whole family is here in Webster County! She isn't a flight risk!"

"Miss Little, you're new to my courtroom. I was just having some fun with you."

"This is not a laughing matter to me or my client!"

Judge Hennebery looked annoyed. "That would have gone over better with me if you'd said 'No laughing matter, *Your Honor,*'" he said. "Bail is set at twenty thousand dollars." He banged his gavel. Cherry turned in her seat to look at Brianna, her lips quivering. Celia sat down and angrily tried to collect her papers, but instead dropped most of them on the floor. At the prosecution table, Carson and his assistant were looking gratified. A bailiff arrived, and after one more anguished look at Brianna, Cherry was led away again and Brianna sat stock-still, trying not to cry.

State Police Officer Carly Leo arrived at Shep's office right after lunch. She was an ambitious young transplant from Portland, with eyes a little too close together and a ponytail pulled so tight it looked painful. Shep was getting caught up on a home invasion case that had taken place in Yarmouth over the weekend that might have some overlap with an earlier one in his jurisdiction, and wondering to himself how much Cherry Weaver knew about handling snakes. Leo stood expectantly in his doorway with a stack of papers printed from an e-mail from the M.E.'s office. Shep looked up and said, "Is that what I think it is?" and Carly Leo took that as an invitation.

"They can rush when they want to." She handed Shep the papers, and moved the stack of files and newspapers from the one unoccupied chair in the room to the floor so she could sit.

Shep pulled out the autopsy report and scanned the first page. He flipped to the second page, then back again. He looked at Leo, then picked up the phone and dialed the M.E.'s office. When he got Dr. Merganser herself on the line, he said "I'm here with Officer Leo. I'm putting you on speaker. Give us the bottom line."

"Bottom line," said the M.E. out of the tinny speaker, "the snake didn't kill him. He was breathing when the fire got him. The lungs were like burned paper."

Shep leaned back in his chair. Bad news for little Miss Firebug.

"And why the fuck was he just laying there?"

"Timber rattlers have a couple of different kinds of venom," said the tinny voice. "The kind that Antippas got was mostly hemorrhagic and worked like a myotoxin, causing internal bleeding and muscle necrosis."

"What's that in English?"

"He couldn't move. In a smaller man the venom would have led to paralysis of the diaphragm, which would have stopped his breathing," Margaret Merganser said. "Antippas was so big that he probably could have survived it, if he hadn't been lying there getting roasted like a weenie."

Shep picked up the report again and paged through it, thinking. So the snake in the bed was assault with a deadly weapon, but the fire was the killer. That meant they had to nail down the arson case and tie it up with a big red bow.

The M.E. said, "Couple of reporters arc dancing around outside my office here, trying not to wet their pants. Okay if I give them a statement?"

"Sure, go ahead," Shep said, and ended the call. He sat thinking. The tech guys would have to test again for traces of ILRs or accelerant. He knew it was there. That little girl had some guts, to bring the snake into it. He could think of some people he'd be glad to see snake-bit, but if he had to handle the snake himself he'd probably rather just shoot them. He had to admit, the scheme was clever. If the snake had burned up with the guy, as she must have thought it would, you could be looking at a perfect crime. Guy smoked in bed, end of story.

The crime tech guys had put their samples into mason jars. He knew that nowadays big city fire forensics thought that heat-sealed nylon bags had a slower leak rate, but he couldn't see it. Still, if there had been a leak, an error in handling the jars let's say, you'd get a false negative. The tech guys hadn't seen a pour pattern of gas, or varsol, and neither had he. But wait—the wastebaskets. He suddenly remembered, there should have been baskets by the desk and in the bathroom, and the baskets had been made of dried grass or some shit. Couple of those filled with tissue, or newspaper, lit with a match and set to travel to the bedding, or left *on* the bed, and it's all she wrote. And it wouldn't leave any suspicious traces.

Man, if that guy was conscious, he must have been fucking terrified.

He picked up the phone again to call Carson. That Weaver family. Some bad genetic juju there, he wouldn't be surprised, like those people who come out of the woods once a year to go to the county fair, with their heads too big or too small, or too many fingers.

Lisa Antippas felt as if she hadn't slept in years. It was an evil-feeling day in Los Angeles, with hot Santa

Ana winds blowing dust and grit, making you feel as if something terrible was about to happen. But everything terrible had already happened, and wouldn't unhappen, ever. Her bed was a restless mess, the sheets damp from night sweats, and she had a drug hangover, richly deserved, as she'd taken double of everything, and still she spent the night in some nightmare twilight waking state, at the mercy of demons. For the first time in her life, she thought, I might not get through this.

I might not get through this.

Her twins had each other and they could cry; they had cried and cried yesterday until Ada's eyes had almost swollen shut. Sometime late in the evening, though, Lisa had realized things had gone quiet at their end of the hall, and went to see what the girls were doing. She found them in pajamas, huddled together under a cashmere throw the decorator had said would never be used, eating ice cream out of the carton and watching *The Daily Show*.

Jeremy, though, was a boy, and alone, and he'd been Jenny's pet. He probably had a tiny crush on her, along with every other boy his age in the first world. He'd still been outside sitting by the pool, drinking and listening to his headphones, when she went to bed, and now he was nowhere to be seen and his door was shut.

Her memories of the day before were an insane jumble. Limousines, camera flashes, microphones, Jenny, eight feet high on the screen at the Staples Center. People wanting to touch, to ask, to hug, to say . . . nothing that would help. By the time they got to the service for Alex, Lisa was feeling nothing, surprised she could remain upright. Thank god her hat had a heavy veil; she needed that scrim between herself and the world. Then the people at the house, whoever the hell they all were, Glory had taken over along with Jenny's ghastly manager, thank god. Drinking, eating, signing memorial books, saying stupid untrue things to the kids, who bravely stood there, being talked to. By that time Lisa was at the end of a long tunnel, watching from her private hell, and after a while she had gone to her room and stayed there.

Glory had been up and out early. She had talk shows to do and had to be at the station for hair and makeup at seven. Lisa wished Glory were here, that they could sit on the couch and watch TV together right now as they had done when they were children. She thought about eating ice cream for breakfast and even went as far as to look in the freezer but found—just as well— that the girls had eaten it all.

She moved as if she were a hundred years old. She sat down before the TV in the breakfast nook and waited for Glory to come on. She got rather fascinated by a guy showing her how to make shrimp fajitas. Then came Glory's segment.

It was excruciating. Footage of the day before, questions about Artemis as a little girl, footage of her glory days on the Disney channel and later, her concerts. They showed one very funny clip from *SNL*, and asked questions about what she was like at home in those years. It was one of those shows where four hosts talk, mostly at once, shouting and laughing, asking obvious questions, then shrieking with astonishment at the predictable answers. Glory was a pro, thank god. Dishing it out smoothly. Until they started on today's new hook, the way they were going to keep the story alive. Where was Artemis's real mother?

"Artemis's real mother is my sister, Lisa Antippas," said Glory.

"Of course she is . . ." said one, and

"Oh that's so true," said another, and

"You know, family is who shows up," said a third. All talking over one other, nobody listening.

When the question had been rephrased, Glory said, "Her mother abandoned her. Lisa and Jenny bonded instantly, that little girl was so hungry for a mother's love."

"Oh that's right, she was called Jenny," said one, while

"Poor little thing, she was how old?" asked another, and the third and fourth said "Imagine leaving that poor little girl."

Glory said, "Alexander said his first wife didn't believe she could be a good enough mother," and the interviewers said, in overlapping voices, "Oh it's like, what was that movie, Meryl Streep, *Kramer versus Kramer.*"

Except for the youngest interviewer who had never seen the movie, and instead whizzed through her mental movie database and said at last, "Dustin Hoffman."

"And where is she now?" asked someone.

"I have no idea," said Glory, with contempt. "We don't know if she's even alive. To be frank. Her daughter's a millionaire many times over. Was. We were always waiting for her to come out of the woodwork."

Lisa found the remote under a pile of newspapers and turned the show off. She sat, staring at nothing, thinking about Jenny, when she and Alexander were first together. The child was absolutely disturbed, in Lisa's opinion, though at the time she knew almost nothing about children except that in many ways she still was one herself. How funny—Jenny had sort of grown up to have the life that Lisa once thought she might have. Back when she was a gorgeous girl barely out of her teens, and before she knew how common youth and beauty were, especially in Hollywood. But those first months—Jenny had nightmares, she'd whine until they let her get in bed with them; then she'd pee in her sleep. Alexander had to take Lisa to a hotel if they wanted to have sex, which they did, more or less all the time. And the tantrums when Alexander tried to leave. Jenny would howl and cling to his legs, face red, eyes streaming and nose dripping snot, getting it all over his pants leg. You'd have thought her life depended on her keeping him all to herself. More than once Lisa had thought she should just move on.

She tried to remember when she was so hot for Alexander that she hadn't done that. Moved on. How had that felt, that level of lust? Like being out of your fucking mind, really. After she married him, and Jenny lived with them, it was years before she would call Lisa Mommy. Lisa's life would have been ten times easier if Alex could have left Jenny behind. She got sick of him doting on gorgeous little Jenny, he was way too attached to her in Lisa's opinion, and it went on until Jeremy was born.

The buzzer rang. Someone out at the gate. More flowers? She heard Manuela go to the monitor in the front hall. Manuela had shown a deceitful gift in the last few days for pretending she didn't speak enough

English to understand what the petitioner wanted. But this time, after a minute or so, she came into the kitchen.

"Mrs. Antippas? It's a man from the police."

Lisa stared, and finally said, "Really?"

"Could you come? I don't know . . ."

Lisa went to the monitor and looked at the screen. She saw a middle-aged man in perma-press slacks and a windbreaker. Didn't look like police to her. The bloodsucking press again.

"What is it?" she said into the intercom, and the man came to life and spoke to the camera mounted on the top of the concrete gatepost. Looking up at the fisheye lens, he became all nose.

"Mrs. Antippas? Detective Prince from LAPD." He held his badge and credentials up to the camera.

Lisa had no idea how to tell if they were real or fake, but she thought that the consequence of refusing to let him in might be more trouble than it was worth to her if he was real. If he was fake, Freddy could handle him. Freddy was more imposing than he looked. She buzzed, and watched as the gate swung open. The man got into his car and drove through, and the gate swung shut behind him. Up on the road, the reporters stared hungrily after him. Clearly *they* believed he was police, or they'd have tried to follow him in.

"**I'm sorry** for your loss," Kim Prince said, once they were seated in the great room. "Losses." The view of Los Angeles draped below them just beyond the rim of the dark blue pool was spectacular, like a subject world.

Detective Prince wasn't bad-looking. He had thick oiled hair and a compact muscular body with a small paunch. Complexion scarred; she assumed he'd had acne as a kid. He'd opened his jacket and Lisa saw a well-defined chest, and no sign of a gun; probably strapped to his leg, she thought. She watched him scanning the room, noticing the framed pictures of her and Alex, young and radiant. Pictures of the children, of her parents at some birthday or anniversary party. The pictures filled one entire bookcase. So many celebrations as Alexander rose in the world. She remembered one night when they still lived in the flats, when she'd been awakened by some kind of racket in the driveway. When she woke Alexander, sleeping heavily beside her, he listened for a moment, then said sleepily, "That's probably the Porsche being repossessed," and rolled over so his back was to her. It hadn't all been easy, though there were no pictures of those parts.

When Manuela had brought in a tray with the coffee service and a plate of cookies, Prince said, "Detective

Gordon, up there in Maine, asked me to come and talk to you. Would it be all right if I ask a couple of questions?" His voice was gentle. Lisa made a weary gesture of assent.

Prince took out a notebook and studied a page or two of scribbled handwriting.

"When you and your husband checked in at the hotel up there, a young lady was on the reservation desk. Do you remember her?"

"Yes."

"There was some sort of problem with your reservation?"

"No, it was all fine."

Prince flipped back a page in his notes and read, then moved on.

"My husband could be impatient. It never meant anything," Lisa said, without animation.

"I see. I understand you were not sharing a room with your husband while you stayed at the hotel."

"That's right."

"Could you explain why not?"

The question seemed to annoy her. "We didn't always share a bedroom. My husband was a noisy sleeper. And he liked to smoke in bed, which I didn't allow."

"I see. Did you have separate bedrooms here?"

"Sometimes. He has a bed in his dressing room."

"So this wasn't unusual, your sleeping apart?"

"No." After a pause she added, "In the great houses of Europe, husbands and wives always had separate bedrooms." Her decorator had told her that.

Prince said, "I didn't know that." He looked at his notes and remarked, "So the hotel has bedrooms where smoking was allowed? So many don't, anymore."

"It must have. He reeked of cigars the whole time we were there, I know that."

Prince looked at her thoughtfully. He had of course seen the website, which specified that the inn was a no-smoking facility.

"I understood there was something about a dog," he said. He looked around, as if just noting that no dog seemed to be on view here.

"Oh. Yes. My dog, Colette. Not all the rooms could have pets. My sister and I stayed in the wing where dogs were allowed."

"The wing that did not catch fire."

"Obviously."

"Is the dog here?"

"Do you like dogs?"

"Well enough."

"Colette . . . ," called Lisa. She didn't think she'd seen her since before the Staples Center. She must be with Manuela or maybe the children.

"Colette, *chérie, viens ici* . . ." She raised her voice. Somewhere beyond the kitchen a door opened and closed, and a scrabble of toenails on bare floor could be heard. Then a mop of white fur rocketed into the great room, began yapping when the presence of a stranger was detected, fell trying to keep from braining itself on the massive glass coffee table, and finally broke clear and propelled itself onto the sofa, and into Lisa's lap.

The detective introduced himself to the dog, who smelled his hand and then licked it. Detective Prince wiped his hand on his little linen napkin and took a cookie.

"So . . . the hotel was welcoming to dogs?"

"They were fine. Very nice. But Colette's a good girl, she never causes trouble."

Prince looked at his notes again. Lisa cuddled Colette and murmured to her in French-sounding baby talk.

"And the young lady on the front desk. Did you ask her to take treats upstairs to the dog at any point?"

"No. Why would I?"

"I don't know. I understood that the chef kept special scraps for the animals in the house."

"She may have. I feed Colette myself."

"Did you have any contact with her after you checked in?"

"Who? Oh the desk girl? She brought me the phone when my son called to say Jenny was . . ." Her voice suddenly went up an octave and her throat filled with tears.

Prince waited for her to compose herself. He ate another cookie.

"I'm told there was some kind of scene between Cherry Weaver—the desk girl—and the hotel manager on"—he looked at his notes—"Wednesday afternoon."

"I don't know anything about that."

"No? I had the impression it was pretty public."

"My daughter was dead. I had just been in a car crash. I have no idea what was going on downstairs."

Prince paged through his notes thoughtfully. "Well thank you very much for your time," he said at last, and stood up. "May I call you again if I need to?"

Lisa had stood up as well, spilling the dog to the floor. "I suppose."

"Is your sister here, by the way? I was told that she's staying here."

"She is, but she's out. Why?"

"I wondered if she had any idea how snake equipment got into her suitcase."

Lisa looked at him, trying to conceal her surprise. "I have no idea what you're talking about," she said coldly, conveying that she thought it a mean trick to sandbag a person in her circumstances.

"They found your sister's suitcase. Someone buried it in the compost heap. It had a snake bag and tongs in it. Did your sister know how to handle snakes?"

After a beat, as he responded to the confusion and hostility she was suddenly radiating, Prince thought *Well there's a sore thumb I just hit with a hammer.* Lisa said eventually, "Why don't you ask her?"

"Good idea," said Prince. "Before I go, could I see your husband's dressing room?"

Lisa stared at him. At last, she turned and started for the back of the house. Prince followed her.

Manuela had made up the king-size bed, put away her pill bottles, and picked up all the clothes and underwear Lisa had left on the floor. Lisa stood, wordless with resentment, letting Prince look at her bedroom. Then she led the way into Alex's dressing room, which was in fact a small bedroom, through which a huge closet could be accessed on one side, and on the other, a separate bathroom. Detective Prince opened each door, murmured something when he saw the yards of beautiful suits and jackets, the wall of shelves and drawers, and many board feet of custom-built cubbyholes for dozens of pairs of shoes, all polished and fitted with shoe trees. He went into the bathroom, where the walls and floor were lined with manly reddish-gray stone tiles, and noticed the special oversize rain forest shower stall with steam heads the decorator had been so proud of. He opened the medicine cabinets, studied the contents, closed them again, and said, "So your husband always slept in there?" Pointing to the "dressing room."

"Not always, of course not," said Lisa irritably.

After a beat, the detective said, "Well thank you very much for your time, Mrs. Antippas. I can see myself out."

It had been a quiet afternoon at the Oquossoc Mountain Inn. Hope and Maggie had been to visit Brianna, and heard about the bail set by Judge Hennebery. Brianna told them of her doubts about the lawyer she'd chosen. Should she start over? Find someone good in Augusta or Portland? Try the public defenders after all? On the way home, they stopped in at Just Barb's, where they found Buster on a stool, nursing a cup of coffee. They took the stools on either side of him and Hope ordered a piece of coconut layer cake and three forks.

"I love cake," she said. "You never get it except at birthdays and weddings."

"When I was a girl we always had coconut cake at Easter," said Maggie. "I think it was in the shape of a bunny, but I may be making that up."

Hope said to Buster, "You know, I could post Cherry's bail." She and Maggie had been discussing this in the car.

"Did you tell Brianna that?" Buster asked at last.

"No, I wanted to ask you first."

He looked relieved.

"Why? Don't you want Cherry out?"

"I'm not sure she'd be safe."

"Not safe? Why?"

"Town's pretty hot about the inn closing."

"But the inn's not closing!" cried Hope, suddenly wondering if it might be.

"You say," said Buster. "But somebody slashed Beryl Weaver's tires last night anyway."

Hope and Maggie stopped eating, giving Buster a chance he took, to eat a big piece of the outside of the cake slice, covered in icing and coconut flakes.

"So that's why she rode to work with Zeke this morning," said Maggie.

Buster glanced at Mrs. Detweiler and thought it was scary, how much she seemed to know when you couldn't figure out how she knew it. Even when he was in fourth grade, they all thought she had eyes in the back of her head.

"I thought that was her car at Lakeview Garage. I noticed as we drove by," said his mother.

Jesus. Both of them.

He knew it would be like this. That if his mother found out he had a girlfriend, before you knew it she'd be in the middle of it. He didn't want her rescuing Brianna. Or Cherry. He wanted to do that himself.

On the other hand, he wasn't getting very far with that. His knees were jiggling and he wished he could go home and play *Grand Theft Auto* for about ten hours.

It was twilight at the Oquossoc Mountain Inn. Hope and Maggie were at the table by the bow window playing honeymoon bridge. The new girl on the desk trotted toward them in her too-tight skirt clutching the retro telephone. She put it down on their cards, then lowered herself to her knees to plug it into the phone jack in the baseboard.

"Phone for you, Mrs. Detweiler," she said from under the table.

"Oh! I thought this would be Lauren, for you," said Maggie as the new girl hauled herself to her feet. "Hello? . . . Oh hello, Bonnie!"

Hope folded her hand and gave the conversation her full attention. The call lasted ten long minutes.

"Bonnie McCue," Maggie said when she had hung up, though Hope had long since figured this out. "She's out at Montauk teaching yoga. According to the local paper, Albie Clark has killed himself."

Hope gave a scream. Then she covered her mouth, as if to take back the unseemly noise in a public place, although they were virtually alone in the room, and she hadn't disturbed anyone.

"*Killed* himself?"

"Yesterday."

"Poor man, I'm so sorry. I thought he was doing better. Didn't you?"

Actually, Maggie hadn't.

"But I mean he got through the whole cooking course. He was taking an interest. I thought he was feeling a little bit of the color coming back into the world."

Maggie thought about it. "I was worried about what would happen if it turned out to make no difference."

"What did Bonnie say, exactly?"

"The paper didn't give much detail and Bonnie's been doing her best, but so far all she knows is he was found on the beach."

"And how did he do it?"

"Cut his own throat with a kitchen knife. Practically cut his own head off."

"Holy mother of God."

"Yes. That knife class he was so interested in. It's Bonnie's theory that he didn't want to make a mess in his wife's house."

"Cut his own throat, is that even possible?"

"Oh yes. Especially with a really sharp knife."

"How awful for whoever found him. Who did?"

"A woman out on the beach with her dog. At sunrise." And off leash at that hour, she didn't have to say.

They both pictured the scene, and what the dog would have done with what was splattered all over the sand, and sat for a bit. One week earlier Albie had been with them at this very table.

"What a terrible way to end," said Hope.

"How terrible he must have felt before it ended," said Maggie.

They were quiet for a while. Finally Hope said, "Did Albie leave a note?"

Maggie's thoughts came back into her body. "Oh! Yes! *The Star* said that he had a note in his pocket but they wouldn't disclose the contents."

"That's maddening."

"But he left another kind of message."

"Really?"

"Guess whose beach he chose to die on."

"Whose beach? No, wait . . . no!"

"Yes. Right below the great big lawn of Alexander Antippas."

"Between those seawalls he was so pissed off about."

"Exactly."

Day Eleven, Wednesday, October 16

On Wednesday morning, Jorge Carrera parked his car near Windmill Lane and walked to the Southampton Village Police Station. He had already cruised around the block twice, so he knew that there were two police cars in front of the station and all was quiet. He was wearing "I'm on vacation" clothes, a bomber jacket, khakis, and a shirt with an open collar. He walked up the stairs and into the station and stood for a minute, relishing the smell made up of floor polish, dead cardboard cups, and a dozen other things that you probably thought had no smells, the paper, the clipboards, the elderly office equipment.

The uniform manning the desk was a young guy with a mullet haircut, wearing big black shoes with soles that looked half an inch thick.

"Is Chief Rideout here? Detective Carrera. He knows me from the NYPD." He knew from a phone call last night that Rideout was in Hartford at a conference, and felt that if the young officer chose to assume he was still with the NYPD, that was not his problem.

"He's out today. Can I help you?" The mullet didn't ask for credentials, and Jorge had counted on that. He'd worked in a backwater station too when he was this guy's age.

"Oh, that's too bad. No, I was out here on some personal business, and I wanted to say hello."

"Are you staying in town? He'll be in by tomorrow lunchtime."

"Damn. No, I'm just wrapping up what I came for." He cracked his knuckles and looked around. "Quiet morning?"

"Like the grave."

"A fine and quiet place," said Jorge, and the kid looked at him uncertainly. "God, it's been a long time since I did your job. You grow up out here?"

"I did. My dad's a cop. Just retired."

"So you've got the local knowledge, it's important. And you've got the standard-issue burnt coffee. Do you mind if I . . . ?"

"I don't *mind,* but if I were you, there's a Starbucks up the street."

"Not my people," said Jorge.

The kid smiled. "How do you take it?"

When he came back with a mug, Jorge had taken off his jacket and pulled a chair over beside the desk.

"My daughter was telling me at breakfast, you had a suicide on the beach yesterday."

"Two days ago."

"Must have been hard on the guy who took the call."

"Yep." He gestured with his head, and Jorge saw over his shoulder a young officer sitting at a desk, talking on the phone and doodling with some intensity.

"Could I talk to him? My daughter, Terry, knew the family."

He was on his feet and moving around the barrier, carrying his coffee, before his young friend could figure out the answer to the question. "Hey, Dylan," the kid called, as if to convey that he was on top of this, that he'd given Jorge permission to go back.

Dylan was getting off the phone and looking up at him, puzzled, as Jorge sat down on the aluminum chair beside his desk.

"Detective Carrera, visiting from New York. I heard you found the guy on the beach the other morning."

He looked surprised and wary. Had he missed something? Done something wrong?

"Oh no, no, nothing official. I just stopped in to say hi to Harry Rideout. How are you doing? That must have been one rough wake-up call."

Dylan's face softened slightly. Jorge did his best to appear avuncular, and his best was pretty good.

"I've been better," Dylan allowed.

"I remember my first time. Homicide in Patchogue, a guy took his baby by the heels and swung her against the wall, because she wouldn't stop crying." He'd never been in Patchogue, but he knew how to pronounce it. "Suppose there's no doubt that he did it himself?"

Dylan shook his head, his lips pressed together, as if sickened by the image in his mind. "Weapon still in his right hand. Angle of wound exactly what you'd expect. Blood pattern consistent. No other footprints on the sand."

"And we know he was right-handed?"

Dylan nodded. They talked about shock, and grief, and how you handled it if you were in blue. Jorge told Dylan his daughter knew the victim, used to help take care of the wife, Mrs. Clark. She was a painter, he understood. It turned out Dylan had responded to that call too, when the wife died.

"You have really been through it," Jorge said sympathetically. Dylan nodded.

Jorge let him sit with this. Then he said "Are you the one who found the note?"

Dylan nodded again.

"Why did he do it?"

The younger officer looked torn. Jorge was a cop; he should have known Dylan couldn't tell him. It belonged to the family. On the other hand, he was a cop, what was the harm? The rest of the guys here had read it.

"Terry, my daughter—she asked me that," Jorge added, "and I didn't know what to tell her. She felt so close to the family. It's eating at her. You ever lose someone like that?"

Jorge waited, thinking of how he could get the properties clerk to hand over the personal effects, if Dylan wouldn't open.

But he did. He looked up at Jorge and said, "I'm not sorry for what I did. I'd do it again. But neither can I live with it." At first Jorge thought Dylan was speaking for himself, but when he got to the "neither" he realized he was quoting.

"That was the note?"

Dylan nodded.

"And what did it mean?"

"Wish I knew."

"Do his children know?"

Dylan shook his head. "They haven't seen it yet. The son said he'd come out here to get the effects on the weekend. Didn't seem to be in a hurry. We still have the body. They haven't bothered to choose a funeral home."

"That's cold," said Jorge.

"Yes," said Dylan.

Maggie was in her room reading *Middlemarch* when Jorge called. It was just before lunch.

"'I'm not sorry for what I did. I'd do it again. But neither can I live with it,'" Maggie repeated.

"That's it," said Jorge.

"You didn't see it yourself?"

"No. But I promise you, young Dylan knew it word for word."

"You got his name in case we need him?"

"Badge number, everything."

"Did he have anything else that struck you?"

He told her that the family hadn't bothered yet to collect Albie's effects or make arrangements for the body. Maggie was thoughtful.

"He had a son and a daughter. The son is called Al and lives somewhere on the island—Oyster Bay, somewhere like that. I think the daughter lives in the city."

"Name?"

Maggie thought. "Serena . . . Selena."

"Married?" Jorge asked.

"Yes. With children. I'll find her and call you back."

She sat for a bit, watching out the window as a pair of Canada geese waddled down the lawn and glided onto the lake. She thought about the evening Albie had talked about Ruth's death and his estrangement from his children, and also about whether geese really do mate for life. How to learn the truth about either? If she were at school, she could have found what she wanted to know about Albie's children in a heartbeat. And Maggie would be welcome if she showed up at Winthrop—too welcome, maybe, which was why she had resolved to stay well away from the whole community in order to let her successor get his legs under him. But she'd already broken the promise by contacting Jorge. One tiny call to the development office wasn't going to hurt.

"Good morning, Adrianna, it's . . ."

But Adrianna was already greeting her with glad cries. After they'd exchanged personal news, Maggie said, "Could you look something up in the stud book for me?" The development office had a shelf full of Social Registers, for obvious reasons. "See if there's an Albert Clark of Manhattan and Southampton, wife named Ruth."

Adrianna was with her in a moment. "Got it. Albert M. Clark, Yale class of '72, wife Ruth Borden. Quite a string of clubs, do you want to know those?"

"Not at the moment. Is there an Albert M. junior?"

"One in St. Helena, California, one in Oyster Bay."

"The second one, please."

Adrianna read her the information, and they spent a little time gossiping about the hubbub of school. The new head was locked in a struggle with the school cook, who wanted an expensive restaurant bagel toaster for the lunch room, and also wanted to grow her own herbs and salad greens on the school's roof, which the athletic department needed for recess. Maggie, dying to question and comment, said instead, "Well I'm sure he'll work it out," and sent her love to Adrianna's husband.

Then she dialed another number.

"Good afternoon," she said into the handset, "this is Mrs. Detweiler from the Social Register. Have I reached the Albert Clark Junior residence?"

"Yes."

"Is Mr. or Mrs. Clark available?"

"This is Mrs. Clark," said the woman.

"Oh good," said Maggie. "Is this a bad time?"

"No, it's all right." Neutral affect, neither annoyed, nor particularly polite.

"I'd just like to update your information," said Maggie. "You are Melody, née Bothwell?" She was. Maggie went through the family's listing, recording Melody's new e-mail address and confirming the children's present ages, and learning in the process that the oldest boy was now at a junior boarding school in Massachusetts. She wondered what that was about, since Americans didn't usually send children away that young, unless there was a behavior or learning problem, or the family was breaking up. She just barely stopped herself from asking.

Then the tricky part. "Now I hope you can help me," she said. "I'm told our computer files in one part of the alphabet have become corrupted—I'm so sorry, don't ask me to explain that, I just know the words—and we have lost our entry for Mr. Clark's sister, Selena." Please let it be Selena and not Serena, she chanted inwardly.

"None of her contact info has changed," said Melody. "Mrs. Richard Sherrill."

"In Manhattan?" said Maggie, pretending to flip pages. "Not the one in Hobe Sound?"

"Manhattan."

"Thank you so much, could you give me that number?" Melody could and Maggie jotted.

"You're welcome. If you don't get her, you should probably know that their father just passed."

"Oh my goodness, I am *so* sorry! I wish you'd told me, I could have called another time!"

"It's fine," said Melody rather flatly.

Maggie sat for a while, thinking.

Hope had had a restless night and gone back to bed after breakfast. As noon approached, she was bathed and dressed for the second time, and feeling ready to greet her public. In the corridor, she knocked on Maggie's door, but got no answer. She tried her key card in Maggie's lock just out of curiosity, and was relieved when it didn't open the door. That at least narrowed things down a tiny bit.

It wasn't quite time for lunch and she knew the papers wouldn't be in for hours. She thought she'd probably find Maggie on the sunporch, struggling with the *Ship of Fools,* but decided to go downstairs the back way, following the route Clarence had shown them yesterday.

There seemed to be no one abroad in the hotel, and she wondered for a moment if something had happened while she was asleep. A neutron bomb or something.

No one was watching television behind closed doors, or typing or singing in the shower; no one was rolling a housekeeping cart down the corridors. It wasn't Sunday so soon again, was it?

No. Wednesday. Well, then, just a quiet morning in the off-season. She crossed the small landing into the back wing, the oldest part of the hotel, and stopped again, thinking. This first room here had been Albie Clark's. Poor man. She knew it was a suite with an extra bay and bank of windows on account of the new wing having been set at an angle to the old one. She tried to remember if she had seen Albie in the hall the night of the fire. She was fairly sure she had; she had a dim memory of yellow pajamas, but again, her memories of the fire were a jumble, as things tend to be when one has been awakened from a sound sleep and frightened half to death.

Next, she thought, came the room that the Poole sisters had occupied, and next to them Mr. Rexroth and Clarence, and then the small room where Mr. Niner lived. There were two more rooms on the other side . . . who had been in those? The Kleinkramers, she was fairly sure, and Teddy Bledsoe. And then at the end of the hall, the turret suite where the Maynards had been. The turret was charming from the outside of the building. A drawing of it served as the inn's logo on the letter paper and promotional bumf, and photographs of it adorned the website's home page. They had spent some time with Martin and Nina in their sitting room, talking over D.C. schools. The sitting room was on the same level as the corridor, while the bed and bath were above, which probably explained why alone among the hall's occupants, the Maynards hadn't seemed to want to kill anyone in the Antippas family. For most of course, the corpse-elect would have been the dog.

How, she wondered, was an FBI agent affording the best digs in the house? Was that something to ponder? Perhaps Martin was a demon investor on the side. Or maybe Nina was an heiress. Or maybe civil service paid better than she'd been led to believe.

Hope heard a door open softly behind her, and turned to see Chef Sarah emerging from Mr. Niner's room.

"Oh, hello, Hope," said Sarah.

"Good morning, Chef!" said Hope brightly. "Visiting Mr. Niner?"

"Visiting Walter, actually," said Sarah. "He loves toast crusts. I bake them extra hard for him."

"He probably got the remains of my breakfast," said Hope. "I never eat the crusts."

"I think perhaps he did," said Sarah, who knew very well what leftovers came back to the kitchen. "I could make some soft rolls for you if you'd prefer that."

"No, I love the bread you make; I just like to eat the middles out."

Sarah smiled. "Just like my daughter."

"Oh! You have children?"

Sarah looked distracted for a moment, then said, "Just the one."

Sensing something sensitive there, Hope changed the subject. "Is Mr. Niner in? I'd love to see Walter."

"No, he's out in the stable."

"Ah. I better wait till he's here, then."

"Yes. Walter's an old grouch with strangers."

Together they walked down the back stairs. "I was wondering," said Hope, "how Walter and Grommet got along. If Walter flew over and perched on top of the snake cage, why wouldn't Grommet strike him?"

"Oh, Walter doesn't fly," said Sarah. "Before Earl got him, some beast cut his flight feathers short to make him seem to be a young bird."

"Why?"

"It's not legal to sell wild parrots. They were trying to make him look as if he wasn't middle-aged. The feathers grew back, but he still doesn't fly."

"So Walter was caught in the wild?"

"We think so."

"Poor creature. No wonder he's grumpy."

"Yes. Will you be in for lunch? I'm making pop-overs for Maggie's birthday."

"You are amazing to remember. She'll love that." They parted at the kitchen door.

Hope was right about Maggie and the puzzle. When Hope found her, she had just succeeded in piecing together the poor soul swimming hopefully alongside the ship with his begging bowl. He was naked except for his hat.

"You are relentless with that thing," said Hope.

"I can't help it. I can't resist making order out of chaos. But look at him. Who goes swimming with a hat on?"

"I would if I had one," Hope said. "It's been a long time since I went more than a week without having my hair done. It feels as if it's going to crawl off and die."

Come to think of it, Maggie observed, her friend was looking a little bedraggled. "Why don't we drive into Ainsley this afternoon, there must be a hair place there."

"What a good idea!" That settled, Maggie told Hope about the note left by Albie Clark, and the heartless behavior of his children. Maybe he *was* capable of real cruelty, if they were that angry. Hope told Maggie about her encounter with Chef Sarah outside Earl's room.

"Well, that gives us plenty to think about," Maggie said. And they went to the dining room to await the popovers.

If you want to know what's going on in a town, a great place to start is the hair parlor. Hope wondered why they hadn't thought of it before. They found Upper Cuts on State Street, just across from the courthouse, beside a diner called the Chowder Bowl. A large woman wearing a pink apron and holding a bowl of something with a powerful chemical smell stopped her work and came to greet them.

"I'm afraid we don't have appointments," said Hope. "Is there any chance I could get a shampoo and set?"

"I got one of my best girls, just waiting for you. Pammie?" she called across to the sinks, where a slim woman with hair the color of a tangerine was leisurely sweeping up cuttings. Pammie stowed her broom and came to them, wiping her hands on her smock.

"You can take a wash and blow out, can't you?"

Pammie looked at her watch, which had a bright plastic band the same color as her hair, and agreed she could.

"And what can we do for you, hon?" asked the big woman, turning to Maggie. She looked at Maggie's no-fuss flurry of white hair and clearly thought, Not much.

"What about a manicure?" said Maggie.

"Dandy," said the large woman, whom they would learn was a Mrs. Pease. "Choose your color and Tina will be right with you. Would you like her to set up her table beside your friend, so you can talk to each other?"

"That would be lovely," said Maggie.

When she had Hope shampooed and draped in a pink plastic smock and towels, Pammie said, "And what brings you ladies to Vacationland this time of year?"

"My son lives in Bergen," said Hope.

"You staying here in town?"

Where? Hope wondered. She'd seen a grim-looking cluster of pastel tourist cabins on the outskirts, but they looked closed for the season.

"No, we're over in Bergen at the inn."

Pammie lowered her dryer and brush. "We heard everyone left after the fire. Were you there?"

Maggie looked up and caught Hope's eye.

"We were."

"Terrible. We heard it's closing," said Pammie, resuming her work.

"It was very upsetting, but really just the one wing was affected. Mostly it's water damage. As I understand it."

"That Cherry Weaver?" said Pammie. "She used to work here."

Their noises of genuine surprise encouraged Pammie. Hope and Maggie had definitely not known this piece of serendipity.

"She came here right out of high school. Mrs. Pease was training her. It was 2009, I think, CHARLOTTE! WAS IT 2009 CHERRY WEAVER CAME?" she called to the large woman above the noise of the dryers.

"July 2009," Charlotte answered. This was not the first time this subject had come up in the last week.

"So you knew her?" Hope asked. "What was she like when she was here?"

Pammie rolled a thick lock of Hope's hair around her brush and gave it a good pull, then turned the dryer on it. "Dumb as a box of hammers," said Pammie.

"Oh dear."

"Well, but come on. You don't need too many brain cells to figure out you shouldn't set your boss's place on fire, right after he gives you the can. We got off easy here, I guess. CHARLOTTE—WE GOT OFF EASY HERE! RIGHT? SHE MIGHT HAVE BURNED YOU DOWN!"

Charlotte's mouth was full of bobby pins; she was giving the old lady in her chair a kind of pin curl set that hadn't been seen since the 1950s as far as Hope knew. Still, it was clear that she'd thought of that, that Cherry Weaver might have burned her whole salon right down and taken the whole block with it. She was nodding a world-weary agreement and so was the lady in her chair.

"Charlotte had to let her go. She kept talking to the tourists about gun control. People from New York! Boston! What does she have between the ears?"

"You know what I think?" said Mrs. Pease, taking the bobby pins out of her mouth. "I think she has one of those complexes."

"Really?" said Hope.

"Like you hear on *Oprah*. About her father. She couldn't get his attention if she set her own hair on fire right in front of him, but she kept trying." Mrs. Pease put the pins back in her mouth, made another tight curl of blue hair with her fingers, then pinned it tight to the old pink scalp in front of her.

"He's a fireman," said Pammie. "And a hunter. Charlotte went to high school with him. Gun nut, you'd probably say," she said grinning, giving Hope's shoulder a nudge.

"Oh no," said Hope. "I'm quite a good shot myself. My husband and I used to hunt ducks in Canada."

This went over extremely well, and impressed even Maggie.

"So this idiot child, Cherry," said Pammie. She now had Hope's hair smooth and dry, the way she normally wore it. Without stopping to ask, Pammie started to back-comb the hair the way you make beehive hairdos when the spring musical is *Grease*. Maggie waited for Hope to scream, but Hope didn't say a word.

"When she was brought in for questioning," said Pammie, "she was in the bathroom, and of course someone has to be in there with her. She was crying, and saying she shouldn't have done it, and talking about how scared she was. It never even occurred to her she was talking to a policewoman!"

The lady with the pin curls was now across the room under a dryer, and Charlotte had come to join their conversation. "Carson Bailey says he's got guys in supermax whose cases weren't as tight as what they've got on Cherry."

"Really?" asked Hope.

"He says so."

"He says everything points one way. There aren't even any other suspects."

"Charlotte cuts his hair," said Pammie. "Carson Bailey."

"Well, when he's in Ainsley. She had motive and opportunity, Cherry did, and the whole family's mean as skunks. She's started fires before."

"And she's an idiot. Kind of kid who'd murder her parents and then want sympathy that she's an orphan."

"She sets fires so she can see her father," said Charlotte.

"She told her lawyer she did it," said Pammie. "Her lawyer's an Indian." She had finished her work with the ratting comb, and was now gassing Hope's head with hairspray. When she was satisfied she handed Hope a mirror and spun her chair around so she could see the back of her head.

I was amazed you let her do that," said Maggie once they were on the street.

"I got sort of fascinated," said Hope. "How do I look?"

"I think your prom date's reaction will be shock and awe."

Hope stopped walking and dug in her purse for her compact. She peered into its small round mirror. "You know, I *wanted* to have my hair done like this for my prom in 1964, but my mother wouldn't let me."

"Now you can cross it off your bucket list."

"I'll say," said Hope, putting away the compact. "But I wanted to hear what she'd say, didn't you?"

"I did. What did you think?"

"I was appalled."

"Yes. No other suspects? They're not even looking for other explanations?"

"I think it's time to call my old friend, the reporter."

"Has he ever seen your hair like that?"

"Nobody has. But it will make him feel young."

"Do you think he'd come up here?"

"He lost his wife last year. Now he doesn't know what to do with himself."

"Sounds familiar," said Maggie, stopping in front of Mr. Paperback. "Look, today's papers." They went in and bought the *Boston Globe* and the *New York Times*, and all the Artemis tribute magazines that had been rushed into print in the last week.

All the magazines wrote up the fire at the Oquossoc Mountain Inn. They reported that a suspect was in custody and two ran interviews with a self-important Carson Bailey pretending to be modest about how quickly they had solved the case. Hope and Maggie sat silently in the library after dinner, reading each article as if studying for an exam. There were pictures of Alexander in his young manhood. Pictures of him and Lisa, posing in evening dress with beakers of wine in their hands, at a gala at the Los Angeles County Museum of Art. Accounts of Alexander's business career, how he'd started as an immigrant carpenter and ended as a megarich developer of shopping malls and suburban office parks. They showed pictures of the funeral cortege arriving at Forest Lawn after the Staples Center. Someone had gotten a shot with a telephoto lens of Lisa being helped into the chapel by her son, her face completely hidden by a veil that concealed her like a burka. She was wearing high heels in spite of the fact that her right ankle was taped and looked like a football. Glory was right behind her, flanked by Sophie and Ada. The girls looked terrible.

A reporter for one of the Artemis Tribute magazines did a piece on her school days, how she'd attended the elite Harvard-Westlake School until sixth grade, when she transferred to Uplands, a school known for accommodating professional children. They'd gotten a copy of the yearbook for the year her class "graduated." In Artemis's case that was a term of art; she had evidently been tutored on the set while she was working more than she'd attended in person. But she had been enough of a presence to leave a record of personality and friendships. Her name was given as Jenny Antippas. Under her picture, along with favorite sayings (*Wait a hot minute . . . blue M&M's . . . rockin' the Cartier!!*) were her nicknames: *Artemis, Goddess,* and *JennyKookla.*

"Look at this," said Maggie. She put the page in front of Hope.

"Cute picture," said Hope. "How do you think they got the yearbook?"

"Bought it from one of her classmates. What do you make of this, though?" she said, tapping the page.

"JennyKookla. Kookla? Kukla, like *Kukla, Fran and Ollie*?"

"Maybe. Some kind of pet name. Does anyone that age even know about *Kukla, Fran and Ollie*?"

"They're show business kids, they might. Does *kukla* mean something? We should Google it."

Maggie took out her phone and looked at the screen. "One bar."

"Sometimes you can get two if you're closer to the antenna," said Hope.

"Is Mr. Gurrell still here? His computer is hard-wired to it." The Internet signal, they now knew, came to the hotel from a transmitter on a hill four miles away, and was a line-of-sight connection, meaning that if fog or heavy rain or anything else obscured the view, the signal blinked out. Out was its condition more often than not, because some trees had grown up since it was installed, whose topmost branches flickered in the way of the signal in any kind of wind. The trees were on someone else's land and the owner declined to remove them. The hardwired computer worked better than the hotel wi-fi, which shouldn't have been true, but was. Places this far from town were supposed to get DSL lines sometime soon, but if you called the phone company to learn when, they would generally admit that it would be around the next ice age.

Mr. Gurrell's door was locked.

"That's frustrating," said Maggie.

"What was Kukla?" Hope asked. "A snake?"

"No that was Ollie. He was a one-toothed dragon. Kukla had the big red clown nose and angry eyebrows."

"Strange nickname for someone you liked."

"Let's go see if housekeeping will let us in."

The door to the housekeeping office was open, but no one was there and the drawer where the skeleton keys were kept was locked.

"Do you think the front desk would let us in?"

"She shouldn't, but it's worth a try."

On their way toward the front of the house, they heard a peal of female laughter from the kitchen, then a low chuckle from a male voice. The door was slightly ajar, and Hope, ever curious, stopped and pushed it open.

In the sink nearest the industrial dishwasher, which was rumbling, was Chef Sarah, holding a long wooden spoon with Walter the parrot perched on the handle. Beside her, Earl Niner was wielding the dish sprayer over the bird, who cooed and chuckled, a portrait of happiness. As the women came in, Walter hopped off the spoon handle into the sink and grabbed the spoon with his beak, which made Sarah laugh again. "You like that, don't you, Wally?" The spray rained over him. Clearly Wally did.

Sarah looked up and said, "Don't call the health department, will you? He's a very clean bird."

"I can see that," said Hope. "I never thought of birds liking water."

"He's from the rain forest. He loves it," she said. Earl turned the water off, and Walter hopped back onto the spoon handle and stretched his wings out like a frustrated god, demanding more water tribute. When none came, he shook himself and began to puff his plumage. He was wet enough to look a little like a plucked chicken. He turned his head so he could fix Earl with one bright orange-rimmed eye. Sarah lifted him, and he stepped off his handle perch onto Earl's shoulder.

"It's very bad of us, but he enjoys it so much." She reached over to scratch Walter's pin feathers, and he leaned in toward her in pleasure and puffed his plumage. He shook himself again, and Earl's shirt began to darken with wet.

"I better get him upstairs and dry him off," said Earl.

"Bye-bye, Walter," Sarah cooed at him. "Say bye-bye?"

Walter uttered a sardonic hahaha sound. It made Hope and Maggie laugh. Earl turned and went out, with Walter chirruping on his shoulder.

"They don't really talk," said Sarah. "African Grays are the talkers. He just goes hahaha when you tell him to say something. He also does a very good smoke alarm."

"What kind is he?" Maggie asked.

"Amazon orange wing. How can I help you ladies? Were you looking for me?"

"No," said Hope. "We were on our way to the front desk when we heard you laughing. We came in because we hate to miss anything."

"You really love animals," said Maggie to Sarah.

"I do. They're so much safer than people."

After a slight pause, Maggie said, "Maybe you *can* help us . . . we wanted to get that new desk girl to break us into Mr. Gurrell's office. I don't suppose you have a key?"

"I think I might. What do you need there?"

"The Internet. We want to find out what *kukla* means."

"Oh!" said Sarah. "I can tell you that."

Maggie, who had been waiting for Sarah to say *Kukla, Fran and Ollie*, said, "You can?"

"Yes. *Koukla* means 'pretty doll,' in Greek."

"Really!"

"What an amazing woman you are," Hope added. "You speak Greek?"

Sarah said, "Not really. I spent a summer on Crete, once."

"I've been to Crete," said Maggie. "I was on the trail of the Minoans."

"You'd just read *The King Must Die*?" Sarah asked.

"Exactly!" cried Maggie. "You too?"

"Fascinating book," said Sarah, smiling.

"Were you studying on Crete?"

Sarah turned and began washing out the sink. "No . . . You know. Just bumming around with a friend."

"Ah. Well thank you very much, that solves one mystery.

"Good night," said Hope.

"Good night," said Sarah, when they were at the door.

Day Twelve, Thursday, October 17

It hadn't taken Jorge long to find out where the Rich-ard Sherrills sent their kids to school. The private school grapevine in New York City could give the CIA intelligence envy. The Sherrill boy, Lucas, who was twelve, was at the Buckley School. The younger daugh-ter, Sally, was at Chapin. Jorge, dressed like a banker, was waiting across from Chapin Thursday morning as the lower school girls were delivered to the school doors by parents and nannies. He knew what Selena Sherrill looked like from Google Images, and from the grape-vine that Richard worked on Wall Street, while Selena was a stay-at-home mom. He figured the odds were good that she did the drop-off.

His plan had been to fall into conversation with Selena if he could, but chance provided a better plan. Selena greeted a friend whose daughter had just run inside, and they left school together, walking west. Jorge followed discreetly. They paused on the corner of Park and Eighty-fourth Street and talked for some time, although it was a crisp morning and a chill breeze had come up. When they parted, Selena to go south, the other woman on toward Central Park, Jorge let Selena go and followed the friend. At the corner of Madison, he caught up with her.

"Excuse me," he said, "but wasn't that Selena Sherrill you were just talking to?"

The woman looked at him, surprised. She'd fished a red earphone wire from her pocket and had been just about to pop in her earbuds.

"George Baker," said Jorge. "I saw you together in front of the school. I was dropping off my granddaughter. I wasn't sure, I haven't seen Selena for years. Which way are you going?"

"Across the park," said the woman, not putting the earphones away.

"I'll walk with you," said Jorge. "I was a friend of Albie Clark, Selena's father. Did you know him?"

"I did," said the woman. Jorge stuck out his hand and said "George," again, and this gave her little choice but to either snub him, or accept the introduction. She did the latter, a touch reluctantly, and said "Jean Chant."

"Great name," said Jorge. "Did you know him from the Hamptons?" He was guessing, but guessing well.

"Yes. That's really how I know Selena. Our husbands were summer friends out there as children." She resumed walking. "I'm going to be late for work," she added, picking up her pace, "if I don't keep moving."

"I don't mind," said Jorge as she took long quick strides down the block. Moving right along with her, he added, "I'd like to pay my respects to her but I wasn't sure it would be welcome."

"Yes," said Jean Chant. "It's complicated."

"Do you think she'd mind a visit from an old friend of her father's? Selena? I'd like to—you know, sit shivah with her or something like that. Sit and remember him. We'd lost touch in later years, and it bothers me."

Jean looked at him without slowing her pace as they hit the Walk light and crossed Fifth.

"I think if I were you I'd write a note," she said dryly.

"They weren't close? I'd gotten that impression, but Albie was private," said Jorge.

"Mr. Baker, I doubt you and Selena have the same view of her father. He was a shit to her mother. There were always other women, and he wasn't such a red hot father, either," said Jean. She said it as if it was something she'd wanted to tell the world for some time.

After a moment to digest this, Jorge said, "You shock me."

"Yes, well. Are you sure you're going this way?"

"It's fine. I'll grab a cab on Central Park West. I never saw that side of him."

"A lot of people are different behind closed doors," said Jean. "He was a very angry man."

"I did know he was very annoyed with some neighbors in the Hamptons."

"Those Greeks? Everyone was angry about *them*. That's not what I meant. Look, I don't want to speak ill of the dead, but Mr. Clark is not a person I feel neutral about."

"I understand. Sorry, I know I'm imposing. I'm just, I guess, puzzled. When Ruth got sick he seemed so stricken."

"Conscious-stricken is more like it."

They were deep in the park now and Jorge was practically running to keep up with her.

"Does Selena's brother feel the same way about him?"

"You better ask him," said Jean Chant. Then she looked at her watch, muttered, "Sorry," and took off race-walking, putting her earbuds into her ears as she went.

Toby Osborne, late of the *Boston Globe,* reached the Oquossoc Mountain Inn on Thursday in time for elevenses. Hope had reserved a room for him in the wing where Earl Niner and Mr. Rexroth lived, partly so he could sniff around there without attracting notice, and partly because Zeke and some boys from the village were starting the cleanup in the wing that had burned and she wanted to protect him from the noise.

Toby was a gorgeous shambling mess, with white hair and a bald spot on the crown of his head, and eyebrows that made every woman he met contemplate pruning shears. Hope saw him drive past the front door and into the parking lot, and she and Maggie watched from the sunporch as he got out of his car and fetched his duffle bag from the backseat. He stood looking up at the site of the fire for a good while.

They were waiting for him in the lobby when he came in the side door with his bag on his shoulder, walking with a cane.

"What are you hobbling about?" Hope asked as she went to greet him.

"Hip," he said. "They say put off a replacement, as long as you can. I may have overdone it. It's not as bad as it looks though, and the cane comes in handy for hailing cabs. What happened to your hair?"

"I'm undercover," said Hope.

They got him checked in and settled, and met at a table in the corner of the dining room to explain where things stood. When they were done, the table was covered with crumbs and empty coffee cups, and drawings of the hallways charting what rooms people were in the night of the fire. Toby said, "Let's review the bidding. Margaux Kleinkramer. Eileen Bachman. I covered the Druid Murder. My first big murder case. I've got my notes somewhere."

"Margaux had no more motive than anyone else on the corridor," said Hope.

"No. But no less, either. And maybe a dicier past than anyone knows. And Albie Clark."

"Motives. Animus. Opportunity if he got hold of a master key."

"And the suicide could be a confession of sorts."

"You'd think they'd at least be looking at that, wouldn't you?" Toby asked.

"We would."

"I did some checking on your key players before I left home. Carson Bailey. Judge Hennebery. They say that Hennebery was made a judge too young, and resents all those years on the bench making civil servant pay, while his old law firm colleagues got rich dragging out divorces among the yacht club set. Pro prosecution, gets impatient if cops don't give the testimony the DA wants. Big ego, foul temper, and he falls asleep during testimony."

Hope and Maggie looked at each other.

"And he likes to gossip about cases."

"To reporters?"

Toby smiled. "Sometimes. Especially if he doesn't know they're reporters." He flipped to a new page on his legal pad and said, "Rexroth."

"He has less motive than Albie, but more opportunity. He's lived here for years and surely knows how to get a key if he wants one. And he's pretty squirrelly," said Maggie. "You could say he got off scot-free after handing his wife a poisonous snake. Who's to say he wouldn't try it again, if someone really pushed his buttons."

After a beat, Toby put a question mark beside Rexroth's name.

"Earl Niner is not exactly mainstream either," said Hope.

"I don't see Earl in this," Maggie said. "He certainly wouldn't have used his own pet as the murder weapon."

Toby raised his vast eyebrows. "I'm still having trouble with the concept of a pet rattlesnake. It goes to character."

"There is that." Toby made some notes.

"The Angelinos?"

"The wife had a screaming fight with her husband that morning. But she was doped up after her accident, and looked pretty lame—I don't see how she could have risen from her bed of pain to incinerate him."

"She would have had a key to his room, though. And the rest could have been an act. The hospital didn't even keep her overnight."

"Do you see her with the snake?" Maggie asked Hope.

"I'm keeping an open mind. All we really have to do is plant reasonable doubt."

" 'Atta girl," said Toby. "What about the sister?"

They agreed that Gloria had more mobility but less motive, as far as they knew. Although in families, there could always be motives that didn't show on the outside. They talked through the other members of the cooking class, but couldn't work up much enthusiasm for any of them as suspects. Then they went through who in the hotel might have a grudge against Mr. Gurrell, and not mind if the place burned down, but that, regrettably, led them only to Cherry.

"All right," said Toby, "make the prosecution's case."

Maggie did the honors. "She had recently been fired. She blamed Antippas and was furious with

Mr. Gurrell. She has a juvenile record for shoplifting a fire accelerant. She shows up in the photographs of fire scenes when there's no reason for her to be there, typical behavior of an arsonist. And as the desk clerk, she knew how to program the room keys. She's got a dead end life and a pretty impressive chip on her shoulder."

"As front desk clerk she could make a key to any room in the house?"

"Presumably."

Toby digested this. "I gotta admit, I see why they arrested her. Now give me the other side."

Hope said, "There are no fingerprints at the fire scene except the housekeeper's and Mr. and Mrs. Antippas's and Miss Poole's. No fingerprints in Niner's room except his, and Chef Sarah's, but we know she goes there to visit the parrot."

"Cherry would have worn gloves," said Toby. "I would if I were stealing a rattlesnake."

"Her sister says she goes to fires to see her father. He's a volunteer firefighter. Cherry says she was at her mother's watching TV that evening until she heard about the fire on the police scanner. She can tell you exactly what she watched."

Toby seemed unsurprised about the police scanner. He probably had his own. "But she was alone?" he asked.

"Well. Yes. But her sister may become the mother of my grandchildren," said Hope. "Brianna says Cherry is innocent and I believe her."

"How does Cherry get around. She have her own car?"

"Some ancient Subaru you could total by losing the keys," said Maggie.

"Got a plate number?"

"Sorry, no. I can tell you where to go see for yourself."

After a thoughtful pause, Toby leaned back in his chair, tapped his legal pad, and said, "Okay. I like a challenge."

Buster pulled his cruiser into the yard of a trailer on blocks at the north end of Beaver Creek Road. He saw the shadow of a figure cross the kitchen window inside as he got out. There had been a light frost that morning and the stumps of long dead geraniums in the planter box on the concrete steps were brown and sad-looking. Buster stood in the weak sun and stretched, then wandered around the side of the house toward the shed in back that served as a garage. When he had seen what there was to see there, he strolled back to the front yard, where a dog on a chain was lying in the dirt, a huge golden-something mix with a gray muzzle, who raised his head and thumped his tail at Buster, but did not otherwise stir himself. Buster walked over to have a look at the dog, and decided to risk scratching its ears. The dog, completely in favor of this development, rolled onto his back.

"Hey, Jasper. You're a good old guy, aren't you?" Buster said as he scratched, and wondered if that was mange in the coat, and how long it had been since this beast had had a bath. At the edge of his vision, he could see a tiny movement of blinds in the back of the trailer, two slats slightly flexed, then closed again.

Buster straightened, looked at the sky, gave a tug at his pants to be sure his pistol could be seen beneath his jacket, and went to the door of the trailer. The morning sun was brighter than it was warm but he was glad to be outdoors.

He rapped at the trailer door, and waited. Silence from within. Outside, he heard a hermit thrush in the woods, and from the road the tocktocktock of a wood-pecker assaulting a Bangor Hydro pole. He waited. He looked at the discarded truck tires lying at the side of the house and a broken child's swing, hanging from one length of rope from a maple someone had planted de-cades ago. The seat of the swing hung vertical. Useless.

He rapped at the door again. "Roy, I know you're in there. I saw you. Open the door."

Again nothing happened. Buster took his time.

The third time he knocked longer and harder, and then he called, "Roy, unless you want to have a talk about that deer hide curing in your shed, you better open this door. I don't want to talk about it, but I will if you make me break your door down."

Then he waited some more, and at last heard movement. The door opened, and Roy said, "I hit it with my car. Jumped right in front of me. You can look and see where it bent the fender."

"I know, Roy. And it shot itself in the chest before it died too."

"I thought you didn't want to talk about it."

"I don't. Will you come out, or will I come in?"

There was a standoff, during which Roy neither moved nor blinked. Buster found this deeply unnerving but he stood as still as he could.

"Hold on," said Roy. "Find my shoes." He had come to the door wearing ancient socks of a gray-beige color that could not be achieved with dye. When he came back, he was wearing his hunting boots. He came out onto the concrete stoop, forcing Buster to step down into the yard, and shut the door behind him.

"Well?"

Buster said, "Your daughter's in trouble. Cherry."

"I know which daughter."

"Well?"

"Well what?"

"What are you going to do about it?"

"Why should I do anything about it?"

"Because you got a fresh deerskin in your shed and it isn't deer season."

Roy stared at him, his expression calculating.

"What is it you think I should do?" he said at last.

"She wants to see you."

"Yeah? Why?"

"To show you care what happens to her."

"And do I?"

"Roy, get in the car before I get ugly."

Roy Weaver looked slightly surprised, then ambled down the steps, past Buster, over to the cruiser. He got into the passenger seat and sat there.

In the car, they drove the first ten minutes in silence. Roy jiggled his legs and looked out the window. Buster was surprised to discover how much the jiggling legs annoyed him, when they weren't his. Finally, to distract himself, Buster said, "You worked the fire at the inn last week."

"Yeah. So?"

"So what did you think of it?"

After a pause Roy said, "Do you want me to rate it or something? I give it three stars out of five."

"I want you to tell me what you think started it."

"Guy was smoking in bed, what the hell do you think?"

Buster slowed down to pass a girl on a bicycle. She was riding on the road, as there was no paved shoulder.

"I don't think anything, that's why I asked you. Brass thinks it was arson."

"Shit for brains."

"Excuse me?"

"Shep Gordon has shit for brains, want me to spell it?"

Roy sounded surprisingly angry.

"I take it you know each other."

"Historically," said Roy.

Buster wondered whether he should press for more on this point and decided there were other ways to find out. "Why do you say it was smoking in bed that started it?"

"Sheets and blankets gone. Mattress half-burned. Carpet all melted on the corpse's side of the bed. No smell of accelerant, no evidence of any, the way the flames had moved . . . seen a dozen of them. They're all like that. Wiring fires are different. Different patterns. Arson different still."

"I see. Would you testify to that?"

Roy barked a laugh. "That's a good one. Shep Gordon asking me to testify about anything."

"I was thinking of the defense."

A pause. "Whose?"

Buster thought of asking him if he'd been living in a cave, and then thought that yeah, he pretty much had. "Cherry's. Cherry is accused of setting the fire."

"Cherry? Weaver?"

"Yes," said Buster.

Detective Kim Prince had a conflicted relationship with the LAPD. Early in his career he'd been partnered with a dirty cop named Hritzko, now in jail himself, who had a great conviction rate because he used paid snitches as witnesses when he knew he had the right man but not enough evidence. As Hritzko had a huge ego, he always knew he had the right man. Prince hated him, but learned quickly how dangerous it is to break the unwritten code. If your partner can't trust you, you can't trust him not to leave you in an alley with three armed gangbangers and no backup. Prince asked for a transfer, made detective, and now worked alone whenever he could.

He didn't know how they did things up in Maine, but he had a feeling it was the same all over. Detective Gordon had gotten up his nose when he'd first called for help on the Antippas case. He'd been a little too full of himself, a little too accustomed to being admired. But since then Prince had worked with Deputy Babbin, and that had gone better. What a deputy from the sheriff's department was doing working with staties he didn't know, but Babbin seemed to actually want to solve this thing, not just convict the first boob his eye fell on. And of course, there was the Artemis piece of it. What the hell had gone on in that family? Separate bedrooms. Silk-covered walls. Where were they when that poor girl was falling down the crapper? He happened to have seen her once, being brought into his station house after a DUI in the middle of the afternoon, about five blocks from the Chateau Marmont. Must have been some lunch. She looked so much younger than she did onstage in all that pancake and garbage. She looked beaten, being hustled inside past the paparazzi, a big bruiser in uniform holding either elbow. She showed no bravado, no anger at the press or the police; she just seemed ashamed. It made him sad.

Which was one reason he was once again at the gate of the Antippas home in the Bel Air hills at nine Thursday morning, holding his shield up to the security camera.

Manuela's voice said, "Mrs. Antippas is not at home."

"That's all right, I think you can help me. That way we won't have to bother her."

After a long silence, the gates swung open. Prince drove through, parked his car, and crunched across warm gravel toward the kitchen door. On his way he passed a stocky man in clean khaki work pants and shirt, standing with a hedge clipper, watching him.

"*Buenos dias,*" said Prince, and Freddy returned the greeting warily.

Manuela opened the kitchen door to his knock.

"Good morning," he said, and offered her his iden-tification. She studied it carefully, then handed it back to him and opened the door wide enough for him to pass.

"I was here before," said Prince.

"I remember."

"I came back for some more of your cookies," he said. He got no response.

"Sorry. I guess no one is in a kidding mood. Your name is Manuela, yes?"

She assented to that.

"Mind if I sit?" He gestured to the table under the window where Manuela and Freddy took their meals. "This is a great kitchen," he added. "Mine is the size of a phone booth. And I like to cook."

Still no response. She followed him to the table, where he pulled out a chair and sat, and she continued to stand.

"Manuela. Do you mind if I call you that?"

She shrugged.

"You are very protective of Mrs. Antippas. I like that."

She tipped her head slightly.

"Tell me this. You went to Mr. Antippas's funeral at Forest Lawn?"

Another nod.

"That had to be a nightmare day for you. For all of you."

Manuela said nothing.

"I know. What would I know about it? More than you might think, but we don't need to talk about that. I'll get to the point. Did Mrs. Antippas have one of those mourners' books there, at the chapel, at Mr. Antippas's service, where people can sign their names so the family will know they were there?"

"I did," said Manuela, slightly startling Prince, who'd become accustomed to her stonewalling. "I bought a book and put it there. She was not thinking."

Prince nodded. "You take good care of her," he said respectfully.

"I take good care of all of them."

"And you brought the book back too?"

"Freddy did. My husband." She tipped her head toward the back door, to indicate he was near; she was not alone. In case he thought she could be bullied.

"And gave it to Mrs. Antippas?"

"Not yet. She isn't ready."

"I can imagine. Where is she by the way? I could wait for her."

Manuela paused, then said, "Lawyer, I think."

Prince nodded knowingly.

"Manuela, could I have a look at that book?"

She looked back, impassive.

"Why?"

"It would be helpful, for the people trying to find out what happened to Mr. Antippas."

"They sent you?"

"They did, yes."

He could see she was trying to figure out how to say no, on general principle. "It would help them do their jobs. They'll keep it private." He saw her glance out the window toward the gates, where today there were only two photographers left from the pack that had been here five days ago. "The press will not get near it, I promise you. You'd be helping Mrs. Antippas."

Reluctantly, she left him, disappearing into a room beyond the kitchen that seemed to be her domain. She returned with a stack of books and set them down in front of him. Then she stood back and crossed her arms. Some of the books were large with gilt edges to the pages. These, he quickly inferred, had been at the Staples Center, since they were filled with messages to Artemis from friends, admirers, and fans, plus drawings and stickers and tear blotches. Another pair were covered in white leatherette that said *condolences* on the covers in silver script. There was one with a silver weeping willow tree against a blue background. The neat script in the front identified this one as being for Alexander Antippas.

Prince opened the book to the first page of signatures, propped it against a melamine sugar bowl to improve his angle, took out his phone, and began photographing the pages. When he was done, he said to Manuela, "By the way, is Mrs. Antippas's sister here? I saw her car in the driveway."

Glory was at a desk in the sitting room of the guest suite. "A second master, really," the decorator had called it. It had been designed for Jenny, when she was still, from time to time, living at home, but those days were long gone, and it had been redone in English chintzes for when the senior Pooles came to visit. Manuela showed Detective Prince in, and wordlessly left them.

"I'm sorry to interrupt, I can see you're busy," said Prince.

"That's all right," said Glory, though she hadn't risen to greet him. "I'm getting started on the envelopes for my sister." She gestured to the piles of notes and letters stacked on one side of the desk, and a stack of fresh envelopes from the stationers at her right. "She'll write the notes herself, but I can do the addresses."

"Must be quite a job," said Prince. "Considering Artemis."

"Not the fan mail. Those are at her manager's office. But the personal ones for Jenny and for my brother-in-law. Lisa's determined to answer those herself."

"Admirable," said Prince. "Do you mind if I sit?"

"Please," said Glory, glancing at her watch. For a moment there was silence as Detective Prince looked at her pleasantly, as if she had called him here and he were waiting to find out why.

Finally Glory gestured to the work waiting on the desk and said, letting her impatience show, "Can I help you?"

"Oh. Sorry," he said. "I was just thinking that you look different in person than on camera."

"Do I?"

"You do."

After a pause, in which Glory waited for the usual compliment, which didn't come, she said, "I hope in a good way," as if reminding him of his lines.

"Oh. Yes. I was just reading up on your career before I came over. My ex-wife was a fan of your talk show."

Glory relaxed slightly, and smiled. "I'm glad," she said. "That makes her and my mom."

"Oh, you had a pretty good audience share, for day-time cable."

Glory looked pleased. "You do your homework." She gave him an impressive camera-friendly smile.

"She liked the shows you did with that animal guy, Cliff . . ."

"Hagerty. Those were fun."

"Some of them are on YouTube, did you know that?"

"They are?" she lied.

"Yes, the one with cheetah cubs?"

Glory preened a little. "They were adorable. They had sharp little needle teeth though." She had made a joke on the show about how good they'd look as a coat, after one of them bit her rather hard.

"They must give you some training before they ac-tually tape the show, when you're working with wild animals."

"They do, of course. My producer wanted me just to be surprised, on camera, he said it would be funnier, but I didn't think it was safe. Cliff didn't either. He taught me how to hold them, and made sure my smell was familiar to them."

"And the time he brought the snakes," said Prince. "That python, that was enormous, that thing."

"Yes," said Glory. Her expression had changed for a moment. "I remember that one. Nineteen feet long or something. They'd found her in someone's swimming pool in Orange County."

"And that little nest of poisonous snakes he brought. Were they drugged or something?"

Gloria was now a little wary. "I don't think so."

"I just wondered. You seemed so calm around them. You must have worked with them before the show too, like with the cheetahs."

Glory glanced at her watch. "I must have," she said.

"Oh, I'm sorry. I'm keeping you. My wife will be so interested to hear all this."

"You said ex-wife."

"Yes. But you know what they say, divorced but never unmarried. I'm told you were very angry with your brother-in-law the night of the fire, up in Maine." Prince took out his notebook and a pencil.

"Oh were you." She was now thoroughly tired of this guy with his Columbo routine.

"I was. Is it true?"

"Of course it's true. He behaved like a pig to my sister. To everybody. He *was* a pig. A fat, selfish, unfaithful pig."

Prince just looked at her, as if contemplating the intensity of her speech.

"Unfaithful? Did your sister tell you that?"

"She didn't have to," said Glory haughtily.

"No? Why not?"

She stared at him. "Everybody knew."

"The children?"

"Not the children. As far as I know. Oh maybe even they knew. What's your point?"

"That not everybody knew. But you did."

After a long moment she said dismissively, "He was my brother-in-law. I'm very close to my sister."

Prince turned to a clean page. "Is it true you said you'd like to stick a knife in him and twist it?"

"Probably. But *I didn't.*"

"No, we know he wasn't stabbed. But you went to his room that night?"

"Of course I didn't!" she yelled at him. From far away in the house Prince could hear footsteps hurrying toward them.

"And we would know that how?"

"I was with my sister. All night! Ask her!"

"How would she know? You said you'd given her massive doses of painkillers."

"Manuela, would you call Freddy? This man is leaving." She looked at Prince with anger and added, "I'm calling my lawyer."

Prince stood. "I'm going. But could you just tell me, how a snake bag and snake tongs got into your suitcase?"

"*Freddy!*" she yelled.

Jorge tried for several hours to reach Selena Sherrill, then gave up and headed east to the younger Albert Clark's house in Oyster Bay. He found a brick Colonial on a lane of handsome houses whose small surrounding yards looked new and raw as barely healed scars. An SUV of a size that probably got about twelve miles to the gallon sat in the driveway. There were two child seats strapped to the bench seat behind the driver, and in the way back there was a mess of comic books, action figures, candy wrappers, and Yu-Gi-Oh! cards.

When Jorge looked up from peering into the car, he saw that the front door of the house had opened and a woman so thin she looked made from bicycle parts stood watching him. She was wearing black yoga pants and a tank top, and a pile of straw-colored hair surrounded her preternaturally narrow face. Her cheeks were flushed.

"Can I help you?" she called, looking as if she really meant *What the hell do you think you're doing?*

"Oh, I'm sorry—did I interrupt your workout?" He walked up the driveway and took the brick walk to where she was standing, rather than walk across the lawn, which looked as if it needed all the encouragement it could get. "Mrs. Clark? I'm George Baker. I called before."

"I didn't get any message."

"No? I'm sorry. I hope this isn't a bad time. I was a friend of Albie Clark, Senior. I wanted to pay my respects." He extended his hand and reflexively the woman accepted it. "You're Melody?"

She was. "My husband isn't here." This suited Jorge fine, as young Albert might have realized more easily than his wife that Jorge and Albie shared few common points of biography.

"May I come in?"

Still wary, she stepped back into the hall, leaving the door open behind her, and let him follow her into a sitting room off the front hall, which was mostly furnished with Lego blocks. There was an elderly armchair however, and a window seat. She took the chair, and he perched at the window.

"I'm sorry for your loss."

She inclined her head.

"I can't get used to it, Albie gone. And Ruth too, she was a sweet woman I always thought."

"How did you know my father-in-law?"

"Oh, way back. College. We didn't see each other as much in recent years, which I regret. I travel a lot."

She wasn't giving him any help, and he was distracted by the thought that he'd like to take her into town and make her eat a bacon cheeseburger and a butterscotch sundae.

She glanced at her watch. "I don't mean to be rude, but I have to pick up my youngest from nursery school in a few minutes."

"Oh," he said, "I *have* come at a bad time. Forgive me."

"But I should tell you that if you came for a warm cuddly love fest about good old Albie, you're in the wrong pew."

Jorge did a good job of looking taken aback. "I'm sorry—there's obviously something going on here I don't understand."

Clearly, Melody agreed with him.

"The Albie I knew was a lot of fun, he . . ."

"I'm sure he was, and lucky you. But he made everyone around him miserable. Look, I'm sorry to be blunt. But this family is having a hard time, and tiptoeing around it isn't helping."

After a stretch of thinking he didn't know what to say, Jorge said, "I don't know what to say."

"No, you don't," said Melody. Jorge thought she was about to order him out, but as often happens with bottled-up anger, hers, uncapped, had a pressure of its own, and she wasn't done.

He stayed where he was, and after another pause, said, "I'm trying to understand. When Ruth got sick Albie gave up everything to take care of her . . ."

"He took her prisoner," Melody snapped. "It wasn't clear that her cancer couldn't be managed. She could have had more time, with us and with her grandchildren." She gestured at the toys around the room. "But Albie had to know best. It was all about him. He couldn't let it be her decision."

"But didn't she love the beach, wasn't it . . ."

"He moved her away from her doctors and everyone who would have been on her side. And when we tried to talk to her about it, he answered for her. She wouldn't say a word against him."

"So maybe it really was what she wanted."

Melody made a rude noise. "She didn't want to spend the last months of her life fighting with him. She'd always taken what he dished out and she kept it up to the end. My little one has no memory of her as a person at all. Just a scary old sick lady in a bad wig, that's all she remembers. I loved Ruth. And now we're supposed to be sorry for Albie's pain because he slit his throat? What a shitty, cowardly thing to do." She glared at Jorge.

Since that seemed to be the last word on the subject, Jorge said, "Well. I'm sorry to have bothered you."

She didn't even offer to see him out. She just stood watching as he left the house and got into his car, and was still at the window as he drove away.

He drove to the Sunrise Highway and headed east.

Visiting hours at the Ainsley Jail were from two to four. The officer on the desk gave Buster and Roy Weaver padlocks, and told them to leave all metal objects, weapons, and anything that could conceal contraband in their lockers. For Roy, that meant the jacket he was wearing over his T-shirt. By the time they were called to go into the security airlock between the prisoners' world and the outside, Roy's pale arms were covered in gooseflesh.

The visitors were crowded into a small square room, like a freight elevator that didn't go anywhere, as the door they had just passed through was locked tight. In with them were an older woman with what looked to be grandchildren, a young man with a small boy, clearly his son, and assorted others. The door on the opposite side clicked and shimmied after the guard with them gave a signal, then rolled back.

Buster and Roy stepped into a large room with tables and chairs and uniformed guards standing against each wall. The wall of windows showed the cheerful sunlight and the parking lot beyond. The floor was linoleum, the walls institutional tile, altogether much like a grade school cafeteria except there was no food and the tables were bolted down.

The other visitors chose tables and sat down in silence, knowing the drill. Buster chose a table and sat, but Roy remained standing as if he didn't want to drop his guard until he knew where he was and what was going to happen next.

What happened was that a door in the back wall opened into the room, and the prisoners who had visitors filed through. In the front were the mothers. The first, a frighteningly skinny blonde dropped to her knees and wrapped her arms around the two girls who had come with their grandmother. Everyone in this group except the mother seemed stiff and uncomfortable. The second woman through the door was stocky and much tattooed, but the man with the little boy wrapped her in his arms with great tenderness. She picked up the boy and buried her face in his neck. They moved to a table far from the rest. Then came a couple of older women greeting brothers, or lawyers or neighbors, and last came Cherry.

She was pale as a slug, and her eyes were dull. She knew only that she had a visitor, and expected Brianna, or the lawyer woman. When she caught sight of Roy, she stopped walking and her lips began to tremble. Roy went to her and after a moment of not seeming to know what to do, he put his arms around her and said, "Cupcake." Behind him, Buster could see Cherry's mouth take on the oblong it made when she cried, and she wrapped her arms around her father.

Toby Osborne had driven out to get the lay of the land. After stopping at Barb's for a crab roll, and at Beryl Weaver's house to take some pictures, he drove on to Ainsley to do some research for Maggie at the library. When he was finished he swung up to the mall to pay a visit to Celia Little, whom he found in her office immersed in an online accounting course she was taking in case the lawyering thing didn't work out. She was discouraged about the Weaver case, she admitted. She knew everyone deserved a defense, even when they were guilty, but she had student loans and bills to pay and had hoped for a case she could win, a chance to make a little name for herself.

"What makes you think you can't win this one?"

Celia shrugged.

"What does your investigator say?"

She looked startled. Was she supposed to have an investigator?

He took out one of his cards from his days at the *Globe,* crossed out the phone number, and wrote the number of his mobile.

"Here. Now you have an investigator."

"I can't pay you."

"Don't worry about it," he said.

She watched him limping with his cane across her ratty yard, tufted with brown crabgrass killed by frost, and noticed the yellow-green half tennis ball that had been lying beside the walkway since June. She really ought to pick that up. But she didn't see how that old guy was going to make much difference to anything.

She turned back to her accounting homework.

Back in his car, Toby placed a call to an editor he knew at the *Kennebec Journal* to ask about public defenders in Augusta. He didn't want to scare the family, but there had to be somebody better for Cherry than

Celia Little. He could see why Hope couldn't interfere here, but there was no reason he couldn't.

Then he turned his car around and drove down State Street, parked in the municipal lot in front of the court house, and wandered into the Chowder Bowl. He sat at the counter and ordered a cup of decaf tea. He chatted with the waitress about business (good, but would be better if they had a big trial going), the judges and lawyers who came in regularly (Judge Hennebery was a favorite, an old kidder), which did she recommend, the chowder or the shrimp roll (both were real good but she favored the shrimp roll), and where in town could he buy a newspaper? (Mr. Paperback across the street.) He thanked her, and told her that if that wasn't decaf she'd served him, he wanted her number so he could call her at two in the morning. She was tickled and urged him to come back for a shrimp roll soon.

It was quiet in the car for some miles as Buster and Roy drove back toward Bergen. The whole visit had been emotional, and Buster had the feeling that Roy would have been happy not to say another word for a week, but too long a silence made Buster antsy. He said, "You and Shep Gordon go way back?"

"Yuh," said Roy.

"How far back?"

Roy looked at him, as if to say *Are you really going to do this to me?* But finally he said, "Grade school."

Buster nodded thoughtfully. Roy's legs were jiggling again.

"He's not a bad cop," Buster said.

"Good for him." Roy looked out the window. Then he took out a cigarette and lit it without asking if Buster minded.

"Were you in the same class?"

Roy stopped jiggling his legs and looked at Buster. You're really going to do this to me, the look said. But with an annoyed sigh, he answered, "No. He's a year younger. But he was always bigger."

What to ask next to keep this going? Buster tried, "Were you on teams together?"

Wrong gambit. Roy gave a hoot of laughter. "Teams!" he said, seeming delighted at the thought.

Oh. Right, thought Buster. Roy Weaver a team player? Roy Weaver going out for basketball?

"I just didn't like him. But things were fine until they bused us to the junior high. Shep liked to walk up and down the aisle and mess with people. Driver couldn't make him sit down. Nobody could."

Buster nodded. This was a very long speech for Roy, and he recognized the pressure behind it. He had known altogether too many kids like that. Especially at that age, they come into their growth, and they thought that meant that somebody died and made them king of the jungle.

"Used to like to take my hat. He'd take it off my head and play keep-away with it. Toss it to his friends. Back and forth over my head."

Buster could picture the scene. Roy, a natural solitary, made the center of attention. People like Shep always knew exactly who would mind most. Everyone laughing, even the ones who liked Roy, because if you didn't laugh with people like Shep, it was your turn next.

"What did you do?"

Roy cut his eyes toward Buster, then back to the road. The pause lengthened. Finally he shifted a little in his seat and said, "Broke into his house on Christmas morning. Took a dump on the living room rug."

Buster let out a guffaw and Roy smiled briefly himself. Buster couldn't help himself, he punched the steering wheel, laughing.

Finally, Buster said, "His parents must have been plenty mad."

"They were not pleased," Roy admitted.

"Did they know who did it?"

"No, but they knew it had something to do with Shep."

"And *he* knew it was you?"

"Kids all knew. I don't know how, I never told anyone. When I'd get on the bus they'd elbow each other and look at Shep."

"What did he do?"

"Left my hat alone," said Roy.

All the way back to Ainsley after he dropped Roy off, the thought of that Christmas morning made Buster laugh again. And then he'd remember Cherry. He didn't think Shep Gordon would railroad a person unless he really thought she was guilty. But if he did think she was guilty, he was never going to budge from his spot. Shep just didn't.

When Buster had docs or images on his phone and needed hard copy, he'd forward them to Janet Torrey in the Bergen Town Hall from wherever he was, and she'd print them for him. He'd swing around to pick them up on his way to Just Barb's, where he was bound to go sooner or later. On Thursday afternoon he reached Janet at about four. She was a large woman with a ready smile and beautiful glossy dark hair. The previous day had been her birthday. Her counter was covered with birthday cards, and she was wearing a circlet on her head made of silver paper covered with colored foil stars.

"I see you've been crowned," said Buster as he strolled in.

"My granddaughter made it. And my grandson made me a cake from scratch, without a recipe. They saw that movie, about the rat that becomes a French chef, the Disney movie? and Nathan started baking. I didn't tell him what I'd do if I found a real rat in my kitchen."

"How old is he?"

"Nine."

"How was the cake?"

"Real good. It took my daughter all night to clean up the kitchen, but that cake was delicious. Chocolate with blue icing and gummy bears. Now what *is* this?" She was looking at the image that had just emerged from the printer.

Buster stood to look over her shoulder. It was a picture of a page of handwritten notes from what was pretty clearly a standard issue police notebook. The writing was large and clear, but in two places, lines had been crossed out and corrections were hand-printed in the space above the original note.

"Are you supposed to have these?" she asked, a crease of worry between her eyebrows.

"Have what?" said Buster, taking the papers and slipping them into a backpack that had seen better days.

"Oh," said Janet. "Right. Lost my head for a minute and thought we'd done some printing. You give Brianna my best."

"I will. You look good in that crown."

"I thought so too. I told the selectmen, I'm wearing it from now on."

On the sunporch at the inn in the late afternoon, Maggie was explaining what Jorge had learned about Albie Clark, at least in the world according to his children.

"Remind me to write a new Living Will when we get home, will you?" Hope said to Maggie.

"I wish you'd met him, Toby. He seemed so normal," said Maggie. "I mean, for a widower in a clinical depression."

"I still don't see that this amounts to his killing her, even if it's all true. And he sure had a grudge against Antippas."

"I know," said Maggie.

"I'd like to know about Mrs. Clark's autopsy report," said Toby.

"Jorge is on it," said Maggie. "Don't you love that expression? I learned it from a television show. Now, what did you find out in town?" Maggie had asked him to trace Antippas back as far as he could. When did he emigrate, did he have a driver's license, how did he earn a living, where did he meet Jenny's mother. Whoever she was.

"Quite a lot," said Toby. "First, Celia Little shouldn't be representing a cocker spaniel. I've made some calls, and we'll get a real lawyer for Cherry by tomorrow."

"Thank you," said Hope. "Maggie wouldn't let me interfere."

"And I was right. But Toby can interfere all he wants."

"Thank you. Second," said Toby, "Alexander Antippas doesn't exist before 1982, the year he turns up in L.A."

"You're kidding," said Hope.

"No visa records, no green card, marriage license, nothing. I notice Maggie doesn't look very surprised."

"No, I must say, I was expecting that."

Just then Buster arrived in the sunroom. He produced his sheaf of papers and laid the first one on top of the jigsaw puzzle, with the sheet that had caught Janet's attention on top. Hope put on her glasses and Toby took his off. The three stood over the puzzle table, reading.

" 'Why would I do that?' is crossed out and he's written 'Why *did* I do that?' " said Toby.

"*She's* written. These are the notes from the policewoman Cherry supposedly confessed to in the bathroom, the night she was arrested. Carly Leo, her name is."

"Shep Gordon is pressing the people who worked the case to make sure their proof supports his theory," said Toby.

"Who told you that?"

He smiled. "I'm a reporter. People will talk to me who would never tell the same thing to the police."

"Carly Leo is a total brown nose," said Buster, then glanced at his mother and added. "pardon my French. She'd do anything Shep asked her to and insist they never discussed it."

"We can use it. What else have you got?"

The rest of the pages were the photographs of the condolence book Detective Prince had sent him from L.A.

"Oh well done!" said Maggie.

"That was fast," said Hope, and gave Buster a proud smile. They each took pages and settled down with them.

In under a minute, Maggie said "Yes!" and pumped her fist in the air.

"What?"

She pointed to a name in spindly old-person hand-writing. "Melina Kouklakis." She put up her hand and Hope slapped it triumphantly.

Toby was next. "Whoa! You are good!"

Buster was trying not to laugh. His mother giving high fives? What was next, fist bumps? Gangsta rap? He said, "I have to admit, Mrs. Detweiler, you are scary."

She beamed. "Can you get your man in L.A. to find out who she is? Sister? Aunt? And—can he check the registry for missing and exploited children? For a Jenny Kouklakis, or Kouklas or Koukla, in case Alexander shortened the name?"

"He can," said Toby, "but that friend of yours from the FBI could do it faster, and he wouldn't attract interference from Shep Gordon's people."

Day Thirteen, Friday, October 18

Jorge had spent the night at The Maidstone in East Hampton. Thought he might as well, since Mrs. Babbin was paying. He had called five hospice care services in Suffolk County before he found the one Albie Clark had used. The woman on duty gave him contact information for three nurses who had been assigned to the case. The first was at home when he called, but said that he never met the patient because she died before his shift began. The second was on vacation out of state. The third was named Valerie Ramos and was pleased when he addressed her in Spanish. He reached her just as she got home from a night shift and had things to do, but would be willing to see him in an hour. She gave him the address.

Ms. Ramos lived in a bungalow in an area of East Moriches too close to the highway to be attractive to developers. Yet. She was wearing street clothes when she came to the door, stretch jeans and a turquoise angora sweater. He tripped over her cat who had threaded itself between Jorge's feet as he came in, so the conversation began with an apology.

"Never mind, he does that to everyone," Valerie Ramos said. The cat indeed seemed unsurprised and unresentful over the incident, but went into the sitting room and hacked at his carpet-covered scratching post, just to show that he was entirely at home and the interloper wasn't. Ms. Ramos and Jorge followed him into the small, dark room, where a TV was playing soundlessly, and the upholstered furniture was covered with fitted clear plastic covers. On the mantel was a photograph in a frilly gilt frame of a white-haired woman with an oval face and dark eyes who looked very much like Valerie. There was a votive candle in red glass burning beside the picture.

Ms. Ramos offered Jorge a seat on the flowered love seat and took a stiff chair near the cat.

"Thank you for seeing me, Ms. Ramos," said Jorge.

"You're welcome. I'm sorry for what happened to Mr. Clark," she said.

"Yes, terrible. I imagine you saw a good deal of him, while you were with his wife."

"He was there, but he didn't want to talk. His wife was in a great deal of pain."

"She was conscious, then?"

"Briefly, when I first got there. But often when we arrive, especially when the patient has planned her final things and knows what it means when we come, they cross over quickly."

"I see." Jorge looked around the room, taking in the picture on the mantel, the cross made from a palm frond, now very dry, tucked behind the frame of a little mirror on the wall, and the small spinet in the corner. He knew rooms like this. He knew there would be a glass jar with hard candies in it, or gumdrops, on the piano, before he saw it. Wait—surprise. Candied ginger.

"You must feel like the angel of death, sometimes," he said.

"Emphasis on angel," she replied calmly. "When someone has suffered so much we bring relief."

"And you felt that with Ruth Clark?"

"I did."

"You were giving—what?"

"Morphine. Pain is pointless, at that stage."

Jorge thought about this. She was so peaceful, this woman.

"And Mr. Clark? Was he ready for it to be over?"

"Her suffering was terrible to him. If she frowned, or made a sound, he'd say 'she can still feel it.'"

"And could she?"

"We don't know. She could just as well be reacting to something she was seeing or hearing inside her head. There is much going back and forth over the line, at that point."

Jorge, a lapsed Catholic since his teenage years, envied her calm certainty. He wondered, though, if he was at the end, if he would be comforted to see her coming, or want to scream for help.

He asked, "When Mr. Clark said she could still feel it, did he mean you should increase her dosage?"

"He never asked me to do that. I followed protocol."

"How was the drug being administered?"

"A drip."

"Did she have one of those buttons? Could she self-administer?"

"She had a button, but she was past using it."

Jorge was trying to think of how to phrase his next question when she added, "Patients react differently. Some keep on fighting, even when you can't imagine how they're doing it. Others slip off quickly, as if someone opened a door to heaven. Mrs. Clark saw the opened door."

After a silence he said, "Were her children with her?"

"Not while I was there. Just the husband."

"And you were there when she passed?"

"No. I like to be there at the end; it's a profound moment. But she was still with us when my shift ended."

"And Hank Armor was the next nurse on duty?"

After a tiny beat, she said, "Yes. Hank."

"And was there an autopsy?"

"I have no idea. But why would there be?"

Martin Maynard called Maggie right before lunch. She was waiting in her room for his call, not wanting to take it in a public place.

"I hope I haven't put you to too much trouble," she said.

"It's been a long time since I got down in the weeds myself, I admit," said Martin, "and this was never my department."

"I don't think I ever asked, what *is* your department?"

"I'm a forensic accountant."

Maggie laughed. "This *was* a bit out of your way."

"It made me feel young. And you'd already done the heavy lifting. Jennifer Ann Kouklakis was born in

1980 in Washington, Pennsylvania. She was abducted in 1982, nonstranger abduction, presumably by the father. He said he was taking the baby to buy her new shoes. Never seen again. You want me to fax you her birth certificate?"

"Could you e-mail it to Buster?"

"Glad to."

Maggie gave him the address.

"Nina sends her best," he said.

"Mine to her too."

They broke the connection.

The address in his GPS had brought Detective Prince to Culver City, to a large, fairly modern apartment block made of white brick. The clerk at the desk never looked at his ID, he just waved Prince toward a bank of elevators.

Melina Kouklakis came to the door on a fancy walker with wheels, a handbrake, and a basket. She was wearing a pink velour tracksuit. Her hair was cut short and had been given the kind of shapeless perm that women get when they don't want to have to look in the mirror more than once a day.

"Detective Prince," he said, presenting his badge, which she studied carefully. "Thank you for seeing me."

She made a dismissive gesture, and led the way to her seating alcove. On the kidney-shaped glass table there was a Sudoku book, Brainteaser level, and a box of tissues. She maneuvered herself into her chair and gestured Prince to the couch, Danish modern with red cushions.

"I'd offer you something," she said, "but the girl isn't back with the shopping. There's water. You want water?" Her accent was slight, but enough to tell him she was foreign-born.

"I'm fine, thank you, Mrs. Kouklakis."

"Miss Kouklakis. Born that way and I'll die that way. Soon, I hope."

In Prince's experience, when old people said things like that, they were asking you to jolly them out of it. "Even on a beautiful day like this?" he said. He pointed at her window, which was right at tree level. "You don't want to look out the window and see those leaves in the sun?"

She looked at him as if trying to see if he were a fool or not.

"You can have your leaves," she said.

There was a silence. Okay, he got it, skip the small talk.

"Miss Kouklakis, I notice that you attended the funeral of Alexander Antippas."

"Oh, you did. And how is that your business?"

"Could you tell me your connection to the family?"

"Not 'connection.' I *am* the family. I'm the closest relative he had left."

"Didn't he have a wife and children?"

She made a disgusted noise and waved a hand in dismissal.

"You aren't close to the Antippas family?"

"That wife. Alexander brought the children to me when they were small. Later he stopped even doing that. That wife didn't want me there at Christmas and birthdays, because then I'd be in the pictures. She didn't want to have to explain some Greek immigrant in the pictures when she was telling the world that her husband sprang full-grown from the head of Zeus. Or Donald Trumpet."

"How about Jenny? Were you close to her?"

The old woman closed her eyes for a moment, as if waiting for a sudden pain to pass.

"*She* came to see me. She kept up."

She sat, looking sad and angry.

"Can you explain that to me?"

"Why should I? It's over now."

"It could help us find out what happened to your—Mr. Antippas. Your cousin?"

"My *nephew,* she said with the disgust of a teacher for a student who hasn't done the reading. "He was my nephew. The only child of my brother who died in the Peloponnese."

"And you were born there, in the Peloponnese?"

"Of course. Born there, raised there."

"And then?"

"Then what?"

"Then . . . how did you come to California?"

"I didn't, I came to New York. I moved to Athens with my mother's sister when I was sixteen, and got a job making ladies' hats. Someone told me I would make better money in New York, so I came. Ladies were not wearing hats so much in Greece anymore."

"And in New York?"

"I got a job right away, at Saks Fifth Avenue." She pronounced it as if it were all one word, Saksfithavenue. "The pay was much better but ladies in New York weren't wearing hats either."

"So . . . then what?"

"This and that," she said, bored with this. "It was a long time ago. You didn't come here to hear my life story." She looked at her watch, a miniature pocket watch she wore on a chain around her neck. Her wrists and ankles were painfully swollen.

"All right. When did your nephew come back into your life?"

"Alexander. Well. He wrote me when he first arrived to say he was married and living in Ohio or someplace. He wrote in English to show me he was a real American. I wrote back to say he should come to pay his respects and *he* wrote to say that he would but they'd just had a baby. He was working very hard, but he'd come and bring the family soon. I hadn't seen him since he was a little guy." She held out her hand to indicate a five- or six-year-old.

"And did he do that? Bring the family to meet you?"

"No. He did come himself, though. He called a year or two later and said he was in Los Angeles. I was living in Tarzana then."

"Making hats?"

"Hats? No. I was in retail. He had some big deal brewing in L.A., he said. He showed up on my doorstep one evening with a bottle of raki." She chuckled.

"Raki. Is that like ouzo?"

"Sort of. They drink it on *Creta*."

"Creta?"

"Crete. But mostly in Turkey. He had changed so much; I wouldn't have known him except he looked just like my brother Stavros. An Adonis. He stayed all evening. We talked about old times and finished the bottle. He had been the last of us in our village back at home. He'd sold the house and land. That was strange to think of. I doubt he got much for it."

"And then?"

"Well, then, some time passed, and then they came to me."

"Came to you."

"Yes, they came to me, Alexander and little Jenny. I guess the raki night was a test, to see if I'd have them. Jenny was a toddler then, just beginning to talk. Alexander's English had improved a lot. He was smart, that one. His clothes were fancy and he said he had a job with some muck-a-muck in Pasadena. He ran because his wife had a mental thing." She twirled a finger beside her temple. "Tried to hurt the baby. He even had to change his name, he was afraid of what she'd do if she found them."

"Change his name? That seems extreme."

She shrugged. "Lots of people do it. Immigrants. We picked something out of an Athens telephone book."

"Never got past the alphas," said Prince.

She made a sour face. "He was in a hurry. Nothing to do with me. Kouklakis was hard to spell, and someone told him it sounded like 'Ku Klux,' so."

"And they lived with you for—how long?"

"A year, year and a half. I had a house then; I had room. I was working of course, so there was a sitter for the baby."

"Nice of you to take them in."

She shrugged. "Least I could do for my brother. Stavros had no luck."

"And why did they leave you?"

"Alexander got married."

"Oh! So he was courting Lisa Poole when he lived with you?"

"Courting both of them, as far as I could tell. We didn't discuss it much but I had the impression he'd already known those girls for a while when he moved here."

"And are you in touch with Mrs. Antippas now?"

She snorted. "That one? The first time I saw her was their wedding day, and the next time was his funeral."

"Was that because you weren't invited?"

"I was invited, once or twice. I wouldn't go. You know what I heard her call me? She was talking to the sister. She called me 'the babushka.' I was a very stylish person! I worked at Neiman Marcus!"

Jorge found 42 Maple Lane in Riverhead in mid-afternoon. He was on his way back to town, but it bothered him to leave a gap unfilled and he decided just to have a quick word with Hank Armor, the nurse whose shift with Ruth Clark was over before it began. What could it hurt, right? Middle of a Friday afternoon, either the guy was at home or he wasn't.

He had his ID in his hand, prepared to flash and then pocket it as he stood on the front step of the small, dark clapboard house. There were cars in the driveway, so he knew someone was home, but he had to ring three times before anyone answered the door.

The man who eventually opened to him was plump and pale, wearing what looked like hospital scrubs. Jorge was just about to say "I hope I'm not interrupting anything" when he realized that down the hall, children were grouped around a table singing "Happy Birthday to You." Just stepping into view was a woman with a cake, blazing with candles, and he was pretty sure, even at this distance, that he recognized a Carvel Ice Cream Cake.

"Jeez, I'm sorry. Bad timing."

"Yes," said the man, getting ready to close the door.

Jorge figured he had about two seconds. He flashed his license to carry a concealed weapon and said quickly, "Detective Carrera. Are you Hank Armor?"

The man glanced down the hall, then stepped out onto the stoop and pulled the door almost closed behind him. He was in short sleeves and it was brisk outside. And inside, the cake was melting.

The man glanced at his watch. "I'm him," he said.

"I'll be quick, I really will. You were scheduled to work with a patient called Ruth Clark, back in March. Do you remember?"

Armor stared at him.

"House in Southampton, terminal cancer patient," said Jorge.

"Look," said Armor. "It was unavoidable. I have . . ." He gestured with his head back toward the house behind him. "I have a special-needs kid, something came up, I texted Nurse Ramos that I'd be there in ten, and I was."

"You were late for your shift."

"The agency knows all about this. What do you want? Ramos had to go, her own mother was sick at home, and I was ten minutes late. That's all."

"Ten minutes?"

"Fifteen," he said. "Look, we're in the middle of . . ."

Something was wrong. The interruption was one thing, but this man was more irritated by the questions than he should have been.

"I know. Really, we're almost done. The patient had passed by the time you got there, is that right?"

"Right. The husband was with her, it wasn't as if she'd been left to . . ."

'I understand. But she was alive and peaceful when Nurse Ramos left."

"Yes."

"Her shift notes were clear."

"Right."

"So what did you do?"

"I called 911, and they came and declared her, and I went home. Missed a day's pay," he added.

That's not what's bothering you, Jorge thought.

By evening Maggie had debriefed Jorge, and Buster had given a full report from Detective Prince. Buster turned out to have a talent Maggie was ashamed that neither she nor anyone else at her school had discovered. He had an incredible memory for the spoken word. He'd given her the whole conversation verbatim, and when she checked them against Prince's notes, which arrived later via e-mail, he'd been letter-perfect.

"Did you know he could do that?" Maggie asked Hope.

"I can't remember," said Hope.

The four of them—Maggie, Hope, Toby, and Buster—were cloistered in the sunroom, doors shut, jigsaw puzzle forgotten.

"I think we've got to fish or cut bait here," Maggie said. "The longer the police and the AG's office spend on Cherry, the harder it's going to be to turn that ship around. If we're right, we're wasting our time on all the other leads, and if we're wrong, we'll be embarrassed and apologize."

"We could go to the AG with what we've got and get him to order Shep Gordon to start over," said Hope.

Toby gave a bark of laughter, and Hope looked at him, wounded.

"What's so funny?" she asked.

"Nothing."

"All agreed then?" said Maggie.

Three assented. Hope seemed to be sulking.

"Buster, you're on," said Maggie. He stood, squared his shoulders, and left them.

In what felt like a very short span of time, Buster had returned with Chef Sarah. He carefully closed the door behind them when they entered, and locked it.

Sarah heard the click of the lock and looked at Buster, surprised. Then she smiled and said, "You need me to help with your puzzle? I've been waiting for you to ask."

"Have you?" said Maggie. "Good. Please sit down." Sarah took a chair with her back to the wall of glass, with Buster beside her on one side and Toby on the other. No one made a move to clear off the jigsaw.

"Buster is going to record this conversation. All right with you?" said Toby. Sarah looked from one man to the other, then said, "Why not?"

Buster set his phone on the table between Sarah and Maggie.

Maggie began, "We've been concerned about Cherry Weaver. According to her, you told her you knew she didn't do anything wrong. Is that true?"

Sarah hesitated, then said, "I did, yes."

"It meant a lot to her. And we agree with you. We think the police have got the wrong end of the stick, and we've been trying to get it the right way around."

"How are you doing?"

"Pretty well, we think. There were a number of people with reasons to dislike Alexander Antippas. Whether those reasons rose to the level of motives for murder is debatable. But in any case they didn't have much in the way of opportunity, except for poor Cherry.

"The case against Cherry we all know about. Then there's Lisa Antippas. She stands to inherit, and she was very angry at her husband. She'd even been over-heard saying she wished him dead. But she was under great strain when she said it, and the night of the fire she was incapacitated. As far as we know.

"Glory Poole. She too had expressed a wish to harm her brother-in-law, but did she have opportunity? Maybe. Albie Clark had reasons to wish Antippas ill, but there too, we can't see that he had opportunity. How would he get a master key? How would he get into all those rooms?

"Mr. Rexroth had snake equipment, and could probably have gotten a key somehow to Antippas's room, but what was his motive? If he had a grudge it was against the wife and the dog."

Sarah listened thoughtfully. Her calm gaze was steady.

"Then," said Maggie, "there is one person who had every opportunity, but no apparent motive."

"I take it that would be me?" said Sarah. "From the fact that you called me in here."

"You have the run of the house. You work with Mrs. Eaton and could get a master key anytime. You've been seen coming out of Mr. Niner's room when he wasn't there, and your prints are all over that room, as well as in Mr. Rexroth's."

"I go up to visit the animals. I take them treats."

"We understand that. But there's something else."

From among her papers, she produced a facsimile birth certificate from Washington, Pennsylvania, dated March 31, 1980. Jennifer Ann Kouklakis, 6 pounds

14 ounces. Parents: Alexander Kouklakis and Paula Kouklakis.

Sarah looked at it. She looked calmly at Maggie. "And?"

"I'm going to tell you a story," said Maggie. "This happened to a colleague of mine, oh, years ago.

"He was running a country day school in Colorado. He had a new child in his school, a fifth grader. Nice little boy. The only thing odd about the family was that the father paid all the tuition in cash, in advance. My friend thought nothing of it until one day a woman arrived on campus with a couple of policemen and all kinds of paperwork. A warrant for the arrest of the father. They had a picture of him, wanted for kidnapping his son from the custodial parent. Totally different name than they knew him under, of course. Court papers, granting the mother custody. Birth certificate, little baby footprint, the whole thing. She'd spent every dime she could earn or borrow for seven years on investigators, looking for them. She clearly had taken no care of herself; her clothes were cheap, she was fat, she looked nothing like the glossy, well-tended people who claimed to be the boy's parents.

"The policemen ordered the child brought to the head's office. The woman burst into tears and ran at him, calling him Darling, and the boy was absolutely terrified. He had no idea who she was."

The room was quiet. Sarah looked at the table, as if her mind were on the jigsaw, whose pieces could be seen here and there beneath their notes and papers.

Toby finally said, "What happened to the boy? Did the mother take him?"

"The court ruled that it was in the boy's best interest to stay with the family he knew."

Sarah said softly, "That's a terrible story."

"I agree," said Maggie.

"What happened to the boy after that?" Sarah asked.

"I don't know. The family moved on and my colleague took a job somewhere else. That's one of the things about being a school person. There are so many stories you never learn the end of."

There was another silence, and Maggie let it stretch. Finally Sarah said, "And you've told me this why?"

"Because you are the Paula Frances Jackson who grew up in Washington, Pennsylvania. You'd never been fingerprinted before last week but it's easy enough to prove."

Sarah's eyes went to the birth certificate. She didn't speak.

"The Paula Jackson who married Alexander Kouklakis in Chania, Crete, in August of 1975."

Sarah stood up. Buster, instantly on his feet, said, "Ms. Jackson, please sit down."

After a long moment, Sarah sat.

"Martin Maynard has been very helpful," said Maggie.

"Lucky you," said Sarah. Oddly she didn't seem particularly angry.

"Why the change to Sarah, by the way? Paula Jackson disappears in California sometime in 1990."

"When I got a job in a kitchen in San Francisco, Chef already had a Paula on the hot line, so he called me Sarah."

"Nice name."

"He liked it."

"Is there anything you want to tell us?" Maggie asked.

"Yes," said Sarah.

"Stop," said Buster. "My phone just ran out of juice. And you have the right to remain silent."

Sarah waved his words away.

Toby took out his phone, poked the settings, and laid it on the table.

Sarah said, "This is the first thing I've been able to do for my daughter in twenty-eight years. It was worth it."

Buster slumped and put his face in his hands. He was thinking: Cherry. Brianna. Even Mrs. Weaver would have to stop treating him like something she found on her shoe.

"Would you tell us about it?" Maggie asked.

Sarah took a deep breath. She looked at her watch, then apparently remembered that the world as she knew it had just ended. What happened to the dinner service was no longer her problem.

They gave her time to breathe and adjust to the new order of things. Hope asked if she wanted coffee, or a drink, and she said yes.

"Which?"

"Both." Hope left for the kitchen. Buster passed a Miranda warning card and a pen across the table. Sarah picked up the card and examined it, front and back, then sat, apparently lost in thought for a minute or two. To everyone in the room it seemed like an hour. Finally Sarah took the pen, signed the card, then raised her eyes to look at Maggie, who was watching her thoughtfully.

"What made you think of me?"

"No one thing. Just a grain of sand that kept accumulating layers."

"Some pearl. Starting when?"

"After the fire, when I was thinking of everything that led up to it, two things about you snagged my attention. Well, three. You changed when you learned the Antippas family was in the hotel."

"Did I?"

"Yes. At first, it was mostly like someone who has to endure a really bad smell. It'll be horrible but it will pass."

"That's about right," said Sarah.

"But when Artemis died, you disappeared. You got sick."

"Migraines. God, I hate them."

"I don't doubt it."

"And that was it?"

"Almost. One other thing. I was struck somehow, the night the class had dinner together and we got to singing fight songs, by the way you quoted the line from *Casablanca*. You remember?"

"Of all the gin joints in all the towns in all the world, they walk into mine."

"Yes. It reminded me of something that happened my first year as a school head, the way people say something out loud that has enormous meaning for them, that they think no one else will understand. There was a math teacher who—"

"Darling, don't tell us another story," said Hope. She closed the door behind her with her foot and set down a large tray with a coffeepot, cream and sugar, two bottles of the best red wine in the house, and cups and glasses. "We're all still recovering from the first one. I want to hear Sarah."

Sarah poured herself coffee and a goblet of wine. She let Hope serve everyone else. Hope suddenly stopped with the wine bottle tipping in her hand and said, "Wait. Why didn't Antippas recognize you?"

"He never saw her," said Maggie. "Sarah made sure of that. There were a couple of times when he wanted to speak to the chef, remember? It was always Oliver who went."

Into the next silence, Buster said, "Did you take treats to the snake?" He waited for his mother to say "Oh, *Buster*," but she seemed to think this quite a sensible question.

Sarah said, "No, but I give Earl bait for his mousetraps in the barn. Peanut butter. Sometimes when he caught one, I'd go up with him to see the feeding. I was a tomboy and always found them fascinating. Snakes. Early in our marriage I found a milk snake in our henhouse in Pennsylvania and put it outside with a stick. Alexander was terrified of it. After that he called me Hygeia."

"What's Hygeia?" asked Toby.

"Daughter of Aesclepius, god of healing," said Maggie. "Snakes were used in medicine in ancient Greece."

"You mean you're a snake handler?" said Tony to Sarah.

"I'm a farmer's daughter. You deal with animals. Grommet liked to be handled. I never meant for him to get hurt."

"Alexander?"

"Grommet."

After a beat, Maggie said, "I think we'd better back up," said Maggie. "Start with Crete."

Sarah met her eyes again. "That was a mistake, wasn't it? Mentioning Crete."

"Yes. And you worried, after you said it."

"I did. I didn't think it would do any harm, but then I saw something in your face."

"And you thought about taking off?"

"I'm all packed. I was leaving in the morning. Don't tell Gabe." She was still more than half in her old life.

"Start with Chania."

"We met in a café on the lagoon. He wanted to practice his English. I had planned to go on to Turkey but I never left. He was . . . well. It was a magical summer and we didn't want it to end. We were both alone in the world. Both orphans, both only children. By September, I was pregnant and in love. He was in love, at least I thought so, and he wanted to come to America. End of story."

"Beginning of story," said Toby. "You have another child?"

"No. I lost the baby. I lost two, before we had Jenny. She was such a wanted child. And Alexander was enchanted with America. To him, everything seemed so big and rich. Even my poor little farm seemed rich. At first.

"We lived in the house I grew up in. He got a job in construction in WashPaw, and on weekends fixed all the parts of the house that were falling apart. I raised chickens and gave voice lessons."

"So it was true," said Maggie, "that you were a singer?"

Sarah looked at her and showed just a glimmer of irritation. "You don't miss much, do you?"

"I try not to."

"So Jenny got it from you, the music," said Maggie.

And Sarah's eyes suddenly shone with tears, though her expression remained stony. Finally she said, "She sure didn't get it from her father."

Toby said, "Go on."

"We were both so happy when Jenny was born. We'd had lonely childhoods. Everything seemed to be going well. Alex was clever about design and systems, and he got a job with a bigger firm, developers, in Pittsburgh. He hadn't traveled much; to him it was Athens or Paris. It was sweet. He was good with clients, and they had him working in the front office. He was meeting fancy people. Doing some business travel. Going to lunch at the Duquesne Club. He was beginning to understand what rich really looked like.

"Then he started taking golf lessons at a public course in WashPaw. That annoyed me; I was alone with the baby all week and suddenly on the weekends too. She missed him and so did I. He said the company wanted him to be able to play golf with clients and he was doing it for us. He spent hours in the evenings at the driving range; at least that's where he said he was. Then one night he announced he was spending the weekend at the Rolling Rock Club in Ligonier with his boss and some other people. I asked if their wives were going along, and he said he thought so. I asked if I was invited and he said that I couldn't go because of the baby. I pushed; I wanted to hear that at least I'd been invited."

She fell silent. Some moments of pain retain their power to hurt, even after decades.

Maggie said gently, "He hadn't told them he was married."

Sarah threw her hands in the air, whether at what that moment had meant in her marriage or at Maggie's seeing it coming, was not clear.

"We had a terrible fight. He claimed it didn't mean anything, he was just more useful to them as a bachelor.

He could flirt with the clients' wives, escort a daughter. Wasn't I pleased with how fast he was rising? I hit the ceiling at that but I think I knew it was pointless. He was ambitious beyond anything I'd ever imagined. He was looking for a rich wife who could help him get where he wanted to go. I wasn't ever going to be that; I didn't even want to be. But I thought at least I'd always have Jenny."

She poured herself more wine and handed the bottle to Toby, who poured for the others.

"Do I have to go on?" she said. "Or can Maggie just tell you the rest?"

"Go on, please," said Buster.

"He moved into Pittsburgh. I had custody of Jenny. One Saturday he picked her up for his scheduled visit and I never saw her again. Well, except once."

"You tried?"

"Of course. I tried everything. I taught, and I worked for a couple of caterers to earn money for detectives, but I couldn't afford very good ones. And we weren't looking in the right places. Then one day I had coffee with a friend whose kids were watching the Disney Channel, and there she was. My Jenny. There she was."

Tears were near again.

Maggie said, "We know you sold your house in 1990."

Sarah nodded. "By then I knew everything. Where she lived, what their new name was. I went out there. Jenny was scheduled to perform on some morning TV show. I went to the studio, and stood in line outside with all these ten-year-olds dressed like her character on the show. I was so filled with happiness I could hardly keep from crying. When it was my turn I handed her a picture for her to autograph and I said, 'JennyKoukla,' so only she could hear. She looked right at me and smiled, and I thought she'd say 'Mama' . . . I waited for her face to light up, I thought the whole nightmare was finally over. I'd imagined that moment so many thousand times." Sarah had to stop speaking. Her lips were trembling. They gave her the time she needed.

Sarah picked up where she had stopped, in that scene she'd relived in despair, so many times, of which she knew every nanosecond. "But what Jenny said was, 'You read that article. Who shall I sign this to?' I was close enough to see the tiny scar below her lip where she'd cut herself falling off a swing."

"No recognition."

"None. Then I went to Alexander . . . Oh you've heard enough."

"All right," said Buster. "But about the night of the fire."

She shifted heavily in her chair. It was as if she'd forgotten where all this was heading. It was a very long time since she'd told anyone her real story.

"Did you intend to kill him?"

"Of course not. I wanted to scare the living shit out of him. I wanted him to know there was no forgiveness, ever, for what he did to our daughter. And me."

"So you went to Mr. Rexroth's room."

"It just started with that coincidence. I was sick—I'd had a migraine for days—and I went to see Clarence. Animals are a comfort when everything's wrong, they really are. Clarence always knew when I was sick or sad; he'd come put his head in my lap and stare up as if he could fix me with his eyes.

"I was disappointed when no one was in the room. But then I noticed the closet door was open, and I saw the snake equipment, lying up on the shelf, like it had been put there for me."

"You knew what it was."

"I knew. There were copperheads on our farm. Garter snakes and milk snakes we handled ourselves because they're not poisonous. When it was copperheads, we called the snake man."

"So you put on the gloves and took the bag and tongs. And then . . . ?"

"Then I went next door. I knew Earl was down in the kitchen having his dinner, and Alexander was in the dining room. Stuffing himself. I picked Grommet up and dropped him into the bag, easy-peasy. Then I went down to Alexander's room. Housekeeping had already turned his bed down, so all I had to do was slip Grommet in under the covers. Snakes like a dark burrow. I figured he'd go down to the foot of the bed, and when Alexander got into it, he'd feel Grommet or see him, and I hoped he'd have a heart attack, or a stroke."

She breathed deeply, then drank a slug of wine.

"The kitchen knew I had a migraine; no one was looking for me. I went down the back stairs, hid the bag and tongs in the storage pantry, and went back to bed. All the while I lay there in the dark, I was thinking about Alexander finding a snake in his bed. The more I thought about it, the more I wanted him to know it was me. To know how much I hate him. Hated him."

"What did you do?"

"When everything was quiet, I went back to his room. The light was on and I could hear the TV was playing. I opened the door with my key. Alexander was lying against the pillows with a burning cigar in his hand and the ashtray beside him. He wasn't wearing pajamas. Just boxers, I think. Fat people are often hot, why is that? It was a disgusting sight. He stared at me, but otherwise he didn't move. I walked very slowly toward him. I could see the absolute terror in his eyes. It was very satisfying.

"I waited for him to speak but he didn't. He only looked at me, as if his worst nightmare had just come true.

"And that was what I'd come for. I had thought about finding the snake and taking it back to Earl, but it was too complicated. Besides, if I left it, Alexander wouldn't be able to get out of bed the whole night for fear he'd step on it. So I turned around and left."

There was a long silence. Finally Buster said, "Paula Jackson, I am placing you under arrest for the felony murder of Alexander Kouklakis a.k.a. Antippas."

Sarah looked at him. Then she picked up her wineglass and drained it.

Toby rode with Buster in the patrol car, with Sarah in the backseat in handcuffs. Hope and Maggie followed in Hope's car. All four of them walked Sarah into the state police barracks in Ainsley. It was quiet; the dinner hour. The first officer to see them and stop in her tracks was Carly Leo, the woman who claimed Cherry had confessed to her in the bathroom the night she was arrested.

"Now what?" she said to Buster with exasperation.

"This is Paula Jackson, the cook at the Oquossoc Mountain Inn."

"Executive chef," said Sarah.

"She has made a full confession to the assault on Alexander Antippas that resulted in his death."

Officer Leo was speechless. After a pause she said, "For god's sake, Buster. What have you done this time?"

"I suggest you call Detective Gordon," said Buster, holding up his phone. "He's going to want to hear this."

There ensued a period of pandemonium in the department as Shep Gordon was called, and Carson Bailey was called, and the sheriff was called to please explain the behavior of his deputy. Maggie, Hope, and Toby retired to the Chowder Bowl for some supper. They were just being served when a state police cruiser went steaming down State Street with siren whooping and blue lights revolving.

"Shep Gordon's in some kind of red hot hurry," said their waitress, who had just delivered their shrimp rolls and coleslaw. "Wonder what that's all about." She went back to the kitchen for the fries they had ordered for the table.

They were just finishing their coffee when the text dinger on Hope's phone went off.

"Carson Bailey has arrived," she said. They paid their check, picked up the takeout bag with Buster's supper that was waiting for them at the register, and went back to the state police barracks.

Shep Gordon, a mountain of a man at the best of times, looked more like Krakatoa than they had ever seen him. He was waiting for them in a conference room. His face was red, and he was pacing. Buster by contrast was sitting peacefully on his side of the table, texting Brianna. His phone and Toby's had both been recharged during the wait. Carson Bailey, standing by himself and fiddling with a clicker designed for use in dog training that he'd found in his pocket, had apparently been interrupted in the midst of a festive evening. He was wearing an unbecoming pair of plaid slacks and smelled of beer.

After everyone in the room had been introduced, Shep took the chair at the head of the table, with Carson beside him. He signaled the others to sit down. Carly Leo came in just as Shep said to Buster, "Let's hear this thing."

"Not yet," said Carson.

"Why? Who are we waiting for?"

Carson paused, as if embarrassed, then said, "The attorney general."

Shep swung his vast bulk around in his chair and looked at Carson. He was grasping both arms of his chair, as if he could pick himself up and throw himself at someone, a portrait of simmering aggression.

"Frannie Ober is coming here? *Tonight?*"

For a moment Carson looked a little frightened. He said, "It's a big case. I had to keep her looped. When I called her to say that . . . Deputy Babbin . . . she said not to start until she gets here."

The door opened and a strongly built woman with keen, dark eyes and expensively cut red hair strode in along with an officer in uniform, evidently her driver.

"Hope I haven't kept you waiting." She extended her hand to each person in the room, introducing herself to those she hadn't met, except for Carson, to whom she gave a friendly slap on the back. It wasn't hard to see what had gotten her elected. She took a seat. "Sorry for the way I'm dressed. Town-and-gown hoops game. Okay, let's do this thing."

Buster started the recording.

Detective Gordon seemed to have ants in his pants throughout the session. He'd cross and uncross his legs, and occasionally seemed to be controlling noises of derision. Carson kept his head down, making eye contact with no one, and taking notes.

When it was over, there was a long silence in the room. Finally Shep said, "Well, we seem to have had some amateur detective work here, haven't we?" He stared at Maggie and at Hope, as if expecting an apology for their interference. When no one answered, he went on, "Of course, this leaves a lot of questions. And I don't see that it changes the case on the arson that actually killed the guy. We—"

But he was interrupted by the sound of the attorney general laughing. The AG was shaking her head and looking at Shep, and from time to time at Carson Bailey, who was staring at his notes and blushing painfully. Then the AG suddenly stopped laughing and slapped the table.

"Detective Gordon," she said. "Here you have a full and credible confession from a suspect with a powerful motive and every opportunity. Your case against Cherry Weaver was always full of holes and to my mind, malice."

"Now wait a minute," said Shep, inflating like a vast puff adder. "Wait a minute. She had motive and opportunity, and she's a firebug for sure, our pictures of fire scenes—"

"Your pictures of fire scenes prove she shows up whether there's been an arson or not. She told you why, and so did her sister and her mother."

"Oh right, her sister and her mother. Well that proves that," said Shep sarcastically. "And Henry Rexroth saw her snooping along the corridor . . ."

"*Says* he saw her," said the AG. "People lie, Shep. Especially when they want to deflect suspicion. Or criticism."

She leaned forward and put her hands flat on the table, glaring at Shep.

"Do you have one shred of physical evidence that connects that young woman to the fire? Even any evidence that there was arson at all?"

"The evidence at the scene strongly suggests—" Shep began, but he was cut off.

"One fingerprint? One shred of DNA?"

"She would have worn gloves."

"Fine. Have you found the gloves?"

"Ma'am, you don't know much about arson, do you?" said Shep, condescendingly. "The preponderance . . ."

"Speaking of evidence." Ober raised her voice and talked over him. "There's the matter of that suitcase. Does the term 'chain of custody' mean anything to you, Shep? Are there any rules that apply to you, any at all? The way you handle evidence, we'll be lucky if we can convict even *with* a confession!"

"Who . . ." Shep roared, looking around in fury, and then stopped. He suddenly remembered that that fussy little crime tech guy from Bangor with his Baggies and his tweezers had seemed a touch ticked off with him, what was that guy's name?

There was a furious silence as they faced each other.

Frannie Ober said finally, in an almost normal voice, "You have a full and credible confession from a suspect who saw the victim, paralyzed by snake venom whether she knew it or not, in bed with a lighted cigar in his hand. He set himself on fire, and you know it." She stood up and started for the door, then stopped and turned back.

Shep Gordon took that moment to insist, "With all due respect, no one has explained the missing wastebaskets! And Cherry Weaver confessed to Officer Leo here!"

Ober was suddenly furious again. "I've seen the notes on that 'confession.' This has gone on in this county long enough. Carson, I want you in my office Monday morning. There will be consequences." Then she was gone, followed by her detail.

There was a stunned silence for a long minute after the door shut behind them. Finally Carson Bailey said, "I guess we're done here," and he followed his boss out of the room.

Saturday, October 19

G abriel Gurrell seemed finally to be a shattered man. Hope and Maggie went to his office to say good-bye to him and found him staring at the television screen where Sarah in handcuffs, on what seemed like an endless news loop, walked down the courthouse steps in Ainsley. The press mob, back in force, crowded around her and shouted questions, shoving microphones toward her impassive face.

Gabe had his elbows on the desk, one hand folded around the other in a way that seemed to signal both prayer and the possibility of his punching someone. The knuckles of his thumbs were pressed against his lips as if to keep him from shouting or weeping, while on the screen the press verbally pelted Sarah. The word *Artemis* kept cutting through the clamor. Sarah's hands were cuffed in front of her and state troopers on each side of her had meaty hands around her arms. She stared straight before her, head up. At times she seemed to be looking out of the screen into the eyes of whoever was watching, the million-headed Hydra of anonymous audience. For so many years, she had been no part of her famous daughter's life. Now at last she was in the middle of it. But still alone.

Gabe noticed his guests at the door and muted the sound from the set. He stood. Hope and Maggie, somewhat embarrassed, said their good-byes, expressing their sympathy for him and sorrow for Sarah. He nodded and hummed in appropriate registers, more than actually speaking. They left him quickly.

"In shock," said Hope as they rolled their bags across the lobby.

"And maybe just a touch ambivalent about us, at the moment," said Maggie as they went out the side door toward the parking lot. They had agreed that the kindest thing they could do just then was to get out of his sight.

Before they left, they had taken apart the jigsaw puzzle and put it back in its box, so it wouldn't be damaged by sun before someone else thought of it. It could well be some time before the staff of the inn was fully back in working order.

"Toby must have checked out early," said Maggie as they settled into the car. "I didn't say good-bye, did you?"

"We had a little nightcap together last night, after the dust settled," said Hope.

"I see, said the blind man." Maggie looked pointedly at her friend, but Hope, feigning nonchalance, was laboring to get the car turned around without backing into Zeke, who was fussing nearby with a leaf blower. There had been a wind in the night, and a drift of yellow leaves that had been dancing in the branches yesterday was now collecting against the curbs of the parking lot.

"Toby knows I'm not a morning person," said Hope.

"Does he, indeed?"

"And he had to be off early." She had the car heading in the right direction now, and the long driveway was before them.

"I take it you were more than friends at one time," said Maggie, buckling herself in and bracing her foot against the floor as Hope took the first curve.

There was a longish silence and then Hope said, "We had our moment," with a little smile. "Before either of us was married, of course."

"Ah," said Maggie.

Buster and Brianna were seated in the corner booth at Just Barb's, where Maggie and Hope had arranged to meet them for lunch on their way out of town. Buster had been asked to take some time off while the sheriff decided whether to discipline him or to recommend him for detective.

"When will they let Cherry out?" Hope asked Brianna as she slid in across from her, wondering how she felt about children, how many and how soon.

"This afternoon, I hope. There's paperwork."

"There always is." Hope started to say that if Cherry needed any help starting over that she would be glad to . . . but Maggie stepped hard on her foot under the table before she got more than a word or two out.

To prevent her friend from making any more noises like a mother-in-law, Maggie asked, "Buster, in the car last night, did Sarah explain about the suitcase? That was the one thing I meant to ask and didn't."

"Toby asked her," said Buster. "She had stowed the snake stuff in the back of that cupboard . . ."

"The one Clarence led us to," said Maggie.

"Yes, just to get it out of sight until she could put it back in Rexroth's room. She didn't want to be found wandering the halls with it."

"No."

"She planned to sneak it back when Rexroth was at breakfast the next morning. Or worst case, just to throw it out. Antippas would have screamed about the snake in his room by then, Niner would be called to recapture it. No one would know how the snake had escaped, no harm no foul."

"Somehow I don't think this story was ever going to come out well for the snake," said Maggie.

"No," said Hope. "Or Mr. Niner. An escape artist rattlesnake in residence wouldn't be something you'd want in your Yelp reviews."

"Risky leaving the stuff in the pantry, wasn't it?" Brianna asked.

"She said it was stuffed way in back behind the scraps bucket. She figured it would be more damning if someone found it in her room," said Buster. "So many people are in and out of the kitchen, it might have been anyone who put it there. But when the fire broke out, she put on her parka and found gloves in the pockets, and that gave her a better idea. She had a pretty good notion where in the building the fire was. So once everyone else was evacuated, she went to Lisa and Glory's room and stole what she hoped was Lisa's suitcase. She ran down the back stairs with it, and put the snake stuff in it. Then she hid the suitcase in the basement tool room and came outside with blankets for everyone."

"And I made her give those gloves to me!" said Hope. "So then when she had to move the suitcase . . . never mind, I know. She was dressed by then. All the cooks have their pockets full of latex gloves."

"Or there were work gloves in the tool room," said Buster. "I didn't ask that. But when we called the meeting in the dining room, that gave her the chance to get the suitcase from the tool room and put it out in the compost heap. It was still dark. No one would be out that way to see her and no one would be surprised that she disappeared during the meeting; they'd assume she was heating something or serving something. And in fact none of us did notice."

Sandra arrived with their food, and their talk turned general. Brianna asked if Maggie would miss the excitement of working on this case and she said by no means—she had a school evaluation to lead starting on Monday. "They're always fraught with drama."

Brianna said after a moment, "You're joking, right?"

"Right," said Maggie. Though a certain amount of drama was inherent in any human community and Maggie was quite looking forward to it.

"What do you think will happen to Sarah?" Hope asked Buster.

"I hope she's not going to hire Celia Little," said Brianna, and covered her face with her hands.

"Not going to be a problem," said Buster. "Toby asked her if she knew a good lawyer and she said one of the greatest defense lawyers in the country was a backer of her San Francisco restaurant. Toby called him from the car last night."

"Are you supposed to do that?"

"*I'm* not. Couldn't stop Toby."

"And?"

"He'll be here Monday. Interesting case, you know?"

"Can she afford him?"

"He said when she gets out she can be his personal chef for a year."

When they said good-bye, Hope gave Brianna a hug, and Buster allowed both his mother and Maggie to do something like embracing him.

Sandra said, "You girls come back, now you know where to find us," and both Hope and Maggie promised they would. The Just Barb's regulars all watched out the windows as the women climbed into Hope's car, which was parked in front of Buster's cruiser. Hope started inching out into the quiet street, then stopped halfway. They could see Maggie gesturing, then Hope strapping on her seat belt. Then they pulled all the way out, took aim at the road out of town, and Hope stepped on the gas.

Sandra gave Buster a pat on the shoulder and headed back toward the kitchen, as Brianna said to him, "That wasn't so bad, was it?"

Buster said "Easy for you to say."

As Hope approached the Bangor Airport, Maggie got a text. She read it with apparent interest, then answered, tapping quickly with her thumbs.

"What's up?" Hope asked.

"Margaux Kleinkramer."

"Née Eileen Bachman."

"Right."

"What does she want?"

"Dunno. She wants to talk to us. Wonder what that's about."

The car whizzed past the sign for the rental car returns, forcing them to do another circuit around the parking lots, but they didn't mind. They had plenty of time.

Acknowledgments

Jessica, Walter, and Emily Weber are my avian consultants and I am deeply grateful to them. Evan Moraitis and Domna Stanton provided invaluable guidance on Greek matters, and Lucie Semler and Pam Loree read early drafts for me and gave feedback that helped enormously. Lauren Belfer once again gave me the benefit of her craftsmanship and wisdom; I treasure her judgment as well as her friendship and hope I never have to do without either. Major Richard Bishop of the Ellsworth sheriff's office, Brenda Campbell in the Major Crimes Office in Bangor, and Katy Young at Troop J of the Maine state police patiently and cheerfully answered my many questions, and I apologize to them all if I have made mistakes in spite of them. Molly Munn is a gold mine of arcane information and the telling detail, as well as a joy in our lives. To my editor Jennifer Brehl and the team at William Morrow, my admiration and huge thanks as always. And to my wonderful agent and friend, Emma Sweeney, thank you thank you thank you.

About the Author

B eth Gutcheon is the critically acclaimed author of nine previous novels: *The New Girls, Still Missing, Domestic Pleasures, Saying Grace, Five Fortunes, More Than You Know, Leeway Cottage, Good-bye and Amen,* and *Gossip.* She is the writer of numerous film scripts, including the Academy Award nominee *The Children of Theatre Street.* She lives in New York City.